Fill the Stadium

by

K.M. Daughters

Fill the Stadium

Cover Art by *Kim Mendoza*

The Wild Rose Press, Inc.
PO Box 708
Adams Basin, NY 14410-0708
Visit us at www.thewildrosepress.com

Publishing History
First Mainstream Women's Fiction Edition, 2016
Print ISBN 978-1-5092-0489-2
Digital ISBN 978-1-5092-0490-8

Published in the United States of America

"It's not funny, Ram.
How dare you hire people to tear up my house without my knowledge? What the hell were you thinking?"

He shrugged. "I don't know. That I'm helping you?"

She dragged her fingers through her hair. His stomach tightened as he yearned to thread his fingers through her silky hair, too. In the next second he questioned his motives, something he had done repeatedly since she had stormed his office the first time. Ram still remained satisfied that he wasn't trying to buy or to manipulate her affections. Whether or not she'd ever see him the way that he saw her, Ram *had* to help Jack. The compulsion had become near obsession. He'd spend his last dime and would have fought anyone who had tried to stop him, including Nikki.

Nikki pinned him with a penetrating glare, tense and unsmiling.

"Say something," he said.

"I can take care of my son."

"I never said you couldn't. No one could give Jack better care than you. I just want you to let me help you."

She wagged her head, no. "It's too much, Ram. I can't accept it."

"I think it might be a little late to refuse." He smiled, but the dark stare she gave him had him back stepping. "Look," he said, holding his palms up in supplication, "let's be honest. I have been paid an obscene amount of money to play football. More than I will ever need. I have the money to fix up your house for Jack, and you don't have money to spare. It's nothing. It's what friends do for each other."

Praise for K.M. Daughters

"[*AGAINST DOCTORS ORDERS* is] An intriguing story, full of detailed scenes and fascinating, believable characters."

~WR Potter, Reader's Choice Reviews (5 Stars)

~*~

"This story [*BEYOND THE CODE OF CONDUCT*] is hot hot hot!"

~Val Pearson, You Gotta Read Book Reviews

~*~

"Plenty of big-Irish-family passion, lush descriptions and lots of emotion…from its exciting beginning to its unexpected ending."

~Between the Lines Book Reviews (Fantastic)

~*~

"The author writes with such a warm, flowing style, it's like visiting old friends [in *CAPTURING KARMA*]."

~Cindy Himler, RT Book Reviews

~*~

"In one word, this book [*ALL'S FAIR IN LOVE AND LAW*] is Awesome!"

~The Book Connection

~*~

"Daughters' last installment of the Sullivan Boys series is a terrific read. There's lots of family interaction and a case that will have readers scratching their heads in frustration as each lead comes up empty. The romance plot is every bit as wonderful as the rest of the story."

~Sabrina Cooper, RT Book Reviews

Dedication

For A.J. and Jaimie
And for Mike…Keep on filling the stadium

Acknowledgments

Many thanks to our precious family. To Deb Werksman at Sourcebooks for invaluable critique. To Brenda Novak for friendship and her work supporting juvenile diabetes research. To Mike Clare and David Cry for their work filling Harvard's stadium funding ALD research. To Nicola Martinez for making that first call. To Joelle Walker, our fairy tale editor and sister of the heart. To Ally Robertson for her gracious work style and for deeming the book wonderful even though we made her cry. And to the parents of "lent" children who, like Jack, changed the world by their very existence. For more information on supporting ALD research efforts, please visit www.aldfoundation.org.

Blessings,
K.M. Daughters

Chapter 1

Summer

Engine rumbles and intermittent flashes of blue light roused Nikki Lambert. The premonition that her husband was dead jolted her into full consciousness. Two distinct car-door thuds had her scrambling out of bed.

She grabbed her robe and stuffed her arms inside the sleeves as panic sweat gushed from every pore. She was halfway down the staircase when the doorbell chimed, a normally gentle sound, but that night it sounded like a wailing siren.

Stumbling down the remaining steps barefooted, she landed on the hardwood floor at the bottom, and a stinging jolt of pain radiated up to her kneecaps. On a race to beat another doorbell ring that, God forbid, might wake the boys, she flung open the front door, panting into the faces of Officer Tony Carlucci and Sergeant Pat McNally.

"Mrs. Lambert." Tony—a tall young man, a few inches shorter due to his lowered head—regarded her through long eyelashes while moths swarmed around him and batted the porch light's yellow globe overhead.

"Yes," she said unnecessarily, as if Tony had questioned her identity instead of simply greeting her by name.

Nikki and her husband, John, shared a twelve-year history with the Carlucci family who lived down the block. Tony grew up in an identical Cape Cod style house as the Lamberts', cedar siding stained blue instead of gray, with one less bathroom since John was a plumber and a wizard with pipes and toilets.

"Nikki, can we come inside?" Pat McNally's voice was soft and deferential, completely at odds with his typical bull-moose personality.

The Lamberts had a history with Pat, too. John frequently downed a few beers with Pat and the guys at the Town Tap and hitched many rides in Pat's squad car when his ancient truck broke down after assorted malfunctions.

"Yes, come in." She stepped backwards woodenly as they entered her house, smelling of citrus aftershave and tangy summer sweat.

"Lights?" Pat's question pierced the shadows that rendered them featureless silhouettes, ghostlike.

She hesitated before she pointed to the wall switch, preferring that they remain shadow-cloaked like apparitions in a dream—and their middle of the night visit wasn't real.

The room lit, triggering a deadening sensation in her limbs. Her chest ached, and despite the heat in her never air-conditioned house, chills coursed through her. Because she suspected that Tony and Pat would tell her that John's history with his guy friends, his sons, and her was over.

Like a rehearsed ballet, Pat and Tony removed their snappy uniform hats and held them in the crook of their left arms.

Pat, ten years older than Tony and presumably

braver in these things, said, "Nikki, John was in an accident. His truck must have broken down in the middle of the railroad crossing. The midnight freight…"

His head dipped, bowed, as he finished his speech. "The engineer couldn't stop. John didn't survive the collision. I'm so sorry. We're so sorry…" His voice trailed off.

"Yes," she whispered, cementing her foreknowledge.

She froze to the spot in her tiny hallway where she had kissed her husband goodbye and hello thousands of times since he had carried her over the threshold wobbly from afternoon champagne at the VFW wedding reception.

Why had she opened the door? And then she had said one word that acknowledged this unbearable reality—yes.

The day before she had reacted to her son's terrifying diagnosis by uttering one word, also. Except then, the only word she could manage, shout out—was, "No!"

John, I should have…Done what? Foreseen that John would ride off in the night after the Tylenol P.M. dose he had suggested finally worked on her? Understood that John couldn't face a life without his son and begged him not to drive his truck onto the tracks and *turn off* the engine? This was no accident. He left her to raise their two little boys and to face Jack's illness alone. The man that she thought she knew had turned his back on her with stunning, cruel finality. She had no idea that her husband was capable of something so monstrous.

Her knees buckled. Hands gripped her shoulders and steered her toward the living room sofa. Numb, she sagged onto the couch.

"Can we call someone?" Tony Carlucci squatted in front of her. "Want me to ask my mom to come over and stay with you?"

Nikki shook her head. "My mother. And John's parents," she stammered, her head spinning, pounding.

"Sure, sure." Tony straightened and left the room while Pat stood near the door, shifting from foot to foot.

When Tony returned, he handed her the portable phone. She gaped at the device vacantly as if needing instructions to use it.

Tony plucked the phone out of her hand. "Can you tell me the number, please, and I'll dial?"

Closing her eyes, she recited her mother's Arizona area code and the rest of her telephone number. Eleven tones sounded in sequence, and then he wrapped her hand around the receiver. She kept her eyes shut as she pressed the phone to her ear and listened to the burring ring twice before a click preceded, "Hi sweetie. You're up late."

"Momma!" she wailed. "Please come…"

Chapter 2

Ram Delaney peered through the glass cutout on the scuffed wood door. Brad looked good standing on the makeshift podium that he had set up in the front of the kids' gymnasium. The press peppered Brad with questions, a cacophony of booming voices. Ram heard the exchanges clearly from his position behind the door. Smooth as silk, Brad calmly addressed each question without ever really answering it. *Damn, he's good.*

He had met Brad during their freshman year at Highland U. The jock and the nerd struck up a friendship that grew more solid each year since. Ramsey Delaney, star quarterback, and Bradford Ferguson, sports agent, had formed a winning team the past ten years. Brad was one of the few people in the crazy pro-football business that had his back.

Maybe the only person besides my parents. Mom always said that Brad was the son that she had without labor pains.

"Have I ever lied to you, Harry?" Brad faced off with the head sports writer for the *Boston Ledger*.

Enough. Time to let my agent off the hook.

The door banged dramatically against the wall as he unintentionally opened it with too much muscle. The broken rubber stopper plopped onto the floor behind the door, a casualty of Ram's entrance into the press conference.

"Gentlemen. Gentlemen, and lady." He winked at the tall, cool blonde who reported for the local cable station as he strolled casually to the podium. *What's her name Beth? Bessie? Bunny? Something like that.* "Stop harassing Brad."

The assembly rapid-fired questions at Ram instead, the clamor echoing like ricochets off the concrete block walls.

"What happened?"

"When did you find out you weren't invited to Dragons camp?"

"We reported that the arm had healed."

"Good afternoon," Ram shouted, and the questioning ceased.

In even tones, he continued, "Welcome to the Good Sports Club. I hope you've had a chance to look around. What do you think?"

He smiled, determined to convey optimism and honesty despite the flagrant issue skirting.

"Cut the crap, Delaney. I don't have all day." Harry stood abruptly and the metal legs on his folding chair scraped the hardwood floor with an ear-splitting screech.

Brad had timed the press conference aiming to own the five o'clock news bites on the local broadcast and the national news later that evening. If Ram had a prayer of keeping his career alive, this was his chance.

But he refrained from spilling his guts because he didn't want to admit that he was as shocked as the press that he was there addressing them instead of out on the Dragons practice field. Or that team management had humiliated him at camp by omitting his name from the active roster.

"Today is all about the Good Sports Club, Harry," Ram insisted.

"Why aren't you in camp?" The weathered reporter leveled his gaze at him.

"Damned if I know." He had a sudden urge to loosen his collar.

"Bullshit, Ram."

"You want the truth, Harry?" He took a deep breath. "I worked harder than any player in the NFL this off-season. My arm is as strong as the day I signed with the Dragons ten years ago. After all the therapy, I honestly believe it's stronger. I planned on playing in camp and demonstrating that the injury had healed. I showed up. I was told that I'm not needed."

Ram's voice cracked on "needed".

For a couple miserable moments nobody said a word.

"Coach Beltzer judges your arm at about seventy-five per cent," Harry piped up.

Well if you talked to Beltzer, Harry, you already damned well know why I'm not in camp.

"Now that's bullshit. I know it, you know it, and he knows it." Ram thumped a fist on the lectern. It didn't satisfy the impulse to crack it in half.

Brad squeezed Ram's shoulder and leaned toward the mic. "Ram's personal physician, Dr. Canavan, cleared the arm a month ago," he announced. "And just last week the team doctor cleared Ram for full practice. No restrictions."

"But you're off the Dragons. You're confirming that?" came the question from a guy in the back row.

"Yes." No point in denying the sad truth.

"Then what about another team? Any interest?

Anything you want to announce?"

Brad shifted as if to take over the mic again, but Ram stopped him with one raised eyebrow and a shake of his head.

"I have no interest in any other ball club. I am a Massachusetts Dragon," Ram said in full voice. "I started my career with the Dragons, and I will end my career as a Dragon."

Brad nodded, apparently satisfied with Ram's strategic comments. For better or worse Beltzer and the suits would get the message.

A bunch of reporters in the back row stowed their gear and headed to the door on the run to beat deadlines.

"What are you going to do until the Dragons come to their senses? It won't be long until they realize Lawrence Whitney is no Ramsey Delaney." The cable station blonde smiled seductively, evidently in no hurry to leave.

"Thank you for the vote of confidence. Don't forget Larry Whitney won the Heisman last year. He proved himself a very capable quarterback." *I would like to strangle that cocky rookie.*

"Would you go back if asked?" An unfamiliar reporter shouted.

"If I felt I could help the organization in any way, I would not hesitate. Until they make that call, I will be here in the community running my Good Sports Club."

"Is it true that you plan on taking the Good Sports Clubs nationwide?" *The blonde has done her homework.*

"I would like that, yes," he responded. "But we haven't begun planning any expansion yet."

"Mister Delaney, are you coming to the game? Everyone is ready. We're waiting on you," a little boy hollered from the gym doorway.

"I'm on my way, buddy." Ram smiled at the boy and then turned his attention back to the dwindling audience. "I can't keep my kids waiting. Thanks for coming."

"Can we watch the game?" Harry asked. "My Features Editor might be interested in running an article."

That stung. Reduced from first page in the Sports section of the *Boston Ledger* week after week from August until February to a feature in the Community Interest section, or some shit.

"Sorry it's a closed field," Ram said as he stepped off the podium.

"Oh, come on, Delaney. Let us cover it. Take a few pictures. Give you some good publicity and all." Harry slung the strap of his briefcase over his shoulder and paced next to Ram toward the door.

"No thanks, Harry. I appreciate good publicity from the *Ledger*, but you can't take pictures of the kids. The GSC is about providing children with a safe place to learn about sportsmanship and, if they choose, learn how to play a sport at their level without self-consciousness or fear of ridicule. Have a great day."

Ram left the gym and exited the building out into the blazing sunshine.

Chapter 3

Nikki's high heels sank into the ground. She stood in front of John's open grave, linked palm-to-palm with her two sons' damp little hands. Fidgeting, Jack and Rocky bopped her on the arms and head with the heart shaped, helium balloons she had bought on the way to the funeral mass.

She felt numb and robotic. Ambient noise sounded muffled to her as if she were encased in a hollow tube that normal sound couldn't penetrate. The priest's deep voice occasionally broke through the haze.

John's mother sobbed aloud.

The kids stiffened at the sound of their grandmother's voice, and Nikki squeezed their hands to comfort them. Her heart constricted with a searing pain anticipating that Jack might be taken from her. Like Kay Lambert, she would have to bury her child.

Her thoughts drifted to the day before John's death.

****

Nikki and John had prepared for the worst since receiving the call that had set the one o'clock appointment with the most highly respected neurologist on the staff of Coastal Regional Medical Center. Jack's headaches had awakened him several times in the past couple months. Their family physician had ordered an M.R.I. that was conducted in the local hospital.

Afterward, their doctor had referred them to

Coastal Regional in Boston to receive the test results explaining only that he had called upon a specialist to diagnose Jack. Nikki and John feared that they would hear that their ten-year-old son had a brain tumor as they sat nervously awaiting their turn in the specialist's waiting room.

John firmly held Nikki's hand anchoring her on the spotless tiled floor as she rose when a nurse wearing a mint green lab coat called out, "John Lambert, Nicole Lambert."

Shuffling alongside John, she approached the woman who propped open the door leading to the inner offices.

"Dr. Warner will see you now. Please follow me," she instructed.

The nurse ushered them into a large office with rosewood furniture and walls painted the same color as her lab coat. A slim blonde woman in a tailored, sleeveless, powder blue dress stood behind a delicate carved wood desk. Kindness beamed from the round blue eyes that followed the Lamberts' progress toward her.

Extending a shapely arm over the desk, she offered her hand. "Mrs. Lambert. Mr. Lambert. I'm Jodi Warner," she said.

Nikki clasped Dr. Warner's warm hand, embarrassed at how cold and clammy her own seemed in comparison. "Please call me Nikki," she said.

Shaking hands with the doctor next, John said, "I'm John. Good to meet you, Dr. Warner."

"I'd like it if you both call me Jodi." She sat, folded her small hands into a ball and rested them on the edge of a mauve colored blotter.

Nikki and John sank down onto twin Queen Anne chairs across from her, holding on to each other's hands. Their arms dangled between the chairs in a vee of solidarity.

Nikki's gaze locked on Jodi. She sucked in a breath and then confronted their terrifying suspicion. "Did Jack's M.R.I. show he has a brain tumor?"

Profound sadness darkened Jodi's eyes although she responded, "No, your son does not have a brain tumor."

John squeezed Nikki's hand and beamed a smile. Spontaneously Nikki exclaimed, "Oh thank God!"

Her right hand over her heart, relief flooded through Nikki.

But Jodi leaned forward, tense and frowning. "Jack has a rare genetic disorder called adrenoleukodystrophy or ALD. ALD is caused by a gene mutation that prevents the production of a protein that breaks down certain fatty acids in the body. These fatty acids accumulate and destroy the protective coating around the nerves. Without this protective coating, the nerves degenerate. Brain sensors basically short out. The M.R.I. shows that Jack's demyelination is extensive. I'm so sorry."

"I…" Nikki's throat clogged and her tongue seemed swollen, useless.

"I don't understand," John intuited Nikki's intended response. "How did he get this?"

"The faulty gene is on the X chromosome. During conception the woman always supplies an X chromosome and a man supplies either an X or a Y, which determines the gender of their child. XX creates a girl, and XY, a boy. Therefore, in genetic terms, ALD in a boy links to mothers while fathers can carry the gene to daughters."

Horrified, Nikki widened her eyes and tugged away her hand from John's grasp. "I gave this to Jack?" she shrieked.

Jodi's eyes closed briefly as she shook her head. Then she gazed at Nikki and stated forcefully, "No, Nikki. Never think that. This happened to Jack. Nobody knows how or why the gene mutation occurs."

Wounded and inconsolable, Nikki wagged her head back and forth in symbolic denial. "Oh God, no," she said, tears streaming down her cheeks.

"Can you give him chemotherapy or something?" John probed. "What's the treatment?"

The woeful expression on Jodi's face dealt another blow to Nikki.

"If you select me as Jack's physician, I'll advise a fat restricted diet, and we'll try Lorenzo's Oil to explore whether or not he derives some benefit from it. However, it's most successful when used before symptoms present. Bone marrow transplant is a slim possibility, but I don't want to rule it out at this point before we thoroughly investigate. Research is ongoing and this hospital is leading edge. But I don't want to mislead you. Jack's prognosis is rapid decline."

"Are you saying…Jack is going to die?" Terrified, Nikki's teeth chattered and her breath caught in her throat.

The lovely woman with the kind, sad eyes replied, "I'm so sorry that my skills and medical science can't offer him more."

Nikki's peripheral vision shimmered and blackened. She slumped in her seat.

Jodi voiced disjointed words. "Diet. Counselors. Support groups. Explain. Written information. Websites. Family bone marrow matching. Family genetic testing."

When John asked, "How long?" Nikki wanted to rewind that instant and cover his mouth.

She didn't want to know the boundaries of her son's limited future—the string of "lasts" that would define her from that moment forward.

"In cases similar to Jack's, as soon as three to six months. It would be highly unlikely to expect more than a year," Jodi said.

John had remained silent as they left the hospital, his tear-tracked face in profile shouting louder than any words he might have said. Nikki had hunkered in the passenger seat and cried freely during the half hour car ride home from Boston. When they had arrived outside the Good Sports Club complex, their boys' day camp during summers, and after-school program site during the school year, John switched off the engine. Tears swam in his eyes, twisting Nikki's heart in knots. This quiet, strong man that she wanted to marry since the moment she first had spied him dropping his sandwich crumbs to sparrows from a park bench thirteen years ago, sobbed out loud in Nikki's presence for the first time.

Holding each other awkwardly over the car console, Nikki and John had wept, a shuddering purge. The boys' pending dismissal prompted Nikki and John to regain composure. She handed him a Handi Wipe, ever ready in her "mommy" purse, and then swabbed her face with a towelette that she plucked from the package. And then she and John had opened their doors and left the car to meet the boys outside the building: normal, everyday behavior, when nothing would ever be normal again for Nikki and her family.

"I tackled when I ought a touched," Rocky reported from the back of the car in his throaty rasp that hinted at the deep bass voice he'd possess as a man.

"Why'd you do that?" she asked, always enthralled when the boys recounted how they spent their days.

"I forgot," Rocky responded.

Jack giggled. "It was awesome."

She smiled and glanced at John in the driver seat. The slight dimple in his cheek revealed that he was smiling, too. *We have this. We have them. John Michael and Peter Rockland Lambert. Our boys. Together. We have now.*

In many ways that evening was bizarrely normal. Jack, his serene, sunny disposition never wavering, played with his brother whose endless physical energy made the simple occupation of space sound like explosive destruction. Dinner, as usual, entailed the boys' shoveling down food so play could resume.

Jack and Rocky fled the kitchen after dinner to switch on *Star Wars: The Phantom Menace*, one of their daily addictions. Rocky "fought" in every battle scene, and Jack sometimes recited the script along with the actors. They highly flattered Nikki in their belief that Queen Amidala looked like her. Light sabers sizzled electronic zoom on the screen and in the TV room.

Nikki cleared the table, her brain fried, her heart a block of wood.

John shouldered up to her to dry the dishes that she washed. "We don't have the money," he said, his mouth close to her ear.

"We'll find it. I'll work extra hours," Nikki assured him, although her heart longed for the opposite with Jack sick.

"There's no work out there. I can't..." His voice was so flat, so defeated.

****

At John's grave, seething fury surged through Nikki. *How could you leave me this way? I need you! He needs you!*

Nikki stopped short of hating John. But it wasn't easy. She detested that John had what she most wanted: to predecease her child.

"May the perpetual light shine upon him," the mourners responded.

John's friends sweated in the searing sun, their dress shirts stuck to their chests in dark patches. Most of the small town's residents clustered in a semi-circle around the flower-covered casket. John had worked in just about every house in Highland Square. As he had always joked, "When you *really* need a plumber, he's the most valuable person you know."

"May his soul and all the souls of the faithful departed rest in peace," the priest recited.

In her numb state, Nikki wasn't fazed by the heat of the day. But the three other adult members of her family appeared wilted: John's mom and dad, Kay and Mickey, and Nikki's mom sat on unevenly situated folding chairs on the grass. The grand total of John and Nikki's extended family equaled four. Nikki's dad wanted to be there, but he couldn't travel after the stroke three months before.

The boys tugged her rubbery arms. "Now,

Mommy?" Jack's sad upturned eyes galvanized her into action.

"Yes, guys, it's time." Flexing each calf to dislodge her shoes from the ground, she then moved forward a couple steps on the balls of her feet, Jack and Rocky in tow.

She freed her fellas' hands and placed her right hand on John's casket. Smiling at Jack she gave him a nod.

"I love you, Daddy," he proclaimed as he whipped his arm upward and set his balloon sailing.

With another nod she signaled Rocky.

"I love you, too, Daddy!" Rocky launched the balloon with a whole body, jack-in-the-box jump.

Necks craned, they followed the balloons' flight in the cloudless sky. Up, up, the red hearts floated, stringed tails wiggling. *They love you, John. I loved you, too.*

When the red splotches against the powder blue sky reduced to specks, she clasped the boy's hands again and steered them away from their father's grave.

"Does Daddy have the balloons now in heaven?" Rocky asked, pure innocence gleaming in his shiny, round blue eyes.

"He sure does," she said.

"Good." His head bobbed up and down, a triumphant "yes." His pensive expression cast a grave maturity on his little boy, freckled face.

She ached, wishing that John had spared his sons the lesson of loss.

Her mom accompanied John's parents toward the casket for their final goodbyes. Nikki walked away from the burial site across the straw-like cemetery lawn bleached and scorched by the dog days of summer. One of John's friends owned a limousine company and as she and the boys approached, he opened the back door of a sleek black, stretch limo, his donated transportation. It was the first time her sons had traveled in a car like that, and the cans of soda, bottles of water and twinkling crystal glassware impressed them. They fiddled with the radio knobs and air-conditioning buttons half-heartedly—curious, but subdued in their dark funeral pants and starched short-sleeved shirts. Despite the sorrowful reason for the classy car ride, Nikki checked off one item on the fantasy wish list that she had created for Jack.

Chapter 4

Brad accompanied Ram through the cool hallway toward the main office. Sweat dripped off Brad's forehead. "Damn it's hot. I'm glad you called the game and sent the kids inside to cool off. I could use a cold drink right now."

He yanked the tails of his once crisp dress shirt out of his pants and wiped his face with his sleeve. "But you know, it was a damned good game of flag. Those kids are really into football."

"You should have been here Monday. One of the younger boys tackled like a bulldozer," Ram said, enjoying the memory. "He reminded me of Bear. Remember Bear, my guard sophomore year?"

"God, I haven't thought of Bear in years. Wonder where he is now?"

"His last Christmas photo card showed him flanked by his five daughters. Little mini Bears—what a contrast. He's probably thirty pounds heavier than he was in school. The card was signed, 'Bear and his Cubettes.' "

Brad chuckled, catching Ram up in the laugh as they entered Ram's office.

"Uh oh. What are you two up to?" Luci Baldwin sat behind her black metal desk. Her arms folded, Ram's assistant regarded the pair quizzically over the reading glasses perched on her freckled nose.

"Nothing. Just reminiscing about college days." Brad leaned over Luci's desk and smacked a kiss on her cheek. "I like what you've done with your desk, Luce." His crooked grin in Ram's direction goaded the Dragons player.

Brad gazed pointedly at the veritable football shrine that was Luci's workspace. Green Bay Packers mementos including three stuffed bears in miniature cheese head hats; a framed picture of her all-time hero, Bart Star; and a recipe book, autographed she proudly informed one and all, by Brett Favre's mother; cluttered her desktop around the extra large computer screen.

"She only does this to drive me crazy," Ram contended.

"Don't flatter yourself, Ramsey. This has nothing to do with you. I have rooted for my beloved Packers since before you were a twinkle in your daddy's eye," she asserted.

Brad choked back a laugh. "Wish I could stay, but I have an appointment. I'll take a rain check on that cold one, Ram," he said. "Good seeing you, Luci."

"Are you bringing Karen to the house Friday night for the opener?" She gazed at Brad, an expectant expression on her face.

"I'm not sure Karen can make it, but I wouldn't miss it for the world. I'll call and let you know. Ram, talk to you tomorrow."

Speechless, Ram waited until Brad closed the door behind him. "Opener? Karen?"

"The Packers preseason opening game. You know, Alan and I always have a party to kick off a winning season." She gave him a defiant smile, always unapologetically siding with the competition.

"Am I invited?" he asked feeling distinctly left out.

"Of course you are." She smiled, and then she frowned. "You have a standing invitation every year, but you…" Luci paused as tears filled her eyes.

"I know, I'm always in camp. It's okay, Luci. Don't cry." Ram patted her shoulder. "Everything is good. I've always wanted to come to your opener. Now I have my chance."

"Liar." She plucked a tissue from a box on her cluttered desk and blew her nose, a far from delicate trumpet blast.

Never able to slip anything past her, he laughed. "Who's Karen?"

"Brad's girlfriend. They've been together"—she hesitated—"gosh, it must be about a year now."

"I didn't know he had a steady girlfriend. He's never said a word about her to me."

"Brad has been very quiet about Karen. They're spending more and more time together. I think she might be the one."

"The One?" Ram asked incredulously, "I haven't even met her. What is she like? Is she good enough for him?"

Luci chuckled. "She's a lovely lady. You'll like her."

"Why didn't he say anything to me?"

"You've been pretty preoccupied the last few months."

"Well, I have plenty of time now. I'll suggest dinner next time I talk to him." He shook his head. "I really have lived in a bubble, haven't I?"

Gazing at him sadly, Luci slumped her shoulders.

We both know I want back into that bubble.

"Time to change that," he declared with forced gusto. "What can I bring Friday night?"

"Just your appetite."

The phone rang interrupting the conversation. As Luci answered the call, Ram walked into his freshly decorated office and sat down at his desk. Framed team pictures lined the wall, eighteen in all, one photo for every year of play since high school. A motivational poster hung on the wall behind the massive wood desk: a solid black background with gold letters that read:

"Character is how a man acts when no one is watching."

A simple sentiment—words painted on a locker room wall by a former coach who excelled in molding men from boys. Ram tried to honor this every day. He dialed Brad's number and left a message on his voice mail to call him.

Luci poked her head through the doorframe. "Ram, you have a minute?"

"Sure. What's up?"

She hurried inside the office and sat on the edge of the chair in front of the desk, a manila folder in her right hand. Frowning, she slid her reading glasses off the top of her head and put them on.

"I think we have a problem," she said.

Opening the folder and placing it on the desk, she continued, "Coach Harriman filled out a formal behavior report concerning one of the boys in his group."

Bowing her head, she consulted a paper in the file. "The boy's name is John Michael Lambert. He's a really great kid. He and his brother have been in the program since we opened. He's never presented problems of any kind before.

"Lately John Michael has tripped several times and Harriman describes his behavior in the report as occasionally disoriented. He asked to sit out of practice three times last week complaining of a headache. The kids stopped picking him for teams this week. He fell once just walking to the sidelines. Harriman is worried about a lawsuit if anything happens to the child on his watch."

"That doesn't sound like Coach."

"I know. He really is worried about this little boy. This started about a month ago." Luci flipped pages in the folder. "I have a detailed record here. He thought he could handle it, but things are getting worse."

"What does he want to do about it?"

"He hasn't made a recommendation. He wanted us to be aware of the situation, and thought it best to document everything."

Ram nodded as he absorbed the information. "What's your gut reaction?"

"It kills me to say it, but I think we have to speak with the family and ask them to keep him home."

"I don't like this."

"Neither do I, but I don't know that we have an alternative."

"Let's talk to his family. See what we can do to help. I'm not going to turn any child away. If something's going on with him, maybe we can make him a junior coach or something. Can you please get one of his parents on the phone for me?"

"Of course." Luci popped up and left his office.

Ram stood and gazed out the window behind the desk. Boys and girls ran around on the fields below despite the scorching heat. Baseball, soccer, and football fields sprawled in the foreground, the huge indoor gym building a massive backdrop. Growing up he would have given anything to have a place like that to play. Ram never spoke about his athletic experiences as a shy and gangly kid. Always the last to be picked for a team in gym class, he hated Phys Ed, and improvised any pretext to be excused. His main goal in establishing the Good Sports Club was to create equal opportunities in team play regardless of ability levels. He believed his methods fostered confidence and allowed youngsters to enjoy competitive sports.

"Oh Ram." Luci rushed back into the office, tears tracking her cheeks.

Alarmed, he rounded the desk and gently held her shoulders. "What happened? What's wrong?"

"I just checked the file for the Lamberts' phone number, and it hit me. Did you hear about the truck that got stuck on the tracks the other night?"

"Sure, it was on the local news channel all week. Why?"

"Oh my God, Ramsey." She dabbed under her eyes with her index finger. "The man killed in the car was John Michael's father."

"The little boy we were just talking about?"

"Yes. The funeral was this morning."

Chapter 5

Nikki and John's mothers had organized a buffet lunch at Nikki's house after the funeral. Exhausted and hollowed out, Nikki hardly noticed their efforts. Her saving grace and only comfort during the unwanted social occasion was her sons' solidarity.

Rocky and Jack shadowed her movements as she drifted among the guests and received expressions of sympathy.

"If there's anything I can do to help."

"Call me if you need anything, okay?"

If I need, if I need, if I need. I need my husband. I need my son to be well.

Sensitive to her in-laws' grief-stricken past few days, Nikki hadn't yet disclosed Jack's illness to John's parents. She couldn't put it off beyond the end of that day.

After the guests left, Nikki allowed the boys to play in the basement on John's workbench when asked, grateful that they seemed more energized. They kept a stash of Tinker Toys and Legos there to "build" things with their dad. Nikki thought their playing in the area of the basement the three of them called the "man room" might console her sons and make them feel connected to John.

"Nikki, if there isn't anything else you need, Dad and I are going to get on the road, okay?" Kay's eyes were rimmed with tears, but bless her, she didn't break down.

Generally Nikki considered Kay a good mother-in-law. To her knowledge, Kay had never said a bad word about her to John. But in the twelve years she'd been Kay's daughter-in-law, Nikki perceived an air of disapproval wafting over her from Kay's direction. In turn, Nikki hadn't liked her much, either.

John certainly had not "married his mother" when he chose Nikki as his wife and the mother of his children. Kay was contained, restrained, strict, and a black-and-white thinker. Back talk was unthinkable and hugs were rare.

Nikki would hug her kids every spare minute if they let her. Despite her lack of fondness for her mother-in-law, Nikki appreciated Kay's considerate attitude the past stressful days. She couldn't bear that she would add to Kay's mountain of grief by relating Jack's diagnosis to her and the boys' beloved Poppy. She had no choice.

"Mom…" Nikki said, gently touching Kay's shoulder. "I need you and Dad to sit down a minute before you leave, if you don't mind."

Mickey's eyes locked on Nikki, and the alarm she read in their pale blue depths stole her breath. John had looked so much like his father, and had worn the same panicked expression on his face before breaking down in the car after meeting with Dr. Jodi Warner.

Nikki's mom sat on the bench of the picnic style kitchen table facing Nikki, her soft brown eyes willing her daughter strength. Kay and Mickey joined her mother. The three sat stiffly in a row regarding Nikki anxiously, as if they were bowling pins and she was about to make the spare.

"There's no easy way to tell you this…"

The door in the kitchen leading to the basement flew open and crashed against the doorstop. Jack and Rocky charged forward and plowed into Nikki.

"Can we go swimming? Please, Mommy," Jack pleaded.

"Please," Rocky echoed. "It's hot."

"Sure. Go put your suits on." She ruffled Jack's soft black hair and Rocky's stubbly, light brown buzz cut.

The boys tramped away and up the stairs, a progression of thudding booming sounds more like an army on the march than two pairs of feet in sneakers. She loved her noisy household, the physicality, and the sheer fun of mothering her children.

Focusing on the adults again, she said, "I have some information that will help me explain."

She opened the junk drawer searching for the pamphlet on ALD that Jodi Warner had provided four days ago. Nikki shoved around packages of batteries, a cardboard with five thumbtacks, some picture hooks, a stray paper-wrapped Bazooka bubblegum and a broken Halloween pumpkin flashlight, but couldn't find the brochure.

"Would it help if I explained to Kay and Mickey for you, honey?" Momma asked in a strained voice.

She slammed the drawer shut and returned to her seat at the table, fixated on her mother's tear filled eyes. "No, Momma. How will I ever confront this thing if I can't even talk about it?"

Kay clutched Mickey's hand. "You're scaring me, Nikki."

"I'm so sorry, Mom. I don't mean to…but Jack is very sick. As soon as the boys go outside I'll tell you everything, okay?"

Kay clutched Momma's hand now, too. "Is it bad?" she rasped.

Nikki nodded, closing her eyes as she experienced the seven stages of grief yet again.

The boys stampeded down the stairs and ran into the kitchen. Barefoot and clad in matching black bathing trunks, they streaked toward the back door. Rocky, the winner of the race, grabbed the handle on the screen door, whipped it open and sped out, Jack on his heels.

The screen door clattered shut. Nikki told Kay and Mickey that Jack had ALD, nearly as gently and clinically as Jodi Warner had related the facts. One eye trained through the window on the boys splashing around in the dilapidated above ground pool, she helplessly absorbed her in-laws' distress.

Training red streaked eyes on Nikki, Kay sobbed out, "How could this *be*? He looks so *healthy*. There must be some mistake."

Nikki shook her head while keeping a watchful eye on the antics in the three-foot high pool. Expecting it to sprout fountains of leaks all around since John had patched it so many times, she was amazed that it still held water.

The boys hopped out of the pool, and Rocky picked up the garden hose while Jack ran toward the house. Several screechy whines sounded as Jack opened the spigot and water flow hummed through the pipes. Rocky tried to encapsulate the gushing nozzle with his mouth and then he pointed the spray at his giggling

28

brother. On the run away from the sprinkling water Jack tripped and sledded along the slick grass.

Nikki leaped off the bench and was out the door in three strides, aware that the adults had followed her when the screen door clattered behind her. Rocky had run over to his brother who spat out muddy grass propped up on one elbow. She sank to her knees on the sodden lawn at Jack's side. Before she could comfort him, he and Rocky burst out laughing.

Hooting, Rocky pointed a finger at Jack's backside. "I can see your butt!"

Jack covered the split seam on his bathing trunks while he stood up, a sheepish expression on his face. "I'm okay, Mommy," he assured Nikki with a grin.

Still kneeling, she flung her arms around him and clasped him to her chest. Wiggling he protested, "Mommy, gee."

She loosened the embrace and he backed up a step, but she still held onto his shoulders apparently needing the connection more than he did.

He gazed at Nikki, an earnest expression on his face. "I tripped a little. It's the 'ah-dree-no' I caught."

"What?"

"I Googled it. From that paper in the drawer."

"Oh, sweetheart…" Struck speechless, Nikki's tears overflowed.

He reached out and patted her cheek lovingly. "Don't cry, Mommy."

"I'm sorry." She swiped a hand under her eyes and sniffled. "I'll stop."

His arm extended palm upward offering her a boost. She placed her hand in his and he heaved backward for some leverage to haul Nikki up to her feet.

"Mommy?"

"Yes, sweetie?" Gazing into his innocent blue eyes, she smiled.

"Don't worry. I'm still going to change the world."

She took a ragged breath as she nodded.

"Hey, kiddos, Grandma and I have to get on the road." Mickey's tremulous voice belied the cheerful expression on his face. "I don't like driving in the dark."

Rocky and Jack scampered toward him and hugged his legs.

"Give me a big old smack." Mickey squatted down to their level, breaking the stranglehold they had on his thighs.

"Bye, Poppy."

"Bye, Poppy."

Mickey closed his eyes as he kissed the crown of the boys' heads, and they buzzed his cheeks with noisy kisses.

Nikki drifted toward the screen door and held it open, waiting for the kids to kiss Kay goodbye. Momma passed in front of her and gave her a warm, encouraging, heart-breaking smile, and then her in-laws filed through the door.

"Five more minutes, guys and then I want you to come inside to change. We have to take Nana to the airport," Nikki called out.

She ducked inside trailing the adults. "Do you need help bringing down your luggage?"

"No, thanks. I can manage." Mickey and Kay headed for the stairs.

"I left my bag at the front door," Momma said. "I

feel terrible leaving. Do you want me to reschedule my flight?"

Nikki's heart swelled. "I'll be fine. Daddy needs you. I promise I'll call every day."

"All right, sweetie." Momma gave Nikki's shoulder a soft pat. "I'll just go freshen up a bit."

"Sounds good. I'll herd the boys."

****

Nikki backed her car out into the street, her mother riding next to her, as Kay and Mickey stood side by side in front of their navy blue Chrysler waving to the boys in the back seat. Nikki tooted the horn twice and then drove down the block.

She didn't rehash recent events or circumstances with Momma on the way to airport, choosing instead to chat about her dad's recovery. Momma shared funny anecdotes about his interaction with medical personnel and patients.

"The man in the bed next to the window in Daddy's room had several large jars filled with liquid and some sort of floating objects lined up along the window ledge," Momma related. "Daddy didn't want to investigate too fully because he was afraid of what he might find out, but he asked his doctor if the guy next to him was incubating the cure for cancer over there."

Nikki and her mom shared a much-needed laugh. Even though Daddy wasn't with her the past few grueling days, his optimistic life view grounded and inspired her.

On the return leg of the drive, the boys hung over handheld video games in the back seat, and Nikki reined in her stampeding thoughts.

I can't think about John anymore. I have to focus

on Jack. I'll be no good to him if I'm feeling sorry for myself. I have to help him get well. Learn everything I can about ALD.

Nikki's internal pep talk halted abruptly the instant she traveled down her home street and spied her in-laws' car still parked in her driveway. As she drove over the driveway apron and shifted into park, she cast a dull gaze on the figure seated on her porch stoop.

Kay stuffed something into her pocket and then sat primly, gazing in Nikki's direction.

The lawnmower's engine droned as Mickey neared the car cutting the grass on a diagonal.

Jack and Rocky squirmed in the backseat, released seat belts with a couple loud clicks, and shoved open the rear doors of the car.

"Poppy!" Rocky shouted, streaking across the front lawn toward his grandfather.

"Poppy's still here!" Jack chorused on a clumsy run toward Mickey.

Kneeling as his grandsons pitched into his open arms, Mickey wobbled on his knees and grinned at Nikki over their heads.

Pushing the button to lower the car window on the passenger side, Nikki waved a hand and returned her father-in-law's smile.

"We thought you left. Can you stay? Can I help mow the lawn?" Jack chattered.

"Want to play catch?" Rocky inquired.

Nikki sat motionless behind the wheel staring straight ahead for several minutes. Like a woman twice her age, she slowly opened her door, swung her legs out and left the car with the driver's and back doors gaping open.

She shuffled toward Kay. "Mom, what are you doing here? Something wrong with your car?"

Kay patted Nikki's knee as she sat down next to her on the brick step. "I hope you don't mind. We just couldn't leave. I straightened up a bit and prepared some things to pop in the oven for dinner. Dad and I thought you might need some help the next few days," she jabbered as she pulled the pamphlet about ALD out of her pocket and held it loosely in her hand.

Nikki eyed the pamphlet and then stared at her lap for a couple, steadying moments. Silent, she leveled her gaze at Kay.

Kay bit her lip and then said, "I'm sorry for being so presumptuous. We'll pack up and leave."

As Kay started to rise, Nikki rapidly clasped her elbow. "Don't go. I'm sorry, Mom. I didn't mean to make you feel unwelcome. Of course I want you and Dad to stay."

Focusing on the ALD pamphlet, she added, "I could use all the help I can get."

"I found this in Jack's room on his computer desk."

Nikki winced at Kay's harsh, accusatory tone and then sighed. "I didn't give this to him if that's what you're thinking. I hid it in the drawer when John..." She closed her eyes and inhaled sharply.

"When John and I got home from the doctor's office," she continued. "We had planned to go over it after the boys were asleep. But I went to bed and John must have gone out for a ride to clear his head and then the police were knocking on my door in the middle of the night. I didn't realize Jack had it until after he mentioned he had Googled adrenlek... adrenole... adrenoleukodystrophy. Shit." Nikki buried her face in her trembling hands. "How can my little boy have a disease that I can hardly pronounce?"

Kay rubbed Nikki's back: gentle, comforting little circles. "While I sat here waiting for you to come home, I thought about the day John brought you to our house for the first time."

Nikki raised her head and smiled. "I was a nervous wreck that day."

"You were? I was so anxious that I couldn't sit still. I drove Dad crazy pacing back and forth from the kitchen to the front window."

"Why were *you* nervous?" Nikki arched her eyebrows.

"I wanted you to like me."

"I never considered for an instant that you might be nervous, too. I just wanted to make a good first impression. I was so tongue tied; I felt like an idiot." Nikki shook her head. "What did you think of me?"

She hastened to add, "Be honest."

"Aren't I always?" Kay chuckled.

Nikki snorted and rolled her eyes.

"I know. Sometimes I'm too honest," she said.

Nikki agreed nodding her head.

Kay narrowed her eyes. "Hmm."

Grinning, Nikki gave Kay's arm a conciliatory pat.

"Honestly, I thought you were the prettiest girl I had ever seen. And I thought John had exaggerated when he told us beforehand that you looked just like that actress. What's her name? She was in Star Wars?"

"Maybe Natalie Portman?" Nikki suggested shyly. "The boys think there's a resemblance."

"Yes, she's the one. Of course I thought he overstated, since he was so besotted with you. John

34

hadn't exaggerated, though. I thought you were stunning. You still are."

Taken aback at Kay's unexpected high opinion of her, Nikki covered her mouth with her left hand.

Furrowing her brows, Kay gazed at the thin band of whiter skin on Nikki's finger where she had worn her wedding ring. She cast Nikki a questioning gaze, but held her silence.

Your son decided that we're not married anymore, not me.

"Thanks for the compliment." Nikki was grateful she hadn't needed to explain why she'd never wear John's ring again. "I remember that after we drove away from your house I burst into tears. I didn't think you liked me."

"I didn't mean to make you feel that way I was so scared."

"Scared? You? Why?"

"Don't take this the wrong way, but I was afraid of losing my son. I could see it in his eyes and hear it in his voice every time he said your name. I knew he was going to marry you and you lived so far away. He'd move and that would be that. I would never see him again."

"Boston isn't that far from New Jersey. He was already in school here."

"You wanted honest. You didn't say it had to be rational," Kay joked.

"And that is exactly what happened isn't it? John and I got married and the boys came and we never seemed to have enough time for anything other than our boys and our jobs. The occasional holiday spent with you and Dad and my parents."

Squinting at the sky, Nikki confided, "I loved John every minute of our life together." Her voice caught.

Tears brimmed in Kay's hazel eyes. "And I loved him every minute since he took his first breath," she said with quiet conviction.

Kay's shoulders trembled as silent tears overflowed. She displayed monumental restraint in not vocalizing her heartache.

Nikki's throat clogged as she identified with Kay's brand of grief. The mountainous dread of losing a child—like her Jack—gave her chills. "How will I be able to go on? How can I handle Jack's illness alone?" Nikki said.

"You're not alone, honey. Your parents and Dad and I are here for you. We will help in any way we can. It's going to be all right." She grasped Nikki's cold hand.

"Do you really believe that, Mom?"

"They say God never gives us anything we can't handle."

"Who are *they*?" Nikki asked.

"People like us, I guess. People who need help dealing with things they never imagined happening in life."

Rocky charged up to the stoop. "Mommy, can I have something to eat?"

"I made some brownies…" Kay hesitated. "Gees, I didn't think about Jack…"

Blood trickled from a cut on Rocky's knee. "Sweetheart, what did you do to your leg?" Nikki dug a tissue out of her purse, spit on it, and then leaned toward him to swab the cut.

Rocky reached down and smeared the blood

around his kneecap. "It's nuthin', Ma. Can I have one of Grandma's brownies?"

"May I have a brownie, *please*?" Nikki corrected.

"Well, sure. You can have one, too, if Grandma says yes."

Nikki and Kay burst out laughing. *Life will go on, and we'll face whatever God has in store for us together. It will be all right.*

Nikki peered at a white, puffy cloud floating overhead. *From my mouth to God's ears.*

Chapter 6

A week later, Nikki's in-laws had settled into an open-ended stay. It was a pleasant surprise that she increasingly welcomed their presence in her home. Kay had every household surface gleaming, and Nikki hadn't cooked a meal or visited the grocery store since John's funeral.

"How about I take charge of your to-do list, Nikki?" Mickey offered at dinner that night.

He picked up a chicken leg and bit off a chunk of meat. Gulping down the mouthful he continued, "You know, fix a squeaky hinge or maybe take on a painting project? Anything to be helpful. A man can't mow the lawn every day."

Dabbing his mouth with a paper napkin, he gazed at her expectantly.

"It's so nice of you to offer, but I can't think of anything that needs doing around the house."

"Can I go outside and catch fireflies, Mommy?" Jack asked putting down his fork.

"Me, too?" Rocky added.

"Sure," Nikki said. "Take your plates over to the counter by the sink, please?"

"I'm going to lie down for a while. Is that okay, Nikki?" Kay covered her mouth stifling a yawn.

"Of course. Thank you for making dinner. It was delicious."

Kay left the kitchen, and Nikki turned her attention back to her father-in-law, chagrined at his crestfallen expression. "I'm sorry, Dad. Did I insult you?"

"No, no, sweetheart. I guess that's how on top of things John was, right?"

She beamed him a smile. "He really enjoyed taking care of the house. And he was teaching the boys a lot, too."

"Passing it on, just like I did with him. I've always been so proud of the way John took care of his house." He widened his eyes and said, "No offense, Nikki, of course it's your house, too. But John worked so hard to keep things up that I always saw him in how nice everything looks. I still do. Like he's with us here."

He bowed his head. Taking the napkin off his lap, he crumpled it into a ball in one hand. "How about I take the boys on an outing? Maybe a Sox game and all the hot dogs they can eat?"

"Of course if the boys want to go, but no hot dogs, please. Jack's special diet?" she reminded him.

"Sure, sure." He tossed the napkin on the table. "I'd give anything if Jack didn't have a special diet. I'd sell my soul to fix him."

Nikki rose and started clearing the table. "I know. Me, too."

The kids loved their grandparents, and Mickey was their favorite. He fixed things; that's what grandpas did in his opinion. She couldn't count how many toys Rocky had broken that had needed patching. Jack was a different story. He took care of his things.

My smart, gentle boy. Convinced he's going to change the world.

One of John's friends sent Nikki a sympathy card

that read, "Each life is a miracle that changes the world and leaves it a better place than it was before."

She prayed that Jack would grow up to be a man who did world-changing things. And that somehow his grandpa could miraculously fix what was broken.

"You know what you could do, starting tomorrow? It would be great if you'd drive the boys to the GSC in the morning and pick them up at five? I could add some overtime at the college," she suggested.

"No problem," he agreed. "You don't think they'd be up for a baseball game tomorrow if I can get tickets?"

"Probably not. They love the summer camp at the Good Sports Club. And Rocky told me that he sees Ram Delaney there every day."

"Wow, Delaney?" The reverence in his voice echoed the same hero worship that Nikki detected when the boys mentioned Ram's name. "I guess he's a major attraction since the Dragons dropped him after he messed up his arm."

"Right. But even if Ram Delaney weren't there, I think I'd still like the boys to go to camp every day just like they did…before everything changed."

"You know, I offered to replace John's old truck many times." Mickey bowed his head. "He was too independent to accept. I was proud of him."

"Yes, I know," Nikki said softly.

"Pride can do you in." He lent her a hand clearing the table.

****

The following evening Mickey rushed through dinner and then gave a head nod to Kay.

Mysteriously, she rose from the table and

requested, "Jack, Rocky, can I help you catch fireflies tonight?"

She hustled over to the sideboard and picked up a Target bag. "I bought you each a firefly house to keep them in."

"Cool!" came the collective reaction as Grandma tailed the boys out the back screen door.

"Nikki, Mom has taken the boys outside so I can talk to you privately. Something happened at the Good Sports Club today that you need to know about." Mickey hurried through the preamble.

His apparent urgency spiked equal parts curiosity and concern.

"I was parked out in front of the main building when a tall, thin redhead knocked on my window. She asked me if I was John Michael Lambert's grandfather and when I said yes, she asked me to come inside because she wanted to talk to me about John Michael's program there.

"As I followed her to her office she told me her name is Luci Baldwin and she's Ram Delaney's assistant. I got the feeling that she had bad news for me and I was right."

"What?" Nikki's pulse spiked. "Jack didn't say anything."

"He doesn't know anything about it...yet," Mickey said. "When we got to her office she opened a file flat on her desk and then told me that the flag football coach there has filled out a bunch of 'incident reports' documenting Jack's spontaneous tripping, complaints of headaches, and such. She said the coach has made two recommendations.

"One, Jack should see a doctor. And two, you have

to keep Jack home until medical treatment corrects the problems he has experienced. Of course I told her he was already in a doctor's care."

Heaving a breath, Mickey gazed at her.

"I don't understand. I have no choice in this?"

"I asked her if she was just making friendly recommendations or if they were prohibiting Jack from participating in the GSC programs."

"Okay, what did she say to that?"

"She said that they think it best that John Michael shouldn't attend sessions there until his medical problems are resolved for his and the other children's safety."

"Oh, God, Dad. Jack will be crushed. How did you leave things with her?"

"Well first I told her that the boys' super hero just went down a bunch of notches in my opinion. And I told her that I disagreed with Ramsey Delaney's decision concerning Jack, that I would inform you of the conversation and that you'd contact them to give them your decision about whether or not you want to follow their recommendations."

Nikki hung her head in her hands. "There's very little chance Jack's physical condition will ever improve," she lamented.

"I felt like she had hit me with a battering ram. Ram son of a bitch Delaney," Mickey spat out. "His good guy image is a load of bullshit. How could this happen to a wonderful kid like Jack?"

"I don't know, Dad…"

The screech of the screen door hinges interrupted the conversation.

Jack ambled inside, a pinched expression on his

face.

"Hi kiddo," Mickey greeted him.

"Did you catch a lot of bugs?" Nikki sang out, her false cheer oily in her mouth. "Doing okay?"

"Not so good," he said.

Rising from her seat, she noted Jack's labored gait. Her heart wrenched as if Ram Delaney himself had grabbed it with his big paw and squeezed.

Jack stopped in front of her, arched his neck and gazed up at her, his huge blue eyes dominating his pale face. "I don't feel good. I don't want to be sick."

Flinging her arms around him, she clasped Jack to her chest. "I don't want you to be sick either. Maybe a hug will make you feel better."

As she kissed the crown of his head Jack's soft hair tickled her face. He smelled like little boy sweat and shampoo. She wondered how many times her heart could break before it shattered completely.

She hugged him gently, careful not to hurt him.

So thin.

His ribs dug into her forearms.

Chapter 7

The elm tree in the corner of the sun-drenched, grassy quad provided Nikki a patch of shade. She rested her back against the trunk, the jagged bark scratchy through her blouse's thin material. Nibbling on a sandwich she observed the late summer activity on campus.

Students lolled on the grass. A symphony of chatter and laughter filled the air. Summer classes had ended and the new semester would begin in a couple weeks. Every school year marked a new beginning. Confused freshmen and confident seniors would descend in droves on the admissions office where Nikki worked.

She had never aspired to a career other than full-time motherhood, but in the declining economy no one had money to spare for home renovations, and new construction seemed permanently stalled. Only broken pipes and emergency repairs had provided John sporadic work.

A year ago he had suggested that Nikki should look for a paying job. Her passion for the dream job of raising her sons and making their home a haven made her unreceptive to the proposition at first. Begrudgingly she had agreed, though, since she hadn't expected John to shoulder the family's financial burdens alone.

An ad for a part-time opening at John's alma mater, Highland University, appealed to her. However, with a ten-year gap in her employment history, she had doubted her chances of securing the position. The offer she had received at the interview surprised her. Even more surprising—after the first month on the job in Highland U's registrar's office, she had discovered that she loved the work.

Who knew how important the ten hours per week job would become? That morning she had asked her boss, Elizabeth, to consider scheduling her to work a forty-hour week. Not only would the extra money help enormously, but also, the full-time status would provide family medical benefits that she now viewed as priceless.

Silver-green leaves fluttered in the welcome breeze. Before long the leaves would change color, flutter down, shrivel, and die. Nikki normally relished the crisp air, apple picking, and football season during the fall months. Autumn used to rank as her favorite time of year. Not this year. She wanted time to stop and rewind—to restore her life to early summer. She couldn't bear thinking about shriveling and death.

Her stomach lurched at the vibration of her cell phone in her pocket, always on edge that ringing phones and doorbells would bring fresh new catastrophe. She grabbed the phone and read the caller ID, calming at the familiar number displayed.

"Hi, Momma," she answered.

"Hi, sweetie. Just got your message. Can you talk? Are you still on break?"

She checked her watch. "About ten minutes into lunch hour. How's Daddy?"

"He's improving every day. He's still in therapy."

"I miss him. Tell him I'll call back tonight."

"He'd like that. He misses you, too. How are you doing?"

"Hanging in there. I talked with my boss this morning about working full time."

"What did she say?"

"She's checking with the big boss but, thank God, she thinks that he'll approve. Enrollment for this coming semester is up fifteen percent. We'll be swamped during the next few weeks as the kids start arriving."

"Can you handle the extra hours?" Her voice quivered, which Nikki interpreted as her mother's lack of confidence in her.

"Do I have a choice?' she barked.

A whoosh sounded in her ear at her mom's sharp intake of breath.

Her conscience stung. "Sorry, you didn't deserve that. After last night, I guess I'm on my last nerve."

"What happened last night?"

"John's dad waited until after dinner to tell me. When he went to pick up the boys at the GSC yesterday the secretary advised him that they would like me to keep Jack home from now on."

"They're expelling him? Can they even do that? What happened? What did he do?"

"He's had headaches, and he fell a few times."

"So they won't let him continue there? You're kidding me."

"I wish I were. Jack loves that place. I want his life to be normal for as long as possible. Plus, I need both boys to go to the after school program when school starts. John's parents won't be here to help out forever. What am I going to do, Momma?"

"Well, honey…" She paused. "The way I see this situation is, you can handle it one of two ways. You can be a passive victim who thinks, why me? Why my boy?" she continued. "*Or* you can be the mama bear who says, 'No *fucking* way will I permit you to treat my baby like this.' "

Nikki burst out laughing. "You just said, 'fuck,' " she gasped. "I can't believe my ears. You've never, *ever* cursed in front of me before."

"I guess not." She huffed a laugh. "And you know what? It felt great. Very satisfying."

Nikki and her mom giggled together—exactly the remedy that lifted her victim fog.

"I won't let anyone force Jack out of that program. I'm going over there right now. Thank you for the kick in the ass. I'll call you tonight to let you know how it goes. And Momma?"

"Yes, honey?"

"You are *the best*. I love you."

"I love you too, Nikki."

Scooping up her purse she crossed her ankles and powered up from a lotus to a standing position. She swept her hand across her backside dusting the seat of her slacks and then stomped to the car before she lost her nerve. She hated confrontations—especially with teachers or authority figures. But she hated Jack's tenuous status at the GSC more.

The scalding vinyl upholstery in her car's interior burned the skin behind her knees through the fabric of her slacks. Sweat beaded her forehead. Opening all the windows, she blasted the air conditioning and turned on the radio. A catchy song played as she steered out of the parking lot. She tapped her thumbs against the steering wheel in time with the music feeling energized by the lively beat.

Her determination to defend Jack's right to a normal life made her feel like she was in charge of her life again. But her confidence was fleeting. She pulled into the GSC parking lot before the song finished, switched off the engine and froze.

She had to overcome her shyness for Jack's sake. Before the onset of his illness, she had fashioned a happy life for her sons and they had thrived. Astonishing, but post-diagnosis, Jack still thrived. If he could view his life as normal, she sure as hell could. *No fucking way, right, Momma?*

Bolting out of the car, she swung the driver's door shut and plowed through the front entry of the Good Sports Club. Children's high-pitched shouts and laughter reverberated within the slate gray walls. Filled with purpose, she hurried toward the main office.

No one occupied the reception desk. The chair was pushed back and a cup of coffee balanced precariously on a pile of folders next to a glass jar filled with red lollipops. Nikki perched on the brown tweed chair in front of the desk, prepared to camp out until the woman to blame for Jack's exile appeared.

The door behind the desk was ajar. A phone rang. "Ram Delaney," a deep bass voice rumbled.

Nikki's breath caught. *The* Ramsey Delaney.

"Luce?" he hollered. "Luce, are you there?"

Before she could advise him that "Luce" apparently was absent, he stood in the doorway, the perfect definition of larger than life. Her heart raced. In person, Ram Delaney made a ridiculously intimidating impression.

"You're not Luce," he said, with a straight face, no less.

The idiotic statement helped banish any prior awe she might have held for his celebrity status. "Uh no," she said, her tone sarcastic.

"Do you know where she is?"

"No again," she said, amazed that he apparently didn't give a damn about her identity or why she sat in his outer office.

"Okay, well...great talking with you." He chuckled, dimples creasing his cheeks, and then he turned his back on her.

Sauntering into his office he leaned over his desk and picked up the phone. "Sorry, Brad. Luce is out of the office, and I don't dare touch anything on her desk while she's gone."

His laughter boomed. "My momma didn't raise a crazy boy. I'll have Luce call you when she gets back. Talk to you later."

He placed the phone back in its cradle and skirted the desk. Heaving that huge body into a king-sized executive chair, he then focused on paperwork on his desk. And ignored Nikki.

She gaped at him. Her boys worshiped this man. He inspired their loftiest ambitions. Rocky had dressed as Ram Delaney every Halloween since he was three. John and the boys spent Sundays during football season on the couch watching his every move. She wondered how John would react to the cold fact that his sports idol deprived his gravely ill son of the one activity that meant the most to him.

Anger bubbled up inside. She jumped up and pushed the door fully open with a bang.

"How could you treat Jack this way?" she blurted out.

"Whoa." Ram held his hands out in front of him. "What do you mean?"

He rose from his seat to his full six foot five inches, one of the many statistics that was common knowledge in Nikki's household.

His aggressive stance, his remarkable muscularity intimidated her again. He was ten times more handsome in the flesh than on TV or the covers of magazines.

Focus Nikki. "How can you throw my son out of your club? You have no idea how important this program is to him, and to me. I don't know what I am going to do once school starts."

Her unfettered irritation blurred his hulking image in front of her. "Where will he go once my in-laws return home? I have to work full time now," she ranted. "Do you want to be responsible for leaving him alone in the house for hours? It's unthinkable. I *can't* leave him alone."

His brow furrowed, a perplexed expression that appeared legitimate enough, as he rounded the desk in one swift movement. Huge hands cupped her trembling shoulders. "Please sit down."

He steered her backward a few steps before she jerked her shoulders and shrugged his hands away. "I don't want to sit down. I want you to reverse your decision."

Frustrated and agitated, tears welled.

"I'm sorry, miss. I don't know what you're talking about. Who are you? Who is your son?" He grimaced and then mumbled, "Where the hell is Luce?"

She balled her hands on her hips. "Do you throw so

many children out of here that you can't keep track of them?"

"Calm down," he commanded. "I have *never* turned away a child in the history of this sports club. There has to be some misunderstanding."

"Don't tell me to calm down. You're a fraud," she accused. "Posing for the paparazzi in front of this place—a *safe* place, and I quote you. The *great* Ramsey Delaney. Helping one child at a time…"

Her legs turned to Jell-O, and she sank onto the chair in front of his desk fuming and exhausted.

"Please…" He crouched in front of the chair. "Give me your name, and I will get to the bottom of this."

His concerned expression, the kindness in his eyes encouraged her. "Nikki Lambert. My sons have been club members for years. John Michael and Peter Rockland Lambert. Jack and Rocky. Five years for Jack and two years for Rocky. Ring a bell?"

The blank look on his face said it all. Her aggression dissolved, replaced by numb acceptance. He didn't know the boys, and he apparently was just a figurehead at the GSC. *He probably doesn't give a shit about any of these kids.*

"Yesterday my father-in-law came to pick up the boys. He was told that we had to keep Jack home because he's had headaches and his coordination is off," she stated flatly.

"Who said this?"

She glared into his blue eyes, their faces inches apart. "Your secretary. Dad was pretty shook up. He mentioned a report from a flag football coach."

Her head spun rehashing the depressing facts.

"Give me a minute to get to the bottom of this. I

never approved this action."

He unfolded upward from the squatting position, stomped through the door and shoved folders around on the reception desk.

"I thought your momma didn't raise a crazy boy." She smiled despite her hollow spirit.

Thumbing through a stack of folders, he selected one midway through the stack.

"John Michael Lambert," he read out loud as he walked to his desk and took a seat in the over-sized leather chair.

His eyes scanned the paperwork. "Yeah, okay. I remember Luce mentioning this to me. John Michael asked Coach Harriman to take him off the flag football team. Harriman is a good man. I trust him. He recommends medical treatment."

He glanced at her rounding his eyes. "There's a notation in the file that John Michael's dad passed away recently.

"I'm very sorry for your loss, Mrs. Lambert."

"Thank you."

"Could this be the reason your son is having problems?"

"No." She lowered her eyes determined to contain her emotions. "My son is very sick. A doctor has evaluated him. Headaches and lack of coordination are all symptoms of his condition."

"What condition?"

"My son has ALD." Her throat constricted. Revealing Jack's illness would confirm the decision to remove him from the sports club rather than reverse it.

"ALD? I have never heard of it. Is it contagious?"

"No." She glimpsed at the clock on his desk. "I

really need to go. I have to get back to work. I'll make other after school arrangements for Jack."

"That won't be necessary. I never approved removing Jack from the club. He can stay in the program as long as you like. When he feels better he can start playing on the team again."

"Thank you, Mr. Delaney." She wouldn't admit that Jack would never play on the team again.

"Call me Ram."

"I'm sorry to take up so much of your time, Ram." She extended her hand. "I apologize for my...unflattering remarks earlier. I appreciate your allowing my son to come here. It means the world to him. And to me."

Ram clasped her hand and squeezed it gently. "Sorry for the confusion, Mrs. Lambert."

"Please call me Nikki."

"Nikki." He continued holding her hand, exuding kindness. "If you need anything just call me."

"Thank you for the offer." She withdrew her hand from his, her cheeks flaming. He had behaved graciously even though she had verbally assaulted him. "Again, I apologize for calling you a fraud."

His hearty laughter caught her off guard. "I've been called much worse," he quipped.

Chapter 8

The little spitfire dissolved in tears. Her shoulders slumped, she bowed her head, and anguish poured out of Nikki like a gusher. At a loss for what to do with the hysterical woman in front of him, Ram tentatively wrapped his arms around her as he would if one of the children in the camp needed a hug. She quaked in his embrace sending tremors across his chest. A delicate floral scent enveloped her, unlike the dirty puppy smell of the sweaty children that he hugged every day.

"Shush," he whispered.

Incapable of expressing anything more meaningful, he added, "Okay now, okay."

Random thoughts flew through his mind during the brief moments that he held Nikki close to his heart. *How do I help this beautiful woman? Have I met her sons? What the hell is ALD anyway? How do I make her stop crying? Why do I want to hold on and never let her go? Why the hell is it so hot in here?*

His temperature spiked along with his pulse. Whether a complete asshole or not for this sudden attraction to a grieving widow, he relished holding her and lightly stroking his hand along her upper back.

Gradually Nikki stopped shaking. She sniffled as Ram reluctantly loosened the embrace.

Huge brown eyes glistening, she stepped back a few steps wagging her head.

"I'm so sorry," she uttered. She bit the corner of her lip.

He reached behind him, plucked a box of Kleenex off his desk and held it out to her.

She tugged a tissue from the box, swabbed her face and dabbed it under her nose.

"I've made a complete fool of myself. I'm so embarrassed."

Clasping her free hand, he gazed into her eyes. "You have nothing to be embarrassed about. I'm sorry for allowing this organization to cause you so much grief. I swear, it will never happen again."

"Thank you for being so kind," she said as she wadded the Kleenex in a ball and stuffed it her pocket.

"I have a bag of M & M's in my drawer if you want some. Usually makes the kids feel better," he offered with a smile.

She grinned and said, "No, thanks."

Her radiant smile transformed her features and lit up his world.

"I better get going. My lunch break is long over." Nikki turned around and left Ram's office, while his thoughts spun in the vain attempt to devise a reason that might persuade her to stay a while longer.

Halting near Luci's desk she faced him as if reading his mind. Beaming she tossed out, "By the way. I ignored your assistant's request. I didn't keep Jack home today."

Her quirky smile caused him to belly laugh. *Damn, he liked a woman with sass.*

Nikki had instantly melted his heart, and he strongly suspected that nothing in his life would ever be the same. For the first time since his injury, he stopped feeling sorry for himself. Powerless to reverse the professional status that Coach Beltzer, the bastard, had foisted on him, he had a hard time avoiding self-pity. Frustrated to the max, he had experienced an identity crisis. Football was Ram Delaney and vice versa. His love of the sport and his personal pursuit of excellence in leading the Dragons had precluded just about everything else in his life. He had never considered that a sacrifice.

His stats as quarterback and win scorecard had established a stellar professional career. Until that summer, he had lived a charmed existence. No door was closed to Ram Delaney, and he hadn't waited in line for anything since his first Dragons game. Women threw room keys and underwear at him. They camped out in front of his hotel rooms and literally slept on the floor. Paparazzi stalked him, and if he had slept with even a quarter of the women the rags claimed he had, he wouldn't have occupied a bed alone the past ten years.

In fact, he had slept alone the vast majority of the time, heeding his father's advice to respect women, conduct himself as a gentleman, and never permit lust to dominate his better judgment.

Pop's exact words were, "Keep your fly zipped. Sex and lovemaking aren't the same things. Both can get you in trouble. But lovemaking is the good kind of trouble."

Taking his dad's advice at face value, Nikki represented the most "good kind of trouble" Ram had ever entertained.

Women had flitted through his life, and he could hardly remember their names, much less what clothes they wore. He closed his eyes and Nikki appeared.

She wore pressed, light weight black slacks; a sleeveless, white blouse; black ballerina flats; a pendant of two hearts with different colored stones on a yellow gold chain; a watch with a thin gold band on her left wrist; and tiny diamond studs set in yellow gold in her pierced ears. Her perfume smelled like gardenias and the skin on her arms was silken, milky white. Her short cap of brown-black hair framed a heart-shaped face dominated by dark brown eyes with amber gold irises.

Ram remained standing in front of his desk after she left his office, flummoxed by the unprecedented depth of feelings for a woman he knew next to nothing about.

"What's wrong?" came Luci's query.

Ram opened his eyes in response. "Come here a minute, Luce. I have a bone to pick with you, lady."

Knitting her brows, she approached him. "What did I do?"

"Why did you expel John Michael Lambert from here without consulting me?"

She leveled a steely gaze at him and asserted, "Wait a minute. I didn't *expel* him, Ram. I advised his grandfather that Coach recommends that the kid should see a doctor and take a break from physical activity until a doctor clears him, that's all."

"You should have checked with me first. I reversed that decision ten minutes ago after meeting with John Michael's mother."

"All right…" Luci frowned. "Can I ask why?"

"Sure." He handed her John Michael's file. "His mom told me that he's already under a doctor's care, and I see no reason why he can't participate here any way he wants. I'll advise Harriman of my decision in a few minutes."

"Whatever you say." She peered at him over her bifocals. "Are you mad at me?"

"Nope."

"Okay. Good." Glancing at the file folder, she asked, "What do you want me to do with this?"

"You can file it for now," he said in a light tone. "I want to do some research on what's going on with him. I'll let you know what I find out."

Luci nodded, pivoted and returned to her desk as Ram sat down and hit the return button on his computer keyboard. The screen flickered and illuminated. He clicked the Safari button and typed ALD on the Google search line. Wikipedia was the first stop. What he read about this rare disease stole his breath. His eyes glued to the computer screen, Ram scrolled, clicked and read more heart-breaking memorials until he couldn't bear absorbing another narrative about the loss of innocent life.

The Stop ALD Foundation website detailed a late 2009 study published in *Science Magazine* with some success in halting the disease through pioneering gene therapy. Conducted in France using stem cells from afflicted boys' own bone marrow, the therapy arrested further brain damage in the patients. Ram scribbled notes on a legal pad and continued searching for more information after sending some money to this foundation.

The only other organization he discovered during his Internet search was the ALD Foundation. At that website he clicked on the bio for the CEO.

"David Cry is the founder and Chief Executive

Officer of the Adrenoleukodystrophy (ALD) Foundation. David's approach toward building coalitions with committed medical professionals interested in finding solutions in the ALD community, led to the formation of the Adrenoleukodystrophy Foundation. The aim of the ALD Foundation is to assist families, raise global awareness, educate physicians, and ultimately, the eradication of ALD."

"Gene therapy seems hopeful," he said.

"Did you call me?" Luce hollered.

"No sorry, just talking out loud." He skimmed narrative on the Foundation's website. "Luce, can you do me a favor, please?"

"Sure." She left her seat and paused in the doorway, her shoulder against the doorjamb.

"I'd like to phone a man named David Cry who heads an organization called the ALD Foundation."

"All right. But why?"

"John Michael Lambert has this disease—ALD. His mother told me when she came in today."

Her brows furrowed, her face pale under the fluorescent light. "Is it serious?"

"Devastating."

"Oh no," Luce groaned.

Ram stood, rounded the desk and walked toward her. He patted the side of her arm. "I'm going out to the field for a while. Can you call my cell when you find David Cry's number, please?"

"I'll get right on it." She returned to her desk and focused on her computer.

Striding down the hall, he yanked open one of the double doors leading outside and squinted in the direction of the flag football field. Harriman stood on the sidelines galloping sideways, parallel to the action on the field. Several kids lazed on the grass near the bleachers, so he jogged toward them hoping to find Nikki's son among the group.

"Hey, guys," Ram greeted the three boys and two girls when he reached their position near the sidelines.

"Wow! Hi Mister Delaney," one kid with dark hair, possibly like Nikki's, piped up.

"Hi there," Ram said extending his hand.

The boy pumped his hand, wide-eyed and open-mouthed.

Ram grinned. "What's your name, son?"

"Jack Lambert, Mister Delaney."

"I'm pleased to meet you, Jack." He released Jack's hand. "But from now on, call me Ram. Deal?"

"You bet," he said.

Plopping down on the grass next to him, Ram watched the flag football game. Harriman's whistle blew shrilly and he waved in the other kids on the sidelines, except for Jack, as the four "men" they replaced shuffled off the field.

"Not playing today?" He threw out the needless question, interested in how Jack would explain his illness.

"Nah," he said. "I feel funny. I caught ALD and it makes me sick. I like sitting here, though," he said as he glanced at Ram.

The innocence in his clear blue eyes pierced Ram's heart like a lance. He scrutinized Jack's face, mystified by what appeared to be his glowing health. How could the relentless disease that he'd just read about apply to this little boy?

"You like football?" Ram asked as the play

resumed on the field.

"Love it." He pointed a finger at a little bruiser, elbowing past an O-lineman. In the clear, the kid hollered, "Over here!" in a raspy voice.

The ball sailed straight into the kid's hands at his midriff. He tucked the ball and barreled into the end zone as Jack cheered, "Touchdown!"

The kid in the end zone stared straight at the sidelines and hollered, "Did you see me, Jack?"

"I did, Rocky! Good job!" Jack hollered back.

"That's my brother," Jack explained with a cockeyed grin, that Ram read as pure pride. "He's seven."

"A fine run," the quarterback complimented Rocky. "You like to be called Jack instead of John?"

"Uh huh. Dad calls me…" His head dipped and then he trained somber eyes on Ram. "…um, called me Jack. I taught Rocky about strategy and how to read the defense."

Ram widened his eyes, legitimately impressed. "Seems like you did a great job."

Jack nodded nonchalantly. "He can read the offense, too. He goes both ways."

"Well, he's one hell… Uh, he's one fine ballplayer. Looks like we have a future NFL'er right here at the GSC," Ram joked as he tousled Jack's black hair.

Soft…I'll bet just like his mother's.

"Wouldn't that be *something*," Jack said, an awed expression on his little face.

Ram's cell phone vibrated in his pocket and the Dragons theme song sounded. "Excuse me a minute," he said as he rose from the grass. "I'll be back after I take this call."

"Hey, Luce," he answered while striding toward the building.

"I have David Cry on the line, Ram."

"Thanks. Put him through." He leaned against the brick facade waiting for the call to connect. A click sounded in his ear and he said, "Mr. Cry?"

"This is."

"Hello. I'm Ram Delaney."

David Cry chuckled. "Then it isn't a prank. I thought someone was punking me. Ram, I'm a huge fan. What can I do for you?"

"Mr. Cry…"

"Call me David, please."

"Thanks. David, I run a children's club in Highland Square, Massachusetts—usually during the off-season. I've become more involved since I have extra time on my hands lately."

"Beltzer is an idiot. The team needs you. How's the arm?"

Ram grimaced, all too aware that the public knew that his off-season had been indefinitely extended. "It's fine." Not wanting to talk about himself, Ram pushed on.

"David, the reason I'm calling is one of the boys in my club has been diagnosed with ALD, and I'd like…"

What is my goal here? "I'd like to help him and his family. Can you spare some time to meet with me?"

"Of *course.* But I don't travel that often and I'm not planning a trip to your area."

"If it's convenient, I could come to you."

"I'm in Slidell, Louisiana."

"No problem. Would next Tuesday be convenient? I'll buy lunch."

"See you then. Oh, hey. Can my son drop by my office to meet you before we go out to eat? He's been diagnosed with ALD…" His voice wavered.

After the research Ram had done earlier he knew the diagnosis was likely a death sentence. Sympathy mushroomed in his chest.

"Meeting you would mean a great deal to him," David continued.

"Is he a Dragons fan?"

"He sure is."

"I'll bring him some team gear."

"Wow, he would love that. Thanks, Ram."

"My pleasure." Heartsick, he disconnected the call and jogged back over to Jack.

Seated next to him on the ground again, Ram tossed out, "You know I've been thinking. You'd make a fine coach. What do you say I talk with Coach Harriman about your becoming his assistant? Maybe you can help me in the office, too."

Jack beamed. "I'd like that a lot."

"Do you want to play football or, maybe coach, when you grow up?"

His blue eyes held Ram's. "I'm not going to grow up."

Ram exerted every ounce of will not to tear up as a silent sob rose up from his core. Speechless, he sat there next to Jack and watched the game until the final whistle blew and the noisy mob stampeded toward the gym. Rising he held a hand down to Jack and hauled him upright, light as a feather.

Today had started out like any other. Ram hadn't a clue that within one brief hour he would fall in love with a woman and two little boys at first sight.

Chapter 9

Jack

"Don't forget to brush your teeth," Mommy called from the kitchen.

Rocky turned off the TV, pitched the remote controller on the couch and zoomed over to the bottom of the stairs. "Come on, Jack, hurry up. I'll race ya."

He took off from the landing like a rocket ship.

We ran up the stairs. Well, Rocky ran, and I limped along behind him. Some days my legs were strong, and some days not. Today was a *not* day. I missed the strong days.

"Hurry up, slowpoke," Rocky yelled when he made it halfway upstairs, not winded at all.

I don't know what made him stop and turn around, but he stared down at me with his hands on his hips. "Good job, Lambert. Keep going strong," he said, sounding exactly like Coach Harriman. He clapped his hands twice, just like the Coach.

I laughed so hard that I had to stop and hang on to the banister to catch my breath.

"Move it. Move it. If you want to run like a girl, then go join the softball team, Lambert." Rocky whirled around and easily finished climbing up the stairs to beat me to the bathroom.

I shuffled into my room out of breath, my legs

shaky, and I slumped over onto the edge of the bed. Last summer Rocky never beat me in a race. I couldn't win anymore even if there was some big prize, like a million dollars.

"Your turn!" Rocky yelled and then he crashed into his room and slammed the door.

Mommy sent him back to the bathroom to *really* brush his teeth and wash his face. Some nights she sent him back three times. Usually on those nights, she wound up in the bathroom with him, sitting on the toilet seat, watching him do a good job. Still, Rocky never quit trying to get out of washing up.

"Rocky. Don't slam the door," Mommy called down the hall and then she stopped in front of my door.

She looked pretty in her PJ's and bunny slippers. Hands down, I had the prettiest mom of all the kids at school.

"How many times will I send him back tonight?" She laughed, even though I bet most moms would be mad at a kid who doesn't follow the rules. It's hard to be mad at Rocky.

Her smile disappeared. "You okay, honey?"

"I'm good, Mommy."

"Go wash up and brush your teeth. I'll be right in after I say good night to your brother."

After I got ready for bed, I went back to my room, crawled under the covers and waited for Mommy. I could hear her and Rocky's voice, but not their words. She laughed at something he said.

Then his door closed softly and she came down the hall, her slippers shush-shush on the floor. The sounds of Mommy coming to kiss me goodnight made me happy. And sad, too.

"Scoot over, sweetie." She squished next to me on the bed.

The sheet and blanket hurt my legs. My eyes felt funny. Like somebody strong stretched my eyelids down like window shades.

"You can say your prayers from your bed tonight." Her cool hand brushed the hair off my forehead. Her sad smile brought tears to my eyes, and I tried to blink them away before she saw them.

"I can kneel, Mommy." I threw the covers off my legs.

"Not tonight, honey. I'm tired and this bed feels so comfortable. Let's just snuggle here and pray together." Gently she covered my legs again and tucked me in. She listened as I said my prayers.

When I finished, she said what Daddy used to say every single night before he died. "Name the best thing and the worst thing that happened to you today." Her voice shook.

I knew why. I missed Daddy all the time, too, especially at bedtime when I told him my best and worst thing. Or when I remembered other special times. Like when we built things in the Man Room. Or when he played ball with Rocky and me after supper. Or that time he built us skateboards, and the birdhouse, and the coolest go-cart ever. Or when he listened to the ideas I wrote in my notebook…and said, "How can I help with that?"

"There were so many good things today," I told Mommy, hoping that Daddy could hear me from heaven.

She smiled and kissed the top of my head. "I'd love to hear them all, but you know Daddy's rules. One of each only."

Daddy always wanted us to tell him the bad first. "Get it out of the way," he said. "You want to remember the good that happened to you during the day right before you go to sleep. That way you will only have good dreams."

"I fell into my locker in school today. I don't know what happened. One minute I was hanging up my coat and the next minute my face was smashed on the back of the locker and my knees were on top of my sneakers in the bottom. Frankie O'Neal laughed at me as I crawled out, and then everyone else laughed at me, too. I dropped my books. Oops, sorry. That was two bad things. But the good thing is just the *best*. Mister Delaney came to Rocky's game and he sat right next to me and everything. He even asked me how I was feeling. Like he really cared."

"I don't think he would ask how you felt if he didn't care, honey." She leaned back against the headboard and closed her eyes. Honestly, she looked real pretty.

"I know, but my teachers ask me all the time and then they don't pay attention to my answer, but Ram did."

"Ram?"

"Can you *believe* it? He told me I could call him Ram. Then he said that Rocky is one hell…"

"John Michael! Watch your language."

"I'm just telling you what Ram said."

"Mr. Delaney should know better than to use that language in front of you."

"I'm sure he will let you call him Ram, too, Mommy. Anyway, Ram told me that Rocky was one fine football player."

Mommy tried not to, but she laughed.

"He could go big time, big college and the NFL. Those were his words not mine."

I pulled my notebook out from under the covers and tapped it with my finger. "I showed him my notes with Rocky's stats; you know the number of yards carried, goals and fumble recoveries. Then it happened."

"What happened?" Mom wrinkled her forehead.

"It's not a bad thing. It's the good thing that happened to me today. Ram asked me if I wanted to help him out sometimes in his office. He likes to keep stats, too and he wants my help."

"Wow. What an honor. Are you sure you're up to the extra work?"

"It won't be work. I can't believe Ram picked me. I wish Daddy was here to meet him. He would really like him. Ram doesn't act like a superstar. He's so normal."

"He's a man just like your dad or grandpa."

"Maybe when Poppy comes back he can get to meet him."

Grandma had promised us they would be back soon after they tied up a few loose ends. I couldn't figure out what ends could take so long to tie. Even Rocky could tie his shoe in a couple of seconds.

"I bet Poppy would love that. Now time for bed." Mom kissed my cheek and straightened the covers. "Want the light on?"

Sometimes my eyes clouded over, and I couldn't see much. It scared me a lot, but I didn't tell anyone. Leaving the light on helped. Mommy always knew how to help me.

"Yes, please."

"Promise you'll go straight to sleep?"

"I will." I had my fingers crossed under the sheet.

She closed the door. When I counted the fourth creak on the very last step before the bottom, I knew the coast was clear. I opened my notebook and took a pencil out of the cup on my bed table. Before I wrote anything down Rocky pushed open the door and climbed into my bed. His warm feet felt good against my legs.

"Want me to sleep with you?" he asked as he took one of my pillows from behind my back and plopped his head down on it.

"I sure do."

Since Daddy died Rocky was afraid of the dark. He never told me. I just knew. He came into my room the night of Daddy's funeral and had come in every night since then. I was pretty sure Mommy knew but she didn't say anything about it. I pretended that I didn't know he was afraid.

That's what big brothers do. I love Rocky.

So many brothers fight, but not Rocky and me. We were best friends. Since my sickness had gotten worse Rocky acted like the older brother. He stood up to the boys when they made fun of me. The least I could do is help him through the dark nights.

"That was way cool Mister Delaney talked to you today."

"I know. And now I get to call him Ram, and he called me Jack."

"Wow! Do you think he will let me call him Ram, too?"

"I'll ask him." I felt very important saying that.

"Thanks."

"You know what he said about you? He said that you were good enough to go big time."

"Well, duh, Jack. We've known that for a long time."

He stretched out on the bed, his arms under his head, and looked up at the ceiling. "I will be Urlacher and you will be Manning. Peyton, not Eli. We'll be like the Palmer brothers playing on the same team. I hope the Dragons draft us, or the Bears. Not Cleveland. Anywhere but Cleveland."

Rocky closed his eyes, and smiled, his dimples like dents in his cheeks. "I can see it, Jack."

"I can see you on the team, Rock. I just don't see me there anymore. But I will be your greatest fan. I won't miss a game. You'll be rich, and you can fly Mom and Poppy to every game. Nana and Grandma, too."

"I miss Poppy and Grandma. Do you Jack?"

I nodded. "Grandma said they had to go back to work."

"I know." Rocky turned onto his side and stared at me. "I miss Daddy even more."

"Yeah, me too," I said. "The four of us were a team, Daddy said."

"We're still a team, Jack. Forever." His voice got louder.

"Shush. Mom will hear," I whispered. "Okay, Rock. Just a different team than we imagined."

Rocky was quiet for a few minutes, so I thought he was asleep. I wrote the first letter down in my notebook, F...

"I hate it," he said all of a sudden, making me jump and squiggle a line on the page.

Erasing the letter and the squiggle I asked, "What, Rock? What do you hate?"

"Your ah-dreeno."

I didn't know what to say. Rocky hadn't acted like he noticed anything different about me. But when I stumbled, he was usually at my side. When I had trouble seeing, he guided me.

"You have to get well, Jack."

"I…It's going to get worse, you know. I've read all about it."

He stared at me, and then he smiled like he knew something I didn't. "No, it's not. You're gonna get better. You can be a superhero. Jack the Whack. You can whack your ALD."

So silly. We laughed, holding our stomachs.

"Boys! To sleep!" Mommy hollered from downstairs.

Rocky wiggled down under the covers and faced the wall away from me. I waited until I heard his even breathing and then I went back to writing in my notebook. I drew a picture of a superhero. A big J and W on his chest with lightning bolts around the letters.

I'm going to color it purple and orange in the morning. The Dragons' colors. Rocky will love it. I have to be "Jack the Whack." I have to try hard.

When I was little I always thought I could change the world. *Maybe.*

On the first line of a new page, I wrote, FILL THE STADIUM FOR ALD. On the second line I wrote, Ram Delaney.

****

71

Chapter 10

Fall

Kay was a godsend. Nikki couldn't believe how much she had grown to love her.

When her in-laws had arrived at the house three weeks before, after the scant break of one week, Nikki had thought she'd explode with frustration. Their car packed to the ceiling with a bungee cord securing the widely gaping overstuffed trunk, Nikki had feared that Kay and Mickey were moving in permanently. She'd have to deal with her mother-in-law's disapproving presence on top of everything else? But Kay continued to surprise Nikki with her patience and unflagging willingness to integrate seamlessly with the new normal in the house.

Mickey had stunned Nikki when he presented the check funded by the mortgage they had taken on their, before John's death, paid-for home. Kay had tsked-tsked away any protests, convincing Nikki that "money is nothing where love is concerned." In the face of their bottomless generosity, she had finally broken down when Dad lifted the motorized chair out of the trunk.

"State of the art," Mickey said as he set the little device down on the driveway.

Festooned with purple and orange bunting and covered with GO DRAGONS stickers, the wheelchair should be appealing to Jack. The cool factor would go far in transforming a handicap into a neat set of wheels.

Nikki had sobbed like an idiot. Kay hadn't flinched. She wrapped her arms around her daughter-in-law and softly asked Mickey to stow the chair in the back shed where Jack couldn't see it, just yet.

"If he ever needs it, you're ready," she said.

If Kay worried about the menacing ALD specter that hovered over the boys, she hid it well. Genetic testing had shown that Rocky's DNA housed the ALD gene, too. The mutation lurked like the big bad wolf, huffing and puffing, the bogie man in Nikki's incessant nightmares. Kay's warm touch soothed her when she cried out in the night, downstairs, gratefully out of earshot of the boys' rooms.

Preferring the couch in the TV room for her couple hours' sleep per night to the bed she and John had shared, Nikki had given her room to Kay and Mickey. She didn't consider sleeping on the couch a sacrifice, and intended to sleep there even after her in-laws left—which they had advised her they intended to do. Nikki detested the marital bed where she had conceived her children. There she had supplied the faulty genetics that had triggered the firing squad of irreversible degeneration in her perfect Jack. The same genetics threatened to devastate Rocky.

She didn't have time to miss John. Nikki resented his everlasting rest in peace while she wandered the first floor during sleepless nights and piloted the course of waking life with the boys without a compass. Certain that the tsunami lay dead ahead, she bobbed like a cork in the water.

That morning Nikki had fixed breakfast for the

boys and kissed them effusively enough to make them squirm before sending them off to school. Then shaky and distracted, she gladly relinquished the wheel to Mickey for the drive to Boston to review Rocky's test results with Dr. Jodi Warner.

The déjà vu that besieged Nikki in Jodi Warner's waiting room intensified her panic as if the cloaked specter of death hovered down the hall in the doctor's office—this time crooking a skeletal finger at Rocky. By the time she entered Jodi's office, Kay and Mickey in tow, her heart drummed in double-time.

Jodi caught sight of Nikki, unsteady in her office doorway, gave a start and raced toward her with outstretched arms.

"Rocky's non-symptomatic. There are no brain lesions," the doctor stated breathlessly.

Nikki gawked at her, light-headed and terrified that she had misheard what she said.

Kay whooped behind Nikki.

"Thank God!" Mickey yelled.

"*Really*?" Nikki stammered. "He's safe? He's not sick? You're sure?"

"Absolutely sure. The tests are conclusive." Jodi grinned as she steered Nikki to a seat.

Her eyes narrowed as she gazed down at her. "You're not sleeping. And you're not eating enough, either."

She automatically denied Jodi's spot-on clinical assessment, "Oh, I'm fine…"

"I'll prescribe something to help you sleep," she interjected. "And you *will* eat three nourishing meals a day starting with lunch on me in the staff dining room now."

"You tell her, doc," Mickey muttered.

"No, no, I'm fine, but thank you," Nikki protested to no avail.

Jodi had already grabbed her purse and then she tugged Nikki's hand with impressive oomph to launch her out of the chair.

Docile, Nikki let her lead, trailed by the pair of delighted in-laws through the hospital corridors. *Rocky is fine, Rocky is fine...* Her emotional roller coaster ascended to elation.

Over lunch, which Nikki devoured ravenously, Mickey proposed, "We have to celebrate and take the boys out to dinner. Rocky may seem calm about the scans and tests, but he's no dope. I'm sure he realizes he might be sick like Jack. That's scary. And a party might help put his fears to rest. What do you say, Nikki?"

She desperately wanted a genuine reason for a celebration. Rocky deserved it. *But how might Jack feel?* "I don't know. Do you think Jack would...resent it? If we made a fuss over Rocky?"

"Are you kidding?" Mickey wolfed down a bite of his cheeseburger with apparent relish since burgers remained conspicuously absent from any of the low fat menus at her house. "If I know that boy, he's been on tenterhooks over his brother's tests. It will do both of them good."

"Then, yes," Nikki happily agreed. "Jodi, would you like to join us? Maybe we can choose a place midway between the hospital and our neighborhood."

Jodi dabbed her lips with a napkin and pushed her chair back from the table. "Thank you for the invitation, but I can't make it this evening. Some other time?"

Nikki nodded as Jodi placed a warm hand on her shoulder. "Make sure you continue to use Lorenzo's Oil, and continue to strictly follow the recommended diets, okay?"

"I will, Jodi. See you soon." Jodi's departing reminder wasn't a complete good-mood killer. But, Nikki knew the next three years with Rocky would be precarious. If symptoms didn't present by age ten, then they'd have a *genuine* reason to celebrate.

Until then she'd grasp at any reason for a celebration to brightly color her all too-frequent gray days.

****

Mickey braked at the curb outside the Good Sports Club complex and started fiddling with his cell phone to search out a restaurant for dinner. Leaving her in-laws to wait in the car, Nikki wove through interior corridors and exited a back door leading to the outdoor playing fields. Happy anticipation filled her as she traipsed across the turf toward the site of the flag football game in progress. A panorama of motion spread before her as the ball was snapped on the line of scrimmage. The players propelled backwards and sideways in both directions like ricocheting children-sized billiard balls.

Smiling, she continued forward as she searched for her sons. Rocky stood out on the playing field, zooming around faster than his teammates and opponents. Nikki's gaze lit on Jack hunkered down along the sidelines, and her heart constricted. Head to head with Ramsey Delaney, boy and man hung over one of Jack's ever-present notebooks. The football star draped a muscled arm around Jack, cupping his shoulder with a huge hand that covered a quarter of her son's back.

"I smell perfume," came Ram's deep resonant voice.

"Uh huh. Smells like my mommy."

Both faced Nikki, presenting ear-to-ear grins.

Their matching dazzling smiles swelled her heart—her customary reaction to Jack, and a jolting, giddy pleasure in the wake of Ramsey's seeming delight at her arrival.

"Hi, Nikki. I'm glad to see you." Ram scrambled to his feet.

Nikki's neck craned upward following his ascent. The man exuded virility and affable grace as he gently tugged Jack to his feet.

Before she returned Ram's greeting, a whistle screeched, and Rocky trundled off the field on a bead for Ram like a mini-truck. As he plowed into the quarterback from behind, Jack teetered and his legs gave way as if deflating. Nikki gasped and her stomach sank.

In a split second Ram's right arm swung outward to circle Rocky's body while his left arm dipped downward toward Jack in perfectly coordinated trajectories. He intercepted Jack's fall and scooped both kids up against his ribs as if he had effortlessly gathered feathers in flight. Giggling, the boys bussed Ram's cheeks and then faced her, their butts propped in the crooks of Ram's powerful arms.

Pleasure ripened into a gathering sensual tug at Nikki's core that left her off center and speechless. Ram's cobalt blue eyes held hers conveying with stunning certainty that this electrifying attraction was mutual.

"Hey, Ma," Rocky rumbled.

"Hi, Mommy," Jack said, snapping her out of the hormonal daze.

She approached them with open arms as Ram lowered the boys down to her level. The encompassing hug she doled out brushed her breasts against Ram's chest and filled her senses with his shower-soap scent for a pulse-revving moment.

Shaken, she back-stepped and stammered, "As soon as Mr. Delaney puts you down, Poppy, Grandma and I are treating you to dinner out tonight."

Jack widened his eyes. "Really?"

I nodded. "Yes. We're celebrating."

Smiling at Rocky Nikki continued, "Your test results were A-OK, Rocky."

"Yay!" Rocky hooted as Ram set him and Jack on the ground and they wiggled out of his arms.

"*Awesome*," Jack asserted. He limped over to Nikki and leaned heavily against her side.

Petting his soft black hair she said, "Rocky, you run on ahead. Poppy and Grandma are waiting in the car out front."

He took off at his usual full-out speed and she strolled slowly at Jack's side as Ram fell into step next to her.

"I'm not inviting myself or anything…" Ram said. "But a couple of my buddies from college opened a string of great restaurants in this area that has gotten stellar press. Deservedly. Their menu is healthy, fresh, homemade and most important—the food is great. It's a twist on fast food. They call it 'real food fast.' I eat there all the time, and I think the boys would love it. Are you interested?"

Jack pre-empted Nikki replying, "Heck, yeah."

"It sounds perfect," Nikki agreed. "What's its name and how do I get there?"

"Why don't you let me treat? We're going to Dedham. I'll lead you there in my car," Ram suggested.

"I…"

Ram lifted Jack back up into his arms. "Want to ride in my Hummer, Jack? We'll go ask Rocky if he wants to ride with us, too."

"Wow, yes!" Jack trained puppy dog eyes on her. "Can we, Mommy? Please?"

"Sure. Thanks, Ram."

Opposition to Ram's proposal seemed futile for the boys' sake, and in her over-stimulated state in Ram's thrall, she couldn't refuse him.

Ram's appeal was universal judging from Mickey's star struck inquiry to Ram, "Mind if I ride with you?"

"Not at all," Ram said.

Mickey winked at Nikki and said, "To keep an eye on them so Ram can keep his eyes on the road."

Apparently all the Lamberts were infatuated with Ram.

Trailing behind Ram's car Nikki spun fantasies in her head. For Rocky: he'd never face ALD despite his genetics. For Jack: Jodi would find an experimental study somewhere in the world, and Jack would receive a miracle cure. For her: She couldn't see past the moment.

Despite her undeniable attraction to a gorgeous celebrity, and she suspected his to her, she still couldn't fantasize for her own benefit. Nikki had to focus on raising her sons without their father, regardless of her needs and wants as a woman. Right then she'd gladly self-sacrifice anything if Jack would continue to live so that she could continue to raise him.

But the impromptu dinner party that night at B.good Restaurant cast Nikki in a special light, too, thanks to Ram. He sat between Jack and Rocky purposely across the table from her.

As she toted her tray to the table, Ram confided under his breath, "Sit across from me? I enjoy looking at you."

Her cheeks flamed. "Uh…that's nice of you to say."

He slid his tray onto the table, took Nikki's tray out of her hands and set it down. Ushering her away from her family, he stood squarely in front of her. "Nikki, I'm really glad you let me come along this evening. I care about your boys very much. They are *great* kids. I'd do anything to help Jack—and you. I've been enjoying getting to know Jack and Rocky. I would like the chance to know you better, if and when you're ready."

Flustered she pressed a hand to her burning cheek. *My husband deserted me in the cruelest way possible and my child is dying.* "Ram, I…" she gasped a breath. "That's out of the question. I'm sorry."

His gaze intense, he stated, "I apologize. I'm out of line. But *if* you're ever ready, I hope you remember this conversation. Maybe you'd enjoy a dinner out sometime. A cup of coffee…I know I would enjoy your company."

She smiled at the compliment despite her discomfort.

"There's that unforgettable smile." And with easy

confidence he headed back to the table.

Ramsey Delaney's reputation as a straight shooter was glaringly intact. Nikki was nowhere near ready. But the possibility that her life as a woman might not have ended at age thirty-three with her husband's suicide and with her baby's diagnosis of a fatal disease provided her with rare comfort.

As she returned to the table she secretly allowed herself to enjoy the view that Ram had engineered. For scattered moments the future didn't seem as hellishly bleak.

The food, as promised, was delicious. Nikki's veggie burgers at home tasted like seasoned Styrofoam compared to the restaurant's preparation. Ram presided over the gathering without hogging the limelight. Mickey hung on his every word concerning Dragons prospects for the season. Ram prodded Jack to pass his "playbook" around the table, and Nikki swelled with pride as her boys talked football as if they were headed toward careers as a pro team coach and a first string player.

The Disney World trip Nikki had secretly considered for Jack paled in comparison to an evening with Ram. Eyes like saucers, her boys gaped as customers lined up at their table for autographs. Ram's easy banter with his fans heaped layer upon layer of hero worship onto the boys' over-flowing plates.

Nikki wasn't immune, either. She relished the rare opportunity for her sons to feel important—lucky. Especially Jack. Anyone who could bless her children with fortune after the loss of their Daddy and the daily losses Jack suffered was Nikki's hero, too.

When the boys and the adults had seemingly licked

their plates clean, Ram said, "We'll have to come back here soon. They're going to have a garlicky-greens eating contest again this year. Anybody up for trying to win the title of 'Champ'?"

Ram consulted a brochure on the table and read, "In our 7th annual Garlicky-Greens Eating Championship, a ninety-five pound, math-teaching vegan chewed the life out of everything and everyone to become the greatest sautéed spinach eater on earth."

He chuckled as he handed the pamphlet to Jack. "Want to be known as the greatest on earth?"

"Spinach is yucky," Rocky opined.

His expression deadpan, Jack quipped, "I'm working on how I'll change the earth. Not with spinach, though. Right, Rocky?" He leaned forward to peer past Ram's muscled torso at his brother, and they both burst into laughter.

"You're Jack the Whack! Not Popeye." Rocky doubled over laughing.

Jack the ALD whack. Nikki's heart twisted, but she went along with the joke, her laughter ringing hollow.

Chapter 11

Jack

Mommy talked on the phone late last night with Nana. She told Nana about Rocky's good news, but after she sounded excited, I heard her crying. I figured it was because she missed Daddy so much. I did, too. And I thought that she was scared about my ALD. I tried to tell her everything would be okay, but I didn't think she believed me. I tried not to be scared, but sometimes I couldn't help it.

The house got quiet after Mommy hung up, but I still couldn't sleep. I was too excited. I pulled my notebook out from under my pillow. I needed to get my plan written down...and soon. I had to wait for my hand to stop shaking before I could write.

The next day we were off school for teachers' meetings and Ram had invited me to lunch. I would meet some of his football pals. I wanted to see if they could help with my plan, too. It was just about ready.

I don't remember when I fell asleep, but I woke up when the mattress shook. Rocky yawned and stretched his hands over his head at the foot of my bed. Lots of mornings I'd wake up and Rocky would be snoozing down by my feet. I didn't know how he got all turned around like that.

I wasn't surprised that Rocky was already awake.

Ram said I could bring him and Poppy with me to lunch. Even Poppy said he was looking forward to it so much he probably wouldn't get a wink of sleep and would be up with the birds.

"Mom said we have to go clothes shopping before lunch today," Rocky said, and then he yawned again. "I don't know why. I've got enough clothes."

"Because our clothes from last year are too small. And we didn't get new shoes for this year yet, either," I explained.

"I don't want to wear shoes. Only dorks wear shoes," Rocky complained. "I want to wear those cool sneakers that Ram has. Racers. They are so sweet."

"Yeah, and too expensive. You know Mommy can't afford them."

Every year Mommy made us wear shoes to school and we could only wear our sneakers on gym day. No one picked on Rocky for wearing shoes, but they sure picked on me. Being different is no fun. I was so afraid of how much worse things might get for me in school. I was *really* different since ALD.

"I'm going to ask Mom if she'll just buy us new sneakers. I don't care what kind, just as long as I don't have to wear shoes." Rocky raised his head and stared at me for a few minutes. His forehead crinkled. "Don't worry, Jack, no one is going to pick on you at school. I promise."

Sometimes Rocky knew what I was thinking before I even said it.

"Boys, are you up?" Mommy yelled. "Better get going. Nana is treating to breakfast at the mall."

The bed shook like an earthquake hit it, and Rocky was out of my room in about a second. The bathroom door slammed shut.

It took me forever to make my legs do what I wanted, but once I got them moving, I threw on my clothes in record time and almost beat Rocky down the stairs. Almost.

****

Even Poppy was in a hurry to get out of the car after he drove into the parking lot at the Good Sports Club. The car had hardly stopped before Rocky crashed out of the back seat and raced to the door. He ran even faster than before in his new sneakers.

I still couldn't believe that Grandma convinced Mommy that we needed the new Racers for school. And she even paid for them with her own credit card. I didn't know Grandma had her own credit card.

I wanted to run with Rocky, but after all the walking in the mall I couldn't make my legs run *at all*. Poppy waited for me and walked slow as a turtle, the way I walked, into the GSC where we met Rocky in the hall.

Miss Luci was at her desk. She stood up and shook Poppy's hand. "Lovely to see you again, Mr. Lambert."

Poppy squinted his eyes and his lips twisted sideways. He said, "My pleasure, Miz Baldwin."

"Please call me Luci."

"Thank you, Luci. And please call me Mike."

I thought Poppy's name was Mickey.

"Ram invited us to lunch." Rocky hopped up and down. Those Racers gave a lot of bounce.

"I know," Miss Luci said, smiling. "All the boys are here already and they are waiting for you in Ram's office. The food was delivered a little while ago. I hope there is something left for you." She laughed as she walked over and opened the office door.

I was pretty disappointed. I thought it was special that Ram invited just me, and let me bring my brother and grandpa to lunch. I didn't know that he invited other boys, too.

"I can't believe that the Dragons have the balls to fu…" A man as wide as a car stopped talking as we walked into the room.

Miss Luci made a loud noise in her throat.

"Uh, sorry, Luci," the giant said.

"I expect you boys to be on your best behavior." She pointed her finger around the room at all the huge men hanging out in Ram's office, and then she snorted a laugh.

"We will, Mom," called out a man who was leaning against the wall. He was even taller than Ram!

"Are you his *mom*?" Rocky asked Miss Luci. He looked at the shiny-skinned black man and then turned back to look at Miss Luci who was even whiter than my Mommy. His mouth hung open a little.

The black man hooted out a laugh. "Miss Luci is our second mom."

Ram stood up and moved around his desk grinning. "When we were at college Miss Luci helped our coach in the athletic office and took care of us." He ruffled Rocky's hair. "Just like she takes care of all of our sportsmen here at the club."

"Now, all of you behave," Miss Luci said as she backed out of the room and closed the door.

"Guys, I want you to meet my friends. This is Jack, Rocky and Mike," Ram said.

I was so proud that I stood up a little straighter. But I felt that funny twitching start up from my back all the way down to my toes, and I prayed that my legs wouldn't cave in on me again.

"Lambert men," Ram said, "This is Neil 'Caboose' Roberts, Casey 'Loco' Mason, Rick 'Tracks' Larkin, Luke 'Diesel' Murphy and Chris 'Engine' Simmons."

As Ram introduced us, each man shook Rocky's, Poppy's, and my hand. Ouch! I thought my bones were gonna crack. I wondered if Rocky's hand hurt as much as mine.

Poppy shook Engine's hand and said, "It is a real honor to meet the original Highland University Train. No O-line at Highland has ever equaled yours. You guys were something. My son John and I were season ticket holders. We never missed a game." Poppy smiled a mile wide.

"Engine, the way you cleared the path for Nicky P in that Penn game? That run was a highlight on ESPN." Poppy shook his head still smiling. "Gees, John and I talked about that for months. I wish John could be here to meet you all today." His voice shook, all quivery.

"Bring him next time. I'd love to meet him." Engine sat down on the couch and patted the cushion next to him.

Poppy looked at the floor as he went over and sat down next to Engine.

"Hey, guys. Grab a plate and get something to eat. I don't think I can keep these hungry vultures away from that food much longer." Ram pointed to the table in the corner of his office.

I had never seen a pile of sandwiches so high. I wondered if more people were coming.

Rocky took three sandwiches. He'd have a stomach ache later for sure, after all the pancakes he ate at the mall. I filled my plate, but I couldn't swallow so good. That was all right. I wasn't hungry anyway.

"Hey, Buddy. Luci can get you a shake if you would rather have that," Ram whispered in my ear. *He is so nice to me.*

"No, I'm good, thank you."

I sat down next to Poppy, and Rocky squeezed in next to me, and I felt even smaller looking up at Ram's buddies. I couldn't believe I was there. I felt like I was in the movie *Honey, I Shrunk the Kids*.

The men sat around drinking coffee.

"Hey, Diesel. Do you remember how many plates of pasta you put down before the game against the Crimson Knights?"

Their laughing shook the floor under my feet. Diesel looked like he weighed a ton and he could sure hold a lot of pasta.

"I still have the record at Luigi's," Diesel said.

"I'm gonna play for Coach Flynn," Rocky said, his mouth bulging with food.

My Racers vibrated again from all the laughter shaking the floor.

"You look like you've got what it takes, my man." Engine clapped his gigantic hand on Rocky's shoulder, and my brother grinned. And then Rocky opened his mouth with all that mess of chewed up sandwich in there and said, "Train wreck!"

Boy oh boy, they laughed crazy loud.

"Loco, remember the time you locked Flynn off the bus?" Ram asked.

"Oh man, do I. You guys will never let me forget that." Loco shook his head. "Probably the dumbest prank of my life."

"What happened?" I asked, all excited to hear the story.

"The football team traveled on two buses, one for offense and one for defense. Coach Flynn always rode on the offense bus. Still does. He goes over plays on the way to the game and rehashes the game on the way home. That leaves the defense bus to…" Loco paused and squinted his eyes saying, "Well, the defense bus always has more fun. Anyway we were on our way back to school after our biggest win ever and I just wanted to have some fun and not listen to a critique of the game. So I paid the bus driver to lock the door."

"What did Coach Flynn do?" Poppy asked.

"He tried the door just once, walked to the defense bus and got on it."

"He wasn't mad at you?" I asked really interested in the story.

"I didn't say he wasn't mad. Just the opposite, Jack. Ever hear the old saying don't get mad get even?"

I nodded, yes.

"He damn, oops sorry, darn near killed us," Track said.

"How?" Rocky piped up.

"He ran us. He made us run before practice and after practice, laps and laps and laps. I must have lost twenty pounds that week." Tracks patted his bulging belly. "I guess I could use a few laps now."

"Ain't that the truth? We all could." Diesel rested his hands on his own fat stomach.

"Speak for yourself." Ram pounded his flat stomach with his fist, and it sounded like smacking a board.

"Good. You have to stay in shape for when that

asshole…sorry, boys." Diesel cringed when Poppy shook his head.

"When Beltzer"—he used the Dragons Coach's name instead of asshole—"and your team management come to their senses and bring you back to camp. The Dragons need you."

"The rookie quarterback is doing well," Ram said in a low voice.

"I don't believe for one minute that he can last the season. They just won't admit they made a huge mistake, and it will just be a matter of time before you are back running the offense right to the Super Bowl." Diesel high-fived Rocky, and then me.

"Do you still play football?" Rocky asked Caboose who was the biggest man I had *ever* seen. I thought Ram was tall, but Caboose was taller, and he must have weighed at least four hundred pounds. But he wasn't fat. He did look like a caboose.

"Nah, I was drafted by the Dragons, but I ruined my knee in an exhibition game. Never played football again. Still try to keep in shape. Wish the wife wasn't such a good cook. I would give my left nu…uh, arm to play again."

"I'm going to play for the Dragons after college," Rocky said with such confidence that I thought everyone in the room believed him. I believed him. He'd make the team, and I sure hoped that I would see him from heaven.

"How about you, Jack?" Diesel asked. "Are you going to play for the Dragons, too?"

"Jack is…" I laid my hand on Poppy's arm to stop his talking, afraid he would tell everybody I was sick.

"No, I'm not as good a player as my brother, so I

am going to be his agent." *Yeah. Guardian agent. I like that.*

"We're going to be the best team." Rocky pumped his fist in the air. "The Rock and Jack the Whack."

"I wish you were my agent," Loco teased. "Maybe I would still be playing."

"You still want to play?" I asked, because Loco could fit into my plan, too.

"I think I can speak for everyone in the room—we all wish we could play again. Football gets in your blood."

"If there was a chance that you could play one more game, would you?" I asked, my brain spinning.

"We'd jump at the chance," Caboose answered and they all nodded their heads.

Ram and his buddies kidded around some more and made plans to play golf. Then the guys left, promising to get together with Rocky and me again.

I took out my plan notebook to write down a few things before I forgot. Really, I didn't think I would forget one minute of that day even if I didn't write it down.

"What's that, Jack? A new stats book?" Ram pointed to my book and sat next to me on the arm of the leather couch.

"Just something I'm working on." I closed the cover quickly and twirled the pencil in my hand.

"He won't let you read it. Don't ask," Rocky said shaking his head. "I've asked a million times and he always says no. But I know what's in it. It's Jack's plan to change the world."

"A plan to change the world? That's a mighty big undertaking." Ram leaned back making me nervous he'd fall on the floor.

Stupid. He's too coordinated.

"Anything I can do to help with your plan?"

It wasn't the right time yet to tell Ram that my plan included him, and now his college friends, too. I needed to draw out everything before I was ready to show it to him.

I knew I was running out of time, but I was excited after meeting the Train. I could make the plan work.

Poppy stood up and held out his hand toward Ram. "Thank you so much for inviting us to lunch. It was an honor meeting your former teammates."

They shook hands.

"We will have to do it again soon," Ram said.

He walked with us to the door and said, "Back to school again tomorrow."

"Yeah, it stinks," Rocky said. "I'd much rather be here."

Ram laughed. "I'm glad we have the after school program, aren't you?"

"Yes, sir."

"Good, then I'll see you after school. Good luck with your studies. Gotta keep those grades up if you want to play college ball."

We left Ram's office and headed outside. I sat in the back seat of the car because Rocky called, "Shotgun!" before Ram even closed his office door.

I knew that if I asked, he would let me sit up front with Poppy. But I was so tired and my head hurt. I just wanted to close my eyes. I had an idea for the team jersey I wanted to draw in my notebook, but it would have to wait. I closed my eyes, and I didn't wake up until I was in my bed and it was night.

Chapter 12

Ram watched the door, twitchy with anticipation as rubber balls whizzed by him helter-skelter. On that and most other rainy days, bombardment was the sport of choice, entertaining the kids no end while spurring low-grade headaches in the supervising adults, including Ram. Jack bent over his notebook in the far corner of the gym, his thin legs folded under him lotus style. Ram shot a quick glance at Jack and then resumed craning his neck in the direction of the door.

He had called Nikki two days ago in the genuine spirit of self-sacrifice and had offered to take the boys alone to B.good Restaurant for dinner that evening to watch the greens eating contest so she'd have a break from care taking. She had delighted him by opting to come along, too. And so Ram waited for her to appear in the gym as skittish as a seventeen-year-old on prom night. His thoughts had centered on her and Jack with such fierce regularity recently that he had difficulty resting day or night.

Spending time with Jack doing the busy work he concocted to create a "job" for him at the GSC were equal measures pleasure and pain. Jack's decline continued in subtle but undeniable changes. His moods swung, his motor skills were spotty, and his attention drifted. Ram had devised ways to snap him back, keep him in the moment, but frequently Ram's creativity tapped out at about the same rate as Jack's vitality.

Unfortunately David Cry had cancelled their lunch date when David's son took a turn for the worse, so Ram never met him face to face. But David made himself available to Ram by phone. Through conversations with David, Ram learned more than he wanted to know about Jack's losing battle.

David's unending dedication and courage in fighting for children like Jack, and unthinkably, in the face of his own son's late stage ALD, humbled Ram to the marrow. Before ending their last phone conversation, Ram made the commitment to help him in any way possible: autographed NFL stuff for auctions, personal appearances, and donations. He vowed to remain at his disposal.

David jumped at the chance to involve Ram in an upcoming fundraiser brunch. Maybe the inactive status on the team had kept Ram from attending training camp for just that reason. Had Beltzer cleared him for play, Ram wouldn't be available. Sometimes the symmetry of the good Lord's plans blew him away.

Ram was foolish enough to feel empowered in gearing up to combat this disease. The sentiment was short lived. Fighting ALD was like facing off with a tank armed with a stick.

Ram's heart wrenched yet again contemplating a world without Jack Lambert. *How must Nikki feel?* Her terror was inconceivable. He yearned to eradicate the looming threat, punch the shit out of it—but couldn't, of course.

He was just as powerless to stop secretly loving Nikki. The timing couldn't have been worse in finding the woman who figuratively brought him to his knees.

He still kicked himself for coming on strong when they all went out to dinner for the first time. But he didn't regret it. *The truth is the truth.*

Paying fleeting attention on the dodge ball game, he maintained his vigil focusing on the door——rewarded when Nikki appeared. She gave him a quick smile that warmed him to the toes. He headed toward her forcing an easy gait despite his impulse to sprint the distance between them, enfold her in his arms, and hold on as long as she'd permit.

She shifted her gaze and scanned the bombardment field.

"Hi," he said halting awkwardly next to her.

Arms dangling at his sides, he regarded her pretty profile while she ignored him, apparently preoccupied with searching out her sons.

Nikki beamed a smile and waved a hand at Rocky. Her eyes darted.

"Jack's over in the corner," Ram informed her, pointing across the gym.

"Where?"

Glancing in Jack's direction, he frowned at the vacant spot on the far side of the gym. "He was just there."

Ram joined Nikki in scanning the perimeter of the gym. *Where the heck is he?*

He must have left the gym through the exterior door. I watched the only other exit like a hawk for Nikki's arrival.

"He must be outside," Ram said.

She widened her eyes. "In the pouring *rain*?"

Already in motion toward the exit he tossed out, "Wait here. I'll go check."

Ram sensed her pursuit close on his heels and by the time he reached the door, he and Nikki barreled through it together. He was drenched in seconds and he blinked repeatedly to peer through the downpour. About a hundred yards ahead Jack paced furiously, spinning on a heel every third step and reversing direction.

Nikki at his side, Ram raced toward Jack, sluicing through the ankle deep water, and churning up frothy sprays while the rain drilled down on his head. Despite his far longer stride, Nikki reached Jack first. Nobody could outrun a panicked mother on a bead toward her baby.

She flung her arms around Jack, and he broke free from her hold with an aggressive shove.

"I have to think!" he screamed, grimacing and obstinate.

Facing Jack, the deluge plastered Nikki's hair to her face and sent droplets dripping off her nose. "Come inside, sweetie. You can think where it's dry."

Nikki extended her hand, and Jack slapped it away roughly. "No! I have to think *now*!" he bellowed.

The rain streaming down her face surely intermingled with her tears. His heart breaking for her, Ram surged forward, captured Jack around the arms at waist level and heaved him up into a vertical carry.

Ignoring his wild bucking and the buffeting sneakers against his thighs, Ram plowed back toward the building. Ram spared his face from the assault of flying hands by pinning Jack's arms at his side.

Nikki opened the door ahead of Ram and he jogged into the gym hollering, "Harriman. Get some dry towels."

Depositing Jack carefully on the gleaming gym floor he witnessed a rapid transformation. Jack's rigid posture relaxed, and he gazed at Nikki blankly.

"Mommy?" he asked apparently bewildered.

Ram couldn't interpret the soft expression in Jack's eyes, but he had no difficulty reading the hopeless expression on Nikki's face. Accepting the two towels Harriman scurried over to him, Ram wrapped one around Jack's quaking body and then he swept the other around Nikki's shoulders.

"Thanks," Ram said as Harriman handed him another towel.

Swabbing his face and briskly scrubbing the towel over the top of his head, Ram stood dripping rivulets of water on the floor.

Rocky skidded to a halt near Ram. He absently ruffled the boy's crew cut and watched Nikki energetically rub down the sides of Jack's arms with a towel.

"Jack's okay, honey," she assured Rocky. Cuddled against Nikki, Jack closed his eyes.

"Did he have a bad moment again?" Rocky's emphasis on "again" had Ram's stomach sinking. The aggressive behavior had happened before.

If I had paid more attention, could I have prevented his ranting in the rain?

"Yes, he did have a bad moment," Nikki confirmed. "But it's over now. He just needs a few minutes. Go back and play. I'll let you know when we're ready to leave."

"I'm sorry," Ram whispered when Rocky was out of earshot.

"It happens more often now." Nikki's eyes filled

with tears but she blinked them away. "Another symptom of ALD."

"Damn," Ram growled.

"You said a bad word." Jack laughed.

Ram and Nikki smiled as Ram ruffled Jack's damp hair.

"Let's get you home," Nikki said gently, pressing Jack to her side. She waved her hand, and Rocky came running back.

Mascara tracks striped her cheeks, and her raven hair glued to the edges of her face. The material of her blouse had plastered to her breasts, and every lacy detail on her bra was visible. Ram's eyes followed her hand as she pinched the hem of her shirt between her thumb and index finger and tugged the sopping material loose.

"Aren't we still going to dinner with Ram?" Jack whined.

"I *really* want to go," Rocky chimed in.

Ram answered the question in Nikki's eyes with a shrug of his shoulders. "Up to you," he mouthed hoping she wouldn't cancel.

Indecision shimmered in her eyes. "We'll have to change first," she said.

"I'll go change into dry clothes, too. How about I pick you up at your house in an hour?" Ram suggested.

"Yay!" Rocky trumpeted—exactly Ram's sentiments.

In a steaming hot shower Ram worried about Jack, and suffered repetitive attacks of guilt that he had let him out of his sight for even a second. He immensely hoped that Nikki wouldn't hold the lapse of supervision against him. Jack's unexpected behavior undid Ram, and he intended to be vigilant and ready for anything in the future.

****

From within the house Nikki admonished, "Look through the peephole."

The front door opened and Rocky rasped, "Hi, they're not ready yet."

And then he barreled up the center stairway.

Ram stepped inside and closed the door, acutely aware that he trespassed on a family life cut short. The welcoming atmosphere warmed him. And something smelled great.

Nikki's melodic voice sounded from above him, and then Rocky charged back downstairs, apparently assigned the role of interim host as well as doorman.

"Come on, Ram, we'll watch TV," he directed.

His husky voice made Ram smile. *Little man.*

He followed Rocky into the cozy family room and sat in a satisfying, man-sized La-Z-Boy recliner/rocker.

The battle raged onscreen. Laser guns pinged, whined, and disintegrated things while Rocky bopped around brandishing an invisible weapon.

"Where are your grandparents? Upstairs?" Ram asked thinking he might enjoy some adult conversation.

"Nah," he replied, still in motion, his eyes glued to the screen. "They went to the movies, I think."

"Oh." Ram nodded—an unnecessary gesture since Rocky didn't divert his gaze from the TV screen. "It really smells good in here. Is your mom cooking some dessert?"

"Nope. She's washing her underwear. It always smells like this."

Ram bit back a grin having learned two fascinating

facts: what Nikki's bra looked and smelled like.

A hairdryer droned above.

"Did you offer Ram something to drink?"

Ram snapped to attention at the sound of her voice behind him. "Hi…"

"I forgot," Rocky said.

Rising from his seat, Ram smiled at her.

Her lips pursed and she wagged her head, amusement dancing in her luminous brown eyes. "Apparently Rocky fell down on the job. Can I get you something?" she inquired. "Jack's almost ready."

"No, thanks. I'm good."

She winced as an explosion sounded in Tatooine, or wherever those storm troopers were duking it out in the video. "I think I'd like a hot cup of tea."

Folding her arms across her chest, she shivered. "I haven't gotten warm yet. Would you like to sit with me in the kitchen so you don't go deaf before dinner?"

"Sure."

Trailing her, their height difference made him self-conscious. Her long skirt flowed gracefully with each step like a runway model. Her trim little figure would suit a model or a dancer. Not one ounce of fat on her petite, perfectly proportioned frame. How would she fit in his arms? How could he fit into her life?

Happy just to watch her fix her tea, Ram sat on the bench at her kitchen table.

Mug in hand, tea bag string dangling, she slipped onto the bench opposite him. She left the teabag in the cup, blew over the surface of the liquid and took a dainty sip before she set the mug down on the table. "Thank you for helping me with Jack today," she said.

"I'm sorry it happened. I never should have let him

out of my sight." He gazed into her eyes, and the bottomless well of sadness he glimpsed sent a chill through him.

She sipped from the mug again, a delicate series of hand movements that transfixed Ram. Her wrist and long tapered fingers were elegant, fragile. But there was nothing fragile about her spirit. Despite her sadness, and he suspected her relentless terror, since Ram experienced those emotions with respect to Jack, too, Nikki was fearless.

Ram folded his hands on the table. "I was waiting for you. I kept staring at the door like a school boy," he confessed.

"Really? You were looking for me?" Her soft hand covered his, warm and illogically pleasurable.

"Yes, I couldn't wait to see your face." He smiled. "It won't happen again, I promise you that."

"You won't be looking forward to seeing me again?" she teased.

"You know what I meant." He chuckled.

Withdrawing her hand, she clasped the handle of the mug, but didn't lift it off the table. "It might happen again."

She hung her head, and then regarded him through her long lashes. "A lot worse might happen than Jack's running around in the rain."

Hoping that she understood the intensity of his resolve he vowed, "I'll be there to help him."

"That is unbelievably kind of you, but…"

Her voice trailed off as a loud noise, like plastic crashing into tile, cracked overhead.

"The hairdryer fell?" Ram posed.

She stiffened and trained her eyes downward as if

straining to hear.

The sickening thud of a body collapsing followed.

"Oh my God." She stood and pushed away from the table. Then she bolted out of the kitchen.

Ram joined her on a race upstairs toward the bathroom.

Nikki gasped and slapped a hand over her mouth when she and Ram reached the open doorway in tandem. Jack was face up, spread eagle on the bathroom floor, his eyes rolled back in his head.

"Call 911, Nikki," Ram said softly, concealing the alarm that screamed through his every nerve ending.

She raced out of the bathroom, and Ram lowered onto all fours bridging Jack's inert body. Then violent tremors wracked Jack, and Nikki's voice grew closer as she provided address info to the 911 dispatcher.

"What's happening to him?" she cried.

Ram didn't turn toward the door to comfort her, but calmly said, "He's seizing. Do you have something he could bite on so he doesn't bloody his tongue?"

"Rocky!" she yelled. "Bring me one of your big pink erasers right now! Jack needs you!"

Ram vaguely registered the chaotic sounds of Rocky in motion as he gathered Jack up and cradled him in his lap. Clasping him to his chest, Jack's spasms echoed through him causing Ram's teeth to clack in sync with Jack's.

Nikki produced the eraser. Ram eased it into Jack's mouth, and then held on to him for dear life. His body temperature felt normal, so Ram mentally ruled out a seizure from a fever. At least, he concluded, Jack's drenching on a fifty-degree day hadn't left him with a fever high enough to launch the seizure.

When Ram was a kid his mother rescued a little Boston terrier that, she was told, had been found chained in a rural barn without food or water for an indeterminate period. The abuse was so severe that the tiny creature was left permanently deaf and blind. About three months after the Delaney family gave Trudy her new home, she remained certainly more comfortable, but resolutely ungrateful in showing any tender emotion to the humans. Then the seizures started. When she was in the throes of one, Ram held her quaking body to his chest, like he was holding Jack. After the attack had subsided, she had licked Ram's hand and he figured that he had done the right thing.

Ram vehemently prayed that the technique was the right thing for a little boy.

Nikki crouched down next to Ram while talking on the cell phone, "Please ask her to call my cell number immediately. Jack's having a seizure."

She dumped the phone in her lap as she sat down on the tiled floor. Her tear-filled, rounded eyes scanned Jack's convulsing form like an M.R.I. "There's a knot on his head."

"It sounded like he hit the floor pretty hard." The words fractured into extra syllables shaking out of Ram as if he sat in a Mixmaster.

The phone rang in Nikki's lap playing the Dragons fight song. *Did she choose that ringtone to entertain the boys? Or...*

She answered the call, "Jodi! He's convulsing."

Her head bobbed. "Uh huh. Yes, a friend has him restrained in his arms, and he isn't thrashing all over. Uh huh. I called the paramedics. They've got to be close by now. Okay, I will."

Jack's jerky movements seemed to lessen and Ram now perceived them as shudders versus convulsions. He glanced at Nikki and said, "I think it's subsiding."

"His doctor wants him to go to the ER, and she'll consult with the doctors there. I just talked with her on the phone."

"Sure," he said as Jack sagged some within his arms. "I'll follow the ambulance in my car and take Rocky with me."

"Oh, Ram. That's too much to ask..."

"No. It isn't."

The doorbell chimed and then all hell broke loose with the commotion of the paramedics' entry and their rapid relief of the small burden of Jack's limp body from Ram's arms.

He rose and almost pitched sideways on his circulation-deprived legs. Pins and needles shimmered up to both thighs as Ram limped down the stairs, collected Rocky and then led him to the Hummer to follow the ambulance.

They didn't use the sirens since they had declared Jack's condition stable after they had examined him, but they hightailed out of there with the lights flashing. Ram thought that Rocky might consider it cool to speed and to ignore traffic signs in a big-ass Hummer, but he sat buckled in next to Ram eerily silent during the fifteen-minute ride.

In the ER waiting room, he climbed into Ram's lap, nestled his head against his chest and remained mute until Nikki appeared about two hours later. He jerked rousing Ram from a blank-minded stare at the TV screen that hung from the ceiling in the corner of the room.

"Where's Jack? Take me to him," Rocky demanded.

Nikki sank into the molded plastic chair next to Ram's and brushed her fingers lightly over Rocky's crown. "They want to do one more test to make sure he doesn't have a concussion," she said seemingly laboring to produce the sentence. Exhaustion lines creased the corners of her mouth.

"What's that?"

"Oh. It means that he might have bumped his head too hard when he fell on the floor. They want to check that. And then they said we could take him home."

"Okay, good." Rocky laid his head back down on Ram's chest and fell dead asleep as if Nikki's reassurances had thrown his off switch.

Ram, Nikki, and the boys arrived back at her house well after midnight. He insisted on carrying both Rocky and Jack up to bed, and Nikki agreed so that she could rummage in the attic in the interim to find a baby monitor to install in Jack's room.

After he helped her set up the audio-video monitor, Ram and Nikki descended the stairs on tiptoes to prevent disturbing her sleeping in-laws.

One hand on the front door knob, she whispered, "I can't thank you enough."

As she opened the door Ram stepped forward and gently closed it, plucking the baby monitor out of her hand. "You go up to bed and get some rest. I'll go sit in the TV room and monitor Jack tonight."

"Absolutely not."

He thwarted her attempt to snag the handheld monitor by swinging it up out of her reach. "Go to bed Nikki," he whispered. "I've got this."

Instead of mounting the steps as he anticipated, she shuffled down the hallway toward the back of the house.

Ram followed her into the TV room.

"I sleep here," she said indicating the couch. "My in-laws have my room."

"Okay." He eased into the La-Z-Boy and propped the hand that held the monitor on the armrest. "Goodnight."

She curled up on the couch and zoned out instantly, similar to Rocky's surrender to slumber in the ER.

Ram alternated watching her sleep and peering at Jack's grainy image on the monitor all night. The house creaked occasionally, the transmitter emitted static and Nikki breathed softly in the dim hush.

Someone awoke upstairs. Footfalls traveled overhead and down the stairs signaling his or her approach.

Ram left the TV room, light-footed as possible, and encountered Mrs. Lambert, clad in a bulky bathrobe and terry cloth slippers, in the hall.

Handing her the monitor he said, "Good morning, Mrs. Lambert. I stayed awake in the chair all night so Nikki could get some rest. Jack had a seizure last night, and we spent some time in the ER."

Her eyes widened. "Oh my God. Is he all right?"

"He was peaceful, and his breathing was even all night. I watched him closely. I'll let Nikki tell you about what went on when she's awake."

Her eyes narrowed, and she peered at him as if sizing him up. He chose not to explain further or to divulge that he intended to give Nikki's mother-in-law plenty of time to figure him out in the future, since he planned to see Nikki as much as she'd permit.

Ram left after wishing Mrs. Lambert a good day.

Chapter 13

"Mrs. Lambert, I just spoke to my mother, and she said she mailed the check yesterday. I *have* to go to class. We're reviewing for our midterm exam. Please. I have to get a good grade on this exam. I'll never graduate this year unless I do. I have to finish school and get a job to help my family. Please help me?"

Nikki stood at the waist-high counter that separated the administrative desks from the outer apron of the university's records office. A fidgeting line of waiting students snaked out the door and continued down the hallway. She and her colleagues had worked extra hours the past week to finish posting financial aid to all active student accounts. Those students with outstanding balances were locked out of their classes until the department received and posted the full difference between financial aid monies and the semester tuitions.

The majority of kids Nikki had assisted earlier that day had checks or cash at the ready to pay their balances, but a few like Tina, the girl who stood trembling on the other side of the counter, had provided excuses or promises. Nikki wasn't supposed to supply anyone a release of the class "lockout" on the strength of promises, but some of the stories touched her heart.

Tina's dad had died serving in Iraq, and her family was barely scraping by. Deep down Nikki trusted that her check would arrive. Each child's excuse, for that matter, seemed to have merit to her.

So what if I'm a sucker for a hard luck story? If I can't create any good luck of my own, at least I might engineer some for those lives I touch at work.

Nikki filled out a form for her, tapped her index finger on her lips and slipped the release slip across the counter.

"I'm sorry, Tina, but I have to receive the check from your mom before I can release." She winked.

Her heart skipped a beat as a smile brightened Tina's pale face, and she mouthed, "Thank you."

The boss, Elizabeth, presided at the opposite end of the counter dealing with locked-out students, too. Her ramrod straight posture and unsmiling, forbidding countenance predicted the negativity that she would continue to dole out. Several kids had left the counter in tears after meeting with her unwavering toughness.

Nikki didn't have tough left in her. Jack's seizure two weeks ago had scared "the tough" out of her emotional repertoire. Work had become her sole form of escape, and she had relished the avalanche of repetitive tasks the job had entailed recently. Sometimes as much as an hour went by during the workday when she didn't have time to think about ALD. When reality reasserted in her consciousness, she felt guilty that she hadn't devoted precious waking minutes to beneficial thoughts for Jack.

Not that any amount of optimistic thinking would create a positive outlook about Jack's situation—except to be grateful each morning at rising for one more day with him. Mostly, Nikki anticipated with mounting trepidation that inevitably, the next shoe would drop.

Jack had wanted to go back to school after only one day home post-seizure. Jodi medically supported Jack's stance believing that his desire to follow a normal routine would preserve his quality of life for as long as possible. But, Nikki was terribly and gnawingly afraid to let him leave the house. Ideally, Nikki would rather wrap Jack in her embrace each precious day, close the blinds and block cruel reality out.

Telephones had chirred various ring tones that Nikki perceived as background noise all morning. But as her coworker, Lynn answered the phone and glanced her way, Nikki sensed that the other shoe had dropped.

Lynn said, "Yes, Mrs. Lambert is in. One moment, please."

For an instant, Nikki considered the happy prospect that Ram was on the other end of that phone line instead of someone bearing dire news. Since the recent crisis in the ER, he had called every morning and every evening to, "check in."

Nikki looked forward to his calls and viewed his seemingly no-strings-attached friendship with her family as a gift. The boys idolized him, and he was as easy to talk with as he was on the eyes. Believing that he stood ready to help if she asked had allowed Nikki to close her eyes at night. Maybe Ram had decided to call in the middle of the afternoon for some reason.

But as Lynn's eyes met Nikki's, her stomach sank. *Something is wrong.*

"Nikki, it's Mrs. Segers from the boys' school on line two," she said.

"Thanks, Lynn."

She scurried over to her desk and connected the call. "Nikki Lambert."

The principal's secretary said, "Mrs. Lambert, can you come to Miss Young's office as soon as possible? Jack is here after an altercation in class."

"Is he hurt? Is anyone hurt?" She'd welcome a disciplinary problem versus a medical emergency any day, but Nikki considered any kind of problem with Jack an emergency.

"No. He's very upset and Miss Young is also upset about his behavior."

Adrenaline shot through her like propellant. She opened her desk drawer and grabbed her purse. "I'll be right there."

She kicked the drawer shut as she hung up the phone and then raced around the counter.

"It's Jack. Something has happened. I have to go," she gasped out to Elizabeth.

Nikki squeezed through the line of students and sprinted out into the hallway.

"Drive careful. Keep us informed," the boss called out.

Bless her, as tough as she is, Elizabeth never gives me flak where Jack is concerned.

Nikki didn't stop running until she bumped clumsily into the driver's door of her car. She yanked the door open, heaved in behind the wheel and screeched out of the parking lot.

What good are you to Jack if you wind up in an accident?

Easing up on the accelerator, she slowed to the speed limit rapping her thumbs against the steering wheel impatiently. Stress-sweat slithered down her back.

She parked with one wheel on the curb in front of

the school and bounded up the concrete stairs. The gleaming white and yellow tiled walls decorated with colorful student artwork created a cheerful atmosphere in the school corridors that neither cheered her nor calmed her mounting anxiety.

An altercation. *My Jack has never been involved in such a thing before. But she said he's not hurt.*

Nikki rested her forehead against a cool wall tile outside the principal's office. She counted to three before she turned the knob and entered the room. Rocky sat next to Jack on the wooden bench outside the closed door to the principal's inner sanctum and in front of the secretary's vacant desk. Jack hunched with his eyes closed and his head hung, his chin against his bony chest. His right arm twitched in his lap.

"It's okay, Jack. Mom's here now. She'll get it." The tenderness in Rocky's voice, and his obvious faith in Nikki's ability to right whatever was wrong touched her.

Jack's red-rimmed eyes popped open. He shot off the bench, crashed into her legs and circled spindly arms around Nikki's waist. Gazing up at her, his expression anguished, he pleaded, "Mommy, please! You *have* to get it back for me!"

She smoothed his hair with her hand. "I'll do my best, honey. What do you want back?"

"That jerk, Coop, took his notebook," Rocky spit out disdainfully. He stood, his fists clenched at his side.

The door opened and Mrs. Segers emerged from the principal's office.

Her face lit with a smile. "Hello, Mrs. Lambert. Thank you for coming so quickly. Miss Young will see you now."

Her expression pleasant, the school secretary focused on Rocky. "You can go back to class. I'm sure your brother appreciated your company."

Rocky accepted the hall pass from Mrs. Segers, mute and scowling. He gave Nikki a head nod and defiantly remained rooted to the spot near the bench.

"Someone took Jack's notebook? Is that what this is all about?" Nikki's arms tightened around Jack as he buried his face in her sweater at her waist.

"Jack had a bit of a tantrum in class. He was very disruptive. His teacher asked him to leave. He accused a boy in the class of taking his book, but the boy denied it," the secretary recited.

Jack raised his head and gazed at Nikki, his blue eyes swimming tears. "Mommy, Rick Cooper stole my notebook. He is a liar. I need it back. He can't read it. No one can read it."

When Jack trembled, Nikki became incensed. "Sit down, boys. I'll be right back."

In three fury-fueled strides she reached the door and yanked it open.

"Mrs. Lambert, where are you going?" Mrs. Segers blurted out in a high-pitched voice.

"To get Jack's notebook." She zipped through the door and out into the hall.

"You can't go up there!" she hollered, a booming echo through the corridors.

Watch me. Nikki climbed the stairs two at a time traveling the route she had taken the week before during Back to School Night.

Outside Jack's class she spied his teacher, Mrs. Spano through the small square window in the door that she promptly yanked open. She stomped inside and sang out, "Where is Rick Cooper?"

Mrs. Spano widened her eyes and bustled over to her. "Mrs. Lambert, you can't come in here while my class is in session. Jack is down in the principal's office."

"I'm sorry for the interruption, Mrs. Spano." Her tone was not apologetic. "I know where Jack is. I need to know which one of your students is Rick Cooper."

Nikki peered at each child's face in rapid succession.

A blond boy slumped in his chair, wiseass written all over his face. He raised his arm half-mast and flipped his wrist a couple times offering Nikki snotty, I could care less about you, lady, waves of his hand. "That would be me," he said, his eyes hooded.

The girls tittered and the boys in the class fixated on him, apparently worshipping their rule-breaking idol.

He bared his teeth affording Nikki a pointedly phony smile and then tightened his lips into a frozen, smug glare. She sized up the class bully, thriving on his classmates' longing to walk in his shadow out of displaced admiration or just plain fear.

"Give me Jack's notebook now." Nikki's voice cracked like a whip.

She pre-empted his denial holding out a flat palm in his direction. "Do not play games with me, Mr. Cooper. Give me the notebook."

She advanced toward his desk opening her hand to retrieve the notebook that she knew he had taken from her little boy.

Her gaze held his unblinking. His eyelashes fluttered twice and he broke the stare.

"*Now*." Nikki's voice blasted in the stillness.

He kicked his backpack out from under his desk, yanked open the flap and extracted Jack's notebook.

"I didn't mean anything by it. I was just teasing him." He handed it over with a shrug of his shoulders as a telltale guilty blush reddened his face.

Nikki jerked the book out of his hand. Tempted to scream at the little brat for the unforgivable act of making her boy's life even more unbearable, she turned her back on him, mute and steaming.

Mrs. Spano tailed her as she marched out into the hallway. "I'm so sorry, Mrs. Lambert, for believing Rick was innocent."

"Has Jack given you any reason to believe that he lies?"

"No, he hasn't."

"I sat with you last week. You know my son is very sick. How could you let that bully torment him?" Nikki stopped and sucked in a breath. "At the very least, why didn't you send Rick Cooper to the office, too?"

"I'm truly sorry. It won't happen again."

"You're right about that." She spun away from her unwilling to listen to another word.

Hell bent on returning Jack's notebook, Nikki raced back to the office. She planned on removing the boys from that unkind environment and taking them home, safe and happy—as far away from the Rick Coopers in their world as possible, for at least an afternoon.

Jack's face lit up when he spied the notebook clutched in her hand.

"Thank you, Mommy. Thank you." He sighed as

he accepted the notebook that she handed him. He pressed it over his heart.

Mrs. Segers sat silent behind her desk.

Nikki flicked her eyes at her and said, "We're leaving."

"But Miss Young is still waiting to speak with you," she said.

"Tell Miss Young to call Mr. and Mrs. Cooper in to deal with the fact that their son lied and stole from my son. She should question Mrs. Spano as to why Rick Cooper isn't sitting outside her office now with Jack.

"Come on, boys, we're leaving." Nikki firmly clasped Jack's hand and left.

Rocky skipped down the stairs in front of Nikki and Jack. He plunged into the back seat of the car without a "shotgun" battle. Behind the wheel Nikki's pulse skittered in the aftermath of confrontation—something she abhorred and had avoided—until ALD had amped up her protective instincts.

"Mom, you were great." Rocky chortled. "You should have seen your face. That was awesome."

His praise stoked her pride, and she momentarily enjoyed the sense of empowerment. Then she glanced at Jack. He sagged in the passenger seat as if defeated, and the bravado seeped out of her. She didn't have a Plan B, and she intuited that Jack needed her to formulate one on the spot.

"Are you okay, sweetheart?" She gently stretched his seatbelt out and buckled it over him.

"I guess." His hands twitched in his lap. "Is Rick going to get in trouble?"

"I don't know." She turned the key in the ignition.

"I guess that's up to Miss Young."

He nodded his head a couple times. "Boy, Rick will really have it out for me now."

"Hmm," she said considering the very real possibility. "I won't let that happen. I promise you," she vowed having no idea how she'd deliver.

"I don't want him to know I'm sick. I don't want anybody to know," he confessed, his voice soft and tremulous.

A silent sob caught in her throat. "Okay."

She braked at a traffic light and gazed at Jack. His face brightened. "I just won't bring my notebook to school anymore."

My God, my God, I hate this.

"How about ice cream?" she proposed, determined in the moment to ignore this damned disease with its unforgiving limitations, erosions and loss.

"Before *dinner*?" Rocky piped up. "This is the best day ever."

In the rearview mirror he bopped in his seat.

"Is your seatbelt on?"

His reflection grinned at her as the buckle clicked.

Jack fell sound asleep and he didn't awaken until she parked in front of the Sweet Shoppe.

Seated on the old-fashioned soda fountain stools between her leg-dangling sons, she dug into a gooey, hot fudge brownie sundae. The identical and absolutely prohibited treat disappeared in minutes under the barrage of her treat-starved duo's flying spoons.

When she trudged into the house behind Rocky and Jack after their "treat stop" her heart and stomach ached.

"Do I smell chocolate chip cookies?" Rocky

sprinted toward the kitchen yelling, "Grandma, can I have a cookie?"

"I'm going to my room." Jack headed toward the stairs.

Pausing at the foot of the staircase he gazed upward and heaved a sigh. His face set in determination and he climbed a step, rested a beat, and then proceeded upward, apparently straining at the effort.

Nikki lingered in the hallway pondering possible home remodeling to make Jack's life easier. If her husband were alive he'd be able to do the construction himself.

John. His suicide made more sense when an insurance check came in the mail a few days before. After tearing the slim envelope open, mildly curious, Nikki had gaped at the amount of the check. John's *accidental* death at the railroad crossing where, unbelievably, the authorities had ruled a malfunction of the crossing barriers, had resulted in the payment of $50,000.00.

Had John rigged the crossing arms machinery? She'd never know, but she suspected that he had.

The irony that she had already accumulated thousands of dollars in medical bills with no end in sight negated whatever good intentions John may have had in orchestrating the "accident" that resulted in his intended windfall for her. She couldn't be grateful for John's assumed sacrifice, and she wouldn't dwell on it.

She rested her head on the banister and closed her eyes. Maybe she had enough money to install a chair lift on the stairs.

"Rocky told me about what happened at school." Nikki startled at the sound of Kay's voice behind her.

"Oh. Sorry to frighten you." She wiped her hands on a dishtowel.

"I guess he told you about the ice cream, too."

"He didn't need to. He had chocolate all over his face." She chuckled. "I figured if you were throwing caution to the wind, a cookie wouldn't hurt him. I'm sorry he caught me baking them. I wanted to give Dad a treat, and I didn't think the boys would be home before I removed the evidence. If it helps, I didn't put any butter in them."

She gave Nikki a melancholy smile and sat on the bottom step. Exhaustion lines creased her face adding ten years to her appearance.

"Are you all right, Mom? You seem tired."

"I'm fine, dear." She patted the space next to her. "I want to talk to you about something important."

The day's events left Nikki wrung out and ill equipped to discuss anything important, but she owed Kay a good deal more than attention, so she sat obediently.

"Dad and I have been talking and we think we have it all figured out. If we take out more on our line of equity, and with Dad's connections with contractors, we think we can remodel our house to be wheel chair accessible. Dad thinks we can have everything completed before Thanksgiving." She stopped and gazed at Nikki's face intently.

"I don't understand. Why would you do that?"

"So you and the boys can move in with us."

Nikki did a double take. "That's very…generous. But no, thank you. I don't want to move the boys to New Jersey. We are not moving out of our home."

"Honey, we can't stay here to help for much

longer. We have jobs and need to get back to them." She wagged her head, the strain of the last few months evident in the grayish pallor in her cheeks and the cascade of wrinkles around her eyes.

"I understand, Mom. And I can't thank you and Dad enough for all you have done. But we can't move. This is the boys' home. All their memories of John are here in this house."

Nikki paused regretting that she caused the tears that welled in Kay's eyes. "I appreciate you and Dad more than you will ever know, but if you need to leave, I'll do anything necessary to manage without you."

"Think this through, Nikki. It's almost impossible for Jack to move around this big old house."

"I know. I'll take care of it."

"How?"

"There's the money from John's life insurance policy…I can work extra hours or even take another part-time job. Maybe something I can do from home."

"What are you going to do when you can't work any longer because Jack needs full time care? What will you live on? How will you survive?"

"I don't know." Her head throbbed and she didn't want to deal with the details.

"The insurance money won't last forever."

The awful looming terror gripped Nikki again. Her throat clogged, but she managed to whisper, "Neither will Jack."

Chapter 14

Standing behind a linen-skirted banquet table, Ram greeted fans that Sunday morning at the ALD Foundation event in Slidell, Louisiana.

"I'll be damned, it's the Engineer!" A bald guy bellowed from across the huge tented space. He lumbered toward Ram, an ear-to-ear smile creasing his pudgy face.

"It's been forever," he wheezed coming to a halt to the left of the line of folks awaiting autographs.

Affording a birds' eye view of his gleaming dome, he extended a hand over the table for a shake while he chattered non-stop, "You're in good shape, Ram. Just as good as when we were in school. Not washed up like the papers say. That Coach Beltzer is a dragon himself, right? There's no stopping the Highland U Engineer. I say that to everybody. Not that there are lots of Massachusetts Dragons fans around in Saints territory. But I am, and proud of it."

Pumping the man's hand, Ram wracked his brain for a connection to someone who acted like an old buddy. "Uh, always good to see a Highland U alum."

"Go Highlanders. Damned straight. I watched you lead that train all four years."

"Ah," Ram said nodding his head dumbly.

Ram estimated the guy's age at about fifty. Either he was a late in life undergrad back then or Ram was his contemporary. If the latter were true, maybe Ram had deluded himself in thinking that he was still in his prime to play football—even more washed up than the Dragons head coach believed.

"Those were the best four years of my life so far," he reminisced, still shaking Ram's hand. "I didn't know you were appearing here today. We could have gotten together last night for dinner or something."

"I elected to participate last minute...after the event flyers were printed." *Who the hell is this guy?* "And I got in really late last night."

"Wow, look at the HU jerseys." With his left hand he fingered a pile of shirts that Ram had hounded the university head coach to donate and had asked his former O-linesmen to autograph. "Caboose, Tracks...shit, the whole train signed it. I have to get a couple of these."

Glancing at the line of people to his right, Ram noticed the disgruntled expressions and overt glaring at his purported former classmate.

"Uh..." He gently pried his hand free from the never-ending handshake, frustrated that he still couldn't fill in the blank with the man's name. "Good to see you again. We could talk longer if you don't mind waiting in line."

He whacked his palm on his forehead. "Sure, sure. Sorry."

Inching back from the table he cast a conciliatory smile at the man at the head of the line who scowled at him and mumbled, "No problem."

As Ram signed the Dragons jersey placed on the table in front of him with a Sharpie, he observed the yet unidentified Highland U alum travel the length of the line and queue into last place. About twenty people queued ahead of him before Ram would have to re-up with this enthusiastic fellow.

Bop, bop, bop sounded from David Cry's taps on the mic. "Friends," he called out, a magnified boom. "If you'd please find your seats?"

Brightening at this temporary reprieve from the embarrassment of potentially dissing an old acquaintance, Ram sat down at the sports "celebrities" table and the autograph line dispersed.

"I'm David Cry, with the ALD Foundation. Thank you all for joining together to enjoy A Big Easy Sunday Morning with us. Special thanks to our Big Easy Sponsors, Coastal Regional Medical Center and Slidell General," David announced as he clapped his hands and spurred audience applause. "Imagine having everything we desire—our taste buds and appetite satiated, and these wonderful children entertained and joyful—all in one place here at the beautiful home of our community hosts, Doctor and Mrs. Gene Rivers."

More applause sounded at David's lead. Ram scanned the faces of the attendees assembled beneath the billowing folds of the lawn tent's canopy. David's amplified southern drawl commanded rapt attention. Clad in dark green chinos and a short sleeve T-shirt screen printed with the ALD Foundation logo and motto, *"Care Today for a Cure Tomorrow,"* the master of ceremonies bristled with excitement and energy. There was something magnetic in the unassuming, prematurely bald man's persona—a charisma that polarized action.

"All proceeds today from attendance donations, sports merchandise purchases, and the silent auction items, benefit the Adrenoleukodystrophy Foundation. We are in for a treat because our celebrity chef, Nick Corello, has prepared a meal that will provide us with the exquisite flavors of a traditional New Orleans Sunday Brunch. We have exceptional children's activities planned for after brunch. Plus…"

He paused clasping his hands in front of him. "We are further blessed to have football, baseball, basketball, and hockey superstars Ram Delaney, Jorge Aiolo, Frank Cruise, and Dennis Chenier with us this morning to sign autographs, pose for photos, or have some friendly conversations with y'all." David elevated a hand. "Guys, you want to stand up?"

Ram and his sports entertainment colleagues rose in place as directed, rewarded by a smattering of applause as David quipped, "Not that they need introduction."

Briefly, Ram gazed into the eyes of his unidentified classmate. Bob McGregor, in school on the GI Bill after several tours of duty. Feeling younger and on top of things having finally remembered the guy's name, he sat back down and tuned in to the remainder of David's speech.

"The foundation's aim is the eradication of ALD. When ALD strikes, children lose their hearing, they become blind, they lose their ability to speak and move. These symptoms give way to a vegetative state where they remain until death. The foundation works with researchers at Harvard, M.I.T., Coastal Regional Medical Center, and other universities in the U.S. and abroad. We have assisted families affected by the tragedies of ALD in over eighty countries, and we will *not* stop until solutions are achieved."

He paused while the audience erupted in thunderous applause. How many of those people knew the full extent of David's dedication considering how personal it had become for the foundation's CEO with his own son's illness?

For the hundredth time, Nikki's beautiful face flashed in Ram's mind. He'd do anything to change Jack's prognosis and snatch him off the one-way rocket toward a vegetative state. A chill ran through him at the thought of that funny, giant-hearted, creative kid losing himself, imprisoned in a neurological limbo. And then...They'd all lose Jack.

"Please. Enjoy the meal and the day. Thank you from the bottom of my heart for supporting the ALD Foundation," David concluded.

"Hey Frank," Ram addressed the power forward for the current world champion Dynamos. "Why don't we divide up," he suggested making eye contact with the other two men at the table, "And go find seats at four different tables?"

"Sure. Good idea."

Rising from his seat Ram smiled up at Frank whose approximate seven feet of height dwarfed him. He rarely felt puny in the general population. Frank casually stretched an arm upward, touched the canvas on the tent's roof with his fingertips and gave Ram a shit-eating grin.

A little boy exclaimed, "Wow!"

Frank ambled over to that kid's table like a two-legged giraffe.

The remaining occupants of the celebrity table scattered toward the other three corners of the space, and Ram carried a chair over to an already full table of eight: four couples, maybe in their late thirties/early forties. "Mind if I join you?"

"Not at all," came one man's hearty voice.

He scooted his chair to the left while the woman next to him opened up an ample gap moving in the opposite direction. As Ram pulled his chair up to the table he smiled at her, and she blushed.

"Thank you," Ram said as he gazed at the smiling faces around the table. "It's great I could be here today." Chuckling he added, "That's kind of a good news/bad news thing. It would be great to be on the field today, too."

"How's th'arm?" the lady next to him drawled. "Y'all think Beltzer will call you up out of injured reserve?"

Ram loved a woman who knew football. "Are you a Dragons fan?"

She snorted. "Lord no. Just want to know what my Saints are up against. No offense, Mister Delaney, but I'd be pleased if Beltzer keeps Larry Whitney in there all season."

Damn him, he probably will.

"No offense taken." Not against her anyway, Ram thought.

"Well, they're six and O for the season now, so Whitney is doing the job," Ram conceded.

"Yeah, but the defense won those games. Whitney didn't do squat."

He burst out laughing. "I love you."

Beaming at him, she touched his sleeve lightly, a wicked gleam in her eye. "You just rest that ol' sore arm, darlin', ya hear?"

In need of a change of subject, Ram posed to the

table at large, "So, why are you generous donors here today? Are you all David Cry's friends?"

As if he had lobbed a bomb into the middle of the table, shell-shocked expressions blotted out smiles.

Fingering her water glass, the woman across from him replied softly, "We've become friends with each other, and with David, because our sons died of ALD."

Their palpable sadness hit him like a sledgehammer. "I'm so deeply sorry. There are no words." He wagged his head as he gazed into the woman's tear brimmed eyes.

"Thank you," she said her chin tilted upward, her huge hazel eyes penetrating. "We are determined to honor our Joe's legacy by eliminating ALD forever."

Marveling at this woman's strength, Nikki's face flashed in Ram's mind again. The seizure, the nightmare trip to the ER. Her unbelievable courage and selfless mother love. Her beautiful smile...The warmth of her touch...

"I know a boy in Highland Square, Massachusetts, who has ALD," Ram said. "I've become close to his family. I'm here today to help David fund research. And to learn as much as I can to help this boy—Jack Lambert."

"The Dragons' loss is our gain," his neighbor lady said. "What do you want to know, honey?"

Before the auction began, Ram excused himself and left the banquet hall. Standing in the parking lot he dialed Nikki's cell phone.

"Hi, Ram." Her voice stirred his heart.

"Hi, Nikki. How's everything?"

"Good. I thought you had the ALD breakfast."

"I do. They're in between events. I thought I would

call and see how Jack is doing." *And I miss you.*

"He's okay. Very tired and seems to be slowing down. That incident at school really took its toll."

"If I had that snot-nosed kid in front of me, I'd teach him a few things about bullying."

"You'd have to get in line behind me, Mickey, and Kay." He could hear the smile in her voice.

"And let's not forget Rocky." He laughed. "We all have Jack's back."

Nikki yawned. He wished he could do something to relieve her from some of her burdens.

"I better get going. They're about to start the auction, and I want to evil-eye donors so they up their bids. I'll talk to you when I get back."

"Thanks for calling," she said.

The call clicked offline. Ram held the phone to his ear a few seconds to stay connected, missing her even more, before stowing it in his pocket.

****

After David drove him to the airport, Ram boarded the charter flight lugging two shopping bags full of autographed gear for Jack and Rocky. He had outbid everyone for V.I.P. experiences for the boys with Frank, Jorge, and Dennis although he had no idea if basketball, baseball, or hockey appealed to either one of them, or if they gave a hoot about the teams those three played on. But if they did, their eyes would pop out of their heads when he presented them with the stash.

With Halloween two days away, they could even use some of the stuff as costumes. And if Nikki would let Jack and Rocky use the V.I.P. experiences that he'd won at the silent auction, the boys would sit on the bench at a Dynamos game, shoot for goal on the ice between periods at Dennis' home rink, and throw out the first pitch of the season at Jorge's opener.

Ram pinched his eyebrows with his thumb and index finger and sighed.

Will Jack still be with us when the baseball season starts next year?

The odds were against him, but Ram remained hopeful. That was his nature. Despite the odds, the underdog could win. He'd done that so many times in his career that he believed if you fought hard and thought positive winning was within reach. He couldn't tolerate his current situation with the Dragons if he thought otherwise. Beltzer would call, and Jack would be cured.

He stared out the porthole as the pilot banked after takeoff. Remembering some of the advice those grieving parents had offered during brunch, his head spun. There seemed no proactive way to keep ahead of the series of debilitating symptoms Jack would likely suffer, but he considered how he could help make things better for him. The V.I.P. experiences represented one way to sweeten Jack's life, but Ram sensed that Nikki was more concerned with sustaining Jack's normal, happy home life than wild, wish list adventures.

The prospect of installing an aquatic center at the GSC appealed to Ram. One mom at his table said that swimming was a tremendous plus for her boy when he had lost his ability to walk. His arms wrapped around her neck as they had twirled around the pool together, he had said, "Mom, this is so great. In the pool there's nothing wrong with me."

Exhausted, he slouched in the leather seat,

considering the logistics of land use on the GSC campus and how fast contractors could complete an indoor pool facility. The testimonies of the parents who had lost children to ALD inched out practical thoughts about building projects. One hand fanned over his eyes, he hung his head and cried.

Chapter 15

The doorbell rang for the umpteenth time since Nikki had rushed home with the boys to change into Halloween costumes.

"Rock, get that for me, please?" she shouted over the banister.

On her way down the hall toward the bathroom, she tugged the purple ribbon and a rubber band out of her hair. Wincing as a few strands ripped out of her scalp, she decided that pigtails didn't work with her choppy-cut hair.

She stepped into the bathroom while undoing the orange ribbon on the other side. Partially closing the door to view her reflection in the full-length mirror mounted on the interior side, she finger brushed her hair and surveyed her outfit.

The vintage Dragons' cheerleader uniform she had found for five dollars in a resale shop fit more tightly over her bust than she liked. She tugged on the hem of the skimpy skirt lowering the elastic waistband down over her hips. That action "lengthened" the skirt enough to cover about half her thighs. Frowning, she stuffed each arm into the sleeves of an eggplant purple cardigan and buttoned up every button concealing most of the vest. But she still showed a lot of leg.

Ridiculously uncomfortable, Nikki regretted having spent the five bucks on the outfit to go trick or treating. Her self-consciousness over her attire wasn't responsible for the stinging tears that welled up. Again, John's permanent desertion of the family left her unanchored and alone.

John and Nikki had dressed up every Halloween with Jack and Rocky. The year before had featured a baseball theme, although Rocky had predictably insisted on dressing as Ram Delaney. A football theme was planned for this year to appease Rocky and to unify the family. Coincidentally Ram had supplied the boys' costumes.

So the football theme lived on without her husband. The first Halloween as a single parent, clad in an uncomfortable costume seemed to symbolize Nikki's attitude about her life. It didn't fit. Rather than venture out into the neighborhood in that get-up, she would rather leave a bowl of candy out on the stoop on the honor system, slip into her pajamas and read a book in bed. Without John's lovable silliness and clowning with the boys, Halloween wasn't for Nikki.

A light tap sounded on the door. "Mom, are you almost ready?' came Jack's voice.

She ran her hands through her hair again resigned to adjust her attitude for the kids' sake. "Coming."

Scooping up the purple and orange pompoms off the floor she flung open the door.

"Wow, Mommy." Jack stumbled a step back, his eyes huge. He beamed a smile. "You look so pretty. Like a *real* cheerleader."

She had never received a better-timed or sweeter compliment.

"And you look like the real Ramsey Delaney," she fibbed.

His calves poked stick-like out of the cuffs of knee length, padded football pants. And the team jersey hung loose on his bony frame. He carried his helmet in a crooked elbow jutted away from his torso as if he avoided contact with a hot kettle.

"Do I have to wear *this*?" His heavy eyelids and the dull sheen in his eyes had lately changed Jack's little boy face. He exuded an old man's weariness with life.

Plodding with him toward the staircase, she relieved him of the heavy helmet. "I'd rather you not wear the helmet, actually. It's already starting to get dark outside and maybe you'd have trouble seeing with it on."

"I have trouble seeing without it on," he quipped with a rueful tense of his jaw.

Jack clamped hold of the banister with his right hand in a white-knuckled grip, and he minced down each step. Weaving while his legs jerked, his supporting hand squeaked as he dragged it along the banister on the descent. Her heart was in her mouth following him downstairs.

"I'm not going to wear mine either, Jack." Rocky, another Ram Delaney clone, stood at the bottom of the stairs.

Nikki read the disappointment in his eyes, but he removed his helmet and placed it on the chair. A quote she loved sprang to mind. *Disappointment is a way of life; character is how you handle it.* Rocky made her proud.

The doorbell chimed again as she reached the first floor. Rocky grabbed the bowl of candy off the hall table and yanked the front door open. Ramsey Delaney,

133

the original, overfilled the doorframe.

"Howdy, partner," he drawled, a hilarious Boston accented "paadnir."

He tipped the child-sized cowboy hat on his superman-sized head, the chinstrap digging furrows on his cheeks. "Hand over all your candy and no one will get hurt."

His hand hovered over the handle of a water pistol that poked out of his belt.

She snorted as Rocky handed Ram the candy bowl in dead serious surrender.

Refraining from laughing in Ram's face she managed, "Come on in, cowboy."

"Why, thank you, Miss Nikki. Mighty kind of you." His far miss attempt at a home on the range accent had the boys giggling.

Ram gave her a mischievous smile and then handed back the bowl of candy. He reversed, sashayed back out onto the stoop, and returned carrying three bulging shopping bags. Inside the house, he set the bags down near the entry and shoved his peewee Stetson back off his head. It plastered to the nape of his neck, the strap a seeming stranglehold over his Adam's apple.

"I come with treats and no tricks, paadnirs." Hoisting the bags up, he requested, "Let's all mosey into this here living room and check out this bounty?"

Grinning, the boys happily complied.

Amused she trailed the three "Rams" and sat on the couch next to the real McCoy. "It's Halloween, Ram. Not Christmas," she commented eyeing the stuffed bags.

Unproductively tugging on the hem of her skirt she gazed at the boys who sat on the floor in front of Ram, mesmerized by the "treat" bags at his feet.

"Here you go." He handed a bag each to Jack and Rocky and then withdrew a baseball mitt and a book out of the third bag.

Sliding that bag on the floor around the side of the couch, he held up the mitt and said, "I asked Jorge Aiolo to sign this for your grandpa. Why he likes the Yankees is a mystery to me."

"Me, too." Rocky nodded his head.

"And a cookbook signed by Chef Nick Corello for your grandma. Are they here?"

"No, they had to go home," Jack said as he peeked into his bag.

"What are you guys waiting for? Go ahead. Unpack your bags." His blue eyes shining, Ram leaned back against the sofa cushion. The couch creaked a groan.

His nearness, the citrus smell of his cologne, and his emanating warmth drew Nikki in, moth to flame. For the first time she was grateful that she could only afford the loveseat when she had furnished the living room.

Delight skittered through her when she noticed Ram's gaze linger on her legs like a thrilling caress.

The boys dipped their hands in and out of the bags, extracting shirts, autographed balls and jerseys from all their favorite players. They heaped items on the floor around them in an excited frenzy.

"Thanks so much, Ram," Jack sang out fingering the Highland U jersey reverently.

Rocky sprang to his feet and flew at Ram, his arms outstretched. Crashing into Ram's chest, Rocky hugged him with his eyes squeezed shut. "Awesome, Ram.

Thanks."

Ram's eyelids lowered a beat as he brushed his lips on Rocky's crown. His arms enveloped her boy.

Her attraction to Ram soared, dizzying. His fondness for her children was genuine, breath-robbing. Everything about Ram Delaney appealed to Nikki.

Jack wore an ear-to-ear grin as he attempted to stand, but caved at the knees twice plopping back down on his butt. Ram casually unlocked one arm out of Rocky's bear hug, extended his hand to Jack and towed him to his feet.

"Thank you. Boy, you weren't kidding when you said you only had treats and no tricks." Jack gave Ram the thin, exhausted smile that split Nikki down the middle.

"My pleasure, boys." Ram set Rocky free and then hugged Jack lightly. "Thanks for taking all this stuff off my hands."

"Mommy, can we call Poppy to tell him about his mitt?" Jack asked. "He won't believe it."

"Sure," she agreed. "But don't talk too long or we won't have time to go trick or treating before dark."

They dashed away leaving their gifts. Suddenly prickly sitting next to Ram on the couch, Nikki kneeled on the floor and settled back on her haunches. Tucking the skimpy skirt securely under her rear end she folded the shirts and put them back in the bags, skittish with his eyes on her.

Ram knelt down next to her and helped load the shopping bags.

Nikki's pulse raced, electrified by the impulse to throw her arms around his neck and immerse in Rocky's brand of uninhibited hugs.

"Your in-laws left?" The bag crackled as he tossed a shirt inside. "Don't you need their help?"

"They have their own lives. They wanted us to move in with them in New Jersey. They made plans to make their house handicap-accessible for Jack. I said, no. They were disappointed. It's a long story."

Thankful that he didn't comment, she continued to collect the boys' gifts off the floor.

"You're spoiling them, Ram. Where did you get all this?"

"At the fundraiser for ALD. I met the most interesting people. David Cry is an amazing speaker."

"I learned about his foundation through Jack's physician."

"I stumbled upon his name when I researched ALD the first day I met you. I called him."

"Really? Why?"

"I wanted to know more about what Jack is contending with, so I contacted David. That's when he told me about the fundraiser he was putting together. I had to get involved."

"You did all of this for Jack?" She faced him. "I don't understand."

"After you came into my office and confided in me about his illness I couldn't stop thinking about him. He is such a special soul."

His eyes glimmered, and he tightened his lips.

"I've worked with lots of kids, but no one has ever touched me like Jack. I *have* to help him, Nikki. I want to help find the cure for this fucking disease," he whispered rubbing his hands over his face.

The obscenity didn't shock her. No adjective was obscene enough to describe ALD.

"And since I met you and the boys…"

Ram's cornflower blue eyes locked on Nikki's. He leaned toward her and she involuntarily tilted her face toward his. Closer. His full lips parted slightly as he drew nearer, inches apart.

"Grandma and Poppy said thank you, Ram." Rocky charged into the living room.

Nikki and Ram separated with whiplash jerks apart.

Rocky grabbed the trick or treat bags off the coffee table and handed one to Jack when he entered the room walking in a hitching gait. "Poppy wants us to call later to tell him how much candy we get. Can we go now?"

Nikki's eyebrows shot up expecting a more courteous request.

"Please."

Ram stretched the chinstrap backward and plopped his cowboy hat on his head. "Let's saddle up, cowpokes."

"Wow. Are you coming with us?" Jack asked.

"If it's okay with your mom."

All eyes trained on Nikki.

It seemed the most natural thing in the world when she responded, "It's more than okay with me."

Ram took Nikki's hand and followed the boys out the door. Comfortable with his warm hand clasping hers and genuinely happy for the first time in so long, she decided not to feel guilty about enjoying this sexy, tantalizing man.

"Let's go to the Nunnos' first. Pauly will poop his pants when he sees Ram trick or treating with us." Rocky hurried across the street as she bit back a laugh.

"And Mrs. Nunno always gives out the big candy

bars," Jack hollered on a beeline for the neighbor's brick front steps behind his brother.

Ram delighted the neighborhood children, most of their fathers and all of their mothers. He flanked the boys at each front door, signed autographs and chatted while the boys' bags grew fat with candy.

Rocky was in his glory. When Jack noticeably tired, stumbling a few times along the sidewalk, Ram lifted both boys up and carried one under each arm like footballs to the next consecutive stop. Nikki couldn't remember her kids giggling like that before.

"Would you like to stay for dinner?" She invited when they finished trick or treating, hoping that the leftover soup would stretch enough to feed Ram.

"I would. Thank you for asking me." He yanked the hat off. "And a gentleman never wears a hat to dinner. Thank God I can lose this thing now."

He grinned as he tossed the hat in the air and pegged it squarely on the coat rack.

"What's for dinner?" Chocolate rimmed Rocky's mouth.

Panic gripped her. VLCFA's—very long chain fatty acids in foods posed a far greater danger than razor blades in apples or unsealed candies that Halloween. "No more candy until I go through your bags. We're having lentil soup for dinner."

"Ugh. Not that again." He clutched his throat and made retching noises. Then he groused, "You used to always order pizza for dinner on Halloween before we ran out of…"

Nikki shook her head at Rocky, and he clamped his mouth shut melodramatically.

"Mommy says we can't afford pizza," Jack said

softly.

Her cheeks burned, and she sorely regretted inviting Ram to dinner.

"I can afford a couple of pies." Ram arched his eyebrow, expectant, and gazed at Nikki. "Would that be all right with you?"

"I can't let you pay for dinner. You've spent too much money already." She pointed to the shopping bags in the living room.

"Let me. I even know a place that can use low fat toppings." Ram reached a hand in his pocket and produced his cell phone. "Okay?"

"I don't want to eat lentil soup again," Jack complained.

"Okay, you win. But you're going to eat the soup tomorrow."

"Any preferences?" Ram asked, frowning as she wagged her head.

"Sausage, please," came Jack's predicted response.

"Hmm." Ram pulled at his chin. "I can't stand sausage myself. I'm a plain cheese man."

"We want what Ram wants," Rocky asserted. "Right, Jack?"

"That's right," Jack capitulated—with a grin on his face.

She let out the breath she was holding and directed, "While we wait for the pizza, go wash up and put on your pj's, guys.

"And, Rocky," she added, "leave that trick or treat bag down here."

"Aw, Ma…"

****

After the pizza demolition, Nikki tucked Jack and

Rocky into bed and changed into comfortable jeans and a soft, sea foam green sweater.

She overheard snatches of Ram's telephone conversation as she padded downstairs barefoot. "I don't care how you get it done. Just get it done. Don't worry about the cost. That's my problem." He belted out a hearty laugh.

"Yeah, I'll sign a few more footballs. Thanks, Brad. I owe you." Ram burst out laughing again. "Sure, you can add it to your very long list."

Nikki drifted into the room. He had set an open bottle of wine and two full glasses on the coffee table.

"Who was that?" she picked up the glasses and handed one to Ram.

"My agent, Brad." He averted her gaze and added, "Just had to go over a few things with him."

He didn't offer further details, so she put her curiosity aside. "Thanks for bringing this, Ram." Taking a sip of the deep red wine, Nikki perched on the couch. "This is delicious. I can't thank you enough for everything you did for us today. I dreaded this first Halloween without John. You made it so easy for all of us. Watching Jack and Rocky sit on the floor sorting their booty and swapping favorites, I thought, this is so normal. The exact same as kids all over town sifting through their candy sitting on the floor with their families. For today, Jack was just a normal little boy. And...you made me feel..." She closed her eyes as prickling tears brimmed.

Ram's arm encircled Nikki's shoulder, and he drew her close against his taut chest. The temptation to bury her head in his shirt and let her emotions loose tempted her. But if she dropped her guard for even a moment, the dam's walls would rupture, and there'd be no stopping the hysteria.

She straightened and gulped down more wine. "What's in that shopping bag?" she asked gesturing toward the vicinity of the couch.

"Oh, I almost forgot." He shifted over to the far edge of the sofa, lifted the bag onto his lap and unpacked things onto the coffee table.

"I brought you your own Dragons jersey, a signed cookbook, and a bunch of tickets to different sports events."

Handing her a stack of envelopes, he placed the bag back down on the floor carefully. "And a couple more bottles of wine are in here."

"Ram, I can't accept all this," she protested, enormously flattered by his thoughtfulness. "It's too much."

His steady gaze riveted her. "It isn't enough."

"Um…then…thank you so much."

Nikki dropped her gaze to her lap and then focused on her glass. Suddenly she wanted to chug it empty. "I don't know much about wine, but this is really excellent."

"I'm glad you like it. I enrolled you in the Big Kahuna Club."

"Huh?" A little wine shot into her nose with her explosive burst of laughter. "Do they make this wine in Hawaii?"

"California. Longboard Vineyards. I met the vintner at the fundraiser. He's a pretty cool guy."

"Exactly what is a big kahuna?"

He chuckled. "A V.I.P. of some sort. I'm not sure how it works, but I'm certain that they send you wine. I gave them my credit card and told them to take care of it."

Sampling the heady stuff again, she still intended to refuse yet another gift. "Please cancel the enrollment, Ram. This is definitely too much for me to accept."

"I have an ulterior motive."

"You do?"

"I'm hoping that when a shipment arrives, you'll invite me over to share it with you." His eyes sparkled and his lopsided grin had her beaming at him.

Ram's overwhelming sex appeal overwhelmed her. *Enough wine, Nikki, before you do something way too impulsive.*

"Tell me more about the fundraiser?" She set her half full wine glass on the coffee table.

"The research that the foundation is helping to fund is breaking new ground. I believe a cure is within reach. We just have to raise enough money to finance the ongoing research. I'm glad that I went to the function. I met some wonderful people, and I learned a lot. Did you know that children with ALD love to swim? They don't feel different in the water. I've already put plans in motion to install an indoor pool facility at the GSC. Jack will love it."

She didn't burst his bubble because she longed to share his hopeful exuberance and pretend, for just part of an evening, that Jack would live long enough to enjoy Ram's pool.

"I feel like I can really make a difference. We're going to help find a cure for this disease, Nikki." He clasped her hand and squeezed it with conviction.

She trusted Ram's intentions completely despite her informed skepticism. If anyone could make a difference maybe Ramsey Delaney could. He had already made an enormous difference to her sons. And to her.

As if he read her thoughts, his penetrating gaze held hers. "And before I go," he said, "I'd like to finish what I started before we went out with the boys."

His huge hands cupped the sides of her face and his fingers gently threaded through her hair. He kissed her softly evoking dreamy, melting sensations in her limbs as she surrendered to the pulse-revving sweetness.

Involuntarily Nikki returned the kiss, and Ram responded by intensifying the fusion of his lips on hers. His hands fell away from her face, and he wrapped his arms around her shoulders and pressed her close to his solid, muscled chest.

Nikki sighed as he released her. Forehead to forehead his gaze bored straight into her eyes. She could stay there, held in Ram's sensual thrall, forever.

He heaved a breath. "Lady, what you do to me," he said softly.

Smiling he rose, his gaze still riveted on Nikki. "I better say good-night."

The temperature in the room suddenly seemed to drop. Standing on rubbery legs Nikki said, "Sure…I'll see you to the door."

The brief trip with him to her front door had the desired outcome. He turned the knob, cracked open the door and swept her into his arms. Ram kissed her fiercely, a mind blanking, stomach sinking pleasure.

Releasing the embrace, he trailed his fingers down her cheek. "Good night, sweetheart," he said as he strode out the door.

"Good night, Ram." Nikki's eyes remained glued

to his back as he retreated down her walkway.

****

On the Saturday following Halloween an explosive sound outside jarred Nikki awake. She scrambled off the den sofa and raced toward the front of the house clad only in a new, extra-large, Dragons jersey and white cotton socks. A semi-truck unloaded heavy machinery in her front yard.

"Excuse me!" She ran out the front door waving her arms. "You have the wrong address."

A man in an expensive suit exited a shiny black Lexus parked in front of the semi. He signaled to the crew to keep unloading the equipment, ran up the front walk and clasped her hand.

"You must be Nikki. I'm Brad Ferguson, Ram's agent."

She let him pump her hand while she gaped at him open-mouthed.

"Let me guess. Ram didn't tell you about this."

"No." She gazed vacantly at the activity on her lawn. "What exactly is this?"

"The renovations."

She shivered, too half-asleep for embarrassment over her scanty dress in full view of the neighborhood. "What renovations?"

"Why don't we go inside and call Ram? I'll let him explain everything."

Chapter 16

"Go right in, Mrs. Lambert. He's expecting you," came Luci's voice from the outer office.

Ram quit pacing when Nikki asserted, "Oh, I'll *bet* he is."

Shoving his office door wider open, Nikki tromped into view, and Ram could almost see steam blasting out of her ears. He grinned—not the most effective strategy, since she narrowed her eyes and regarded him as if calculating the most vulnerable spot on his body to land a punch. He must have had an insane death wish because her formidable expression and combative posture tickled him and he busted up laughing.

"Exactly what is so funny?" she spit out stopping in her tracks a few feet away from him.

"You." He lowered his eyes and stared at the floor for a moment smiling to regroup. "You look so adorable right now. All full of piss and vinegar."

He had anticipated the inevitable confrontation because he had sent the construction crew out without consulting her first. Ram had deemed taking lumps for that decision the lesser of two evils since she'd likely refuse the help otherwise.

"It's not funny, Ram. How dare you hire people to tear up my house without my knowledge? What the hell were you thinking?"

He shrugged. "I don't know. That I'm helping

you?"

She dragged her fingers through her hair. His stomach tightened as he yearned to thread his fingers through her silky hair, too. In the next second he questioned his motives, something he had done repeatedly since she had stormed his office the first time. Ram still remained satisfied that he wasn't trying to buy or to manipulate her affections. Whether or not she'd ever see him the way that he saw her, Ram *had* to help Jack. The compulsion had become near obsession. He'd spend his last dime and would have fought anyone who had tried to stop him, including Nikki.

Nikki pinned him with a penetrating glare, tense and unsmiling.

"Say something," he said.

"I can take care of my son."

"I never said you couldn't. No one could give Jack better care than you. I just want you to let me help you."

She wagged her head, no. "It's too much, Ram. I can't accept it."

"I think it might be a little late to refuse." He smiled, but the dark stare she gave him had him back stepping. "Look," he said, holding his palms up in supplication, "Let's be honest. I have been paid an obscene amount of money to play football. More than I will ever need. I have the money to fix up your house for Jack, and you don't have money to spare. It's nothing. It's what friends do for each other."

"You're out of your mind." Her chest heaved.

She sighed and he detected a slight softening in her eyes and a minuscule slackening of her shoulders.

Encouraged Ram paced a step closer. "What can I

say? I'm just a dumb jock."

Her eyes danced as she snorted a laugh.

He grinned at her. "Did you send the crew home?"

"Not exactly. Brad took them to breakfast while I dressed and drove the boys here for Saturday sports."

"All right. Did Brad tell you what I've contracted to do at your place?"

"Uh uh. He convinced me to hear you out before I decided anything."

Ram closed the distance between him and Nikki to inches. Gazing down at her, his senses filled with the alluring scent of her soft perfume and the magnetizing aura that surrounded her like a gravitational pull. "Will you?"

Her brow furrowed. "Will I what?"

"Hear me out?"

At her nod, he clasped her hand gently and steered her toward the desk. "Come see the blueprints."

He had unrolled and spread the prints out on his desk earlier, anchored at the corners with NFL paperweights. The paper crackled beneath Ram's index finger as he leaned over the desk and pointed at the drawing.

"Wheelchair ramps will be installed here in front, in back and also, here at the exit of the addition they will construct. The new room comes off your TV room, right here at this wall. They'll put in oak pocket doors and either paint them or stain them…whatever you want. This room will house a modular pool with a heater and I've found a special lift that will help you get Jack in and out of the pool if he can't do it himself or if he's too heavy for you to manage alone. The room is big enough to use as a playroom for now or as a downstairs bedroom for Jack if he needs that."

"You've thought of everything."

He took a ragged breath, hating the wisdom in preparing for that day. "A motorized chair will be delivered next week…"

"He has one already," she interjected. "My father-in-law bought it for him."

Leaning heavily on her hands flattened on the desktop, she continued, "I wanted to get it out of the shed a couple weeks ago for Jack to use, but it's impractical in my house."

He placed his hands on her shoulders and kneaded gently. "I know. Now it won't be. And he can use the wheelchair I ordered on the second floor. They'll install a one-person lift on your staircase. If they need to change the banister to support it, they will."

Standing erect, Ram promised, "They will disturb your household as little as possible. I'm paying bonuses for them to get the work done within two weeks and only working inside when you and the boys aren't there. They can schedule outdoor work when you are.

"So…" He trailed off scrutinizing her face.

She focused on the blueprints several moments and then her gazed locked on him. "I'll never be able to repay you."

"I wouldn't accept it even if you could," he said.

His breath hitched as he faced the raw emotion that her luminous eyes projected. He sensed that the tears brimming were equal measure happiness and heartbreak. And deep in his soul Ram believed that she saw him in that moment the same way that he saw her.

He seized the apparent opportunity and wrapped her in his arms, hugging her tightly. The rise and fall of her chest, the soft tickle of her breath on his collarbone triggered soaring joy and utter completion. He tipped a finger under her chin and raised her head upward. Her lips parted and he lowered his lips, achingly slowly.

Spun into dizzying, elevating flights and rollercoaster free-fall, he feasted on her soft, sweet lips. She clung to him, hungrily returning the kiss, and for exhilarating, tumultuous seconds, that union with Nikki was all Ram needed in the world.

Ending the kiss as softly and slowly as he had begun, Ram rested his chin on her silken crown, closed his eyes and held her in his arms, relishing the rightness of loving her and hoping that she had no regrets. She stirred, and he immediately loosened his hold.

"I will never be able to thank you for what you are doing for Jack, for me."

"I would do anything for you, Nikki." Ram debated declaring his love and telling her that she had just given him a priceless gift, but his intuition had him silent. Nikki had too much to deal with already. He didn't want to burden her with worrying about his feelings. She struggled so fiercely to manage her own feelings, always considerate of Jack and Rocky.

Also, Ram didn't want to tempt fate and wind up slammed with a rejection.

"I want to kiss you again. I don't want to rush you." He kissed her soft black hair.

Her head jerked up. An odd gleam reflected in her slightly squinted eyes, a strange fierceness in the hard set of her jaw. "He killed himself," she said dryly.

Ram did a double take at her out of left field pronouncement. "What?"

"I believe that my husband committed suicide the

night after we found out about Jack's prognosis. He couldn't handle it." She gritted her teeth and her chest heaved. "I don't forgive him. But the boys miss him."

"I…" Damn, he thought as sympathy over what she had been forced to withstand paralyzed him. "Nikki, I'm so very sorry. I didn't know."

"No one knows how I feel." Her eyes softened. "Except you."

Ram moved to kiss her again, but she impeded his advance, touching her index finger to his lips lightly.

"I don't have anything to give you." She cast him a rueful smile.

Relief bloomed and he retorted, "I don't need much." Ram winked. "Let me take care of giving to you. When the time is right you can take care of me."

"Why do you want to do this, Ram?" she insisted.

"Just because." He glanced at the blueprints on the desk. "Can I give the construction crew the go ahead?"

A tender smile bloomed on her lips. "If you insist."

"I insist."

"All right." She kissed him softly on the lips, a fleeting contact that he yearned to repeat over and over. "Thank you," she said.

Exhilarated he said, "You're welcome."

"I should go home…Tell Brad what I've decided."

"I'll call him."

"Okay. See you."

"Yeah."

He watched her leave, happy to the core that his intentions for Jack, for her, might have hit the mark.

After she left, the morning's activities were a blur. Ram hung around at the GSC for hours mostly thinking about Nikki. Her loss weighed on his mind, and the deep respect he held for her grew to iconic proportions. Ram faltered each time Jack exhibited symptoms of decline. Where did she find her strength?

At three o'clock Luci announced that Brad was on the phone.

"Hey, superstar," Brad greeted him when Ram answered the call.

"Yeah, starring in the green, green pasture," Ram retorted sarcastically.

"How about on the green, green turf of Lambeau Field, champ?"

"Have you been drinking, buddy?"

"Beltzer called you up out of injured reserve. His rookie quarterback broke the pinky on his throwing hand." Brad guffawed before he erupted in bawdy laughter.

His jaw dropped. "I can't believe I'm on the roster again."

Beltzer's stunning reversal had Ram's pulse racing. "So who's going in as starter from down the string?" Foggy-brained he attempted to recall the opening season roster. "Sanders? Or Denton?"

"Hmmm…nope, I doubt he'll go with either of them. Guess again."

His gleeful tone penetrated the fog. "You're shitting me. He'll start me?"

"I implied that you're not interested in suiting up to sit the bench."

Ram cracked up and then declared, "You are ballsy, my friend."

"Easy to be brave on the telephone. He didn't just roll over. But he agreed that if he sees what he wants from you this week in practice, you'll start next Sunday against Green Bay. Dragons have a bye this weekend, so report to the practice field tomorrow at eleven AM. Since I have full confidence in you, pack your bags for the Wisconsin trip, Ram."

The impossible long-yardage kick sailed straight between the goalposts. "Jesus, that's great," Ram yelled.

"Everything okay in there?" Luci sang out.

Ram grinned from ear to ear. "Yeah, everything's good, Luce.

"Sorry, Brad. Celebrate over a beer with me tonight?" Ram invited.

"I'll let you know later. Beers are on me when we do get together."

Ram hung up the phone and paced around his desk a couple times, gleeful about the turn of events. Pop would normally be the first person he called with stellar information about his career. His father would hand the phone over to Mom so she could hear whatever Ram had to say first hand, and then they'd launch the phone tree alerting the rest of the immediate family and assorted relatives. Mom and Pop had often eagerly used his comp tickets to watch him play in person. Maybe they'd want a trip to Wisconsin to witness their boy's vindication the following Sunday.

But Ram reached for the phone and dialed Nikki's number first.

"Hello," she answered, breathless. Mechanical saws whined in the background.

"I have unbelievable news," he said.

"Really? What is it?" The happy lilt to her voice made him envision her soul-stirring smile.

"I'm back on the team, Nikki. I start against the

Packers next Sunday in Wisconsin."

Hammers plopped and a truck's reverse signal beeped. "That's...wonderful, Ram. I'm so happy for you. The boys will be thrilled."

"Do you want to go to the game? Take Jack and Rocky? I'll pay all expenses."

"Oh, um..." Another pause left him listening to construction sounds.

"It might be good to escape the renovations, too," Ram added.

"That's very generous of you. But Jack isn't doing that well. He's having difficulty seeing."

"I know," he said, his spirits sinking. "I talked with him a while this morning after you left. He seemed depressed."

"He is. I think it's best that we stay home next weekend. But we'll watch you play, and I'll do a blanket tailgate in the TV room to make it fun. Dad paid for the NFL package on satellite TV for Rocky's seventh birthday in April. We'll definitely be able to get the telecast. Maybe we can come to a home game some time?"

"Of course you can," he agreed. "But..." *I'll miss you.* "Mind if I tell Jack and Rocky the news myself? I'll drive them home when they're done here." Spontaneously Ram proposed, "How about a celebration dinner?"

She paused long enough for him to worry that he had misinterpreted her kissing him back. "I'd like that," she said softly. "But Jack is so down today that I think I'd like him to rest tonight. Another rain check?"

"Sure. I'll call you after I beat the hell out of Green Bay."

She chuckled. "You do that. Good luck, Ram. Go Dragons."

When she followed with, "I'll miss you," he hung up feeling euphoric.

Ram sauntered out of his office, plopped down into one of the chairs in front of Luci's desk, and eyed her Packers shrine smugly. "I'm not coming to your football party next Sunday, Luce."

"Well, duh." She peered at him over her reading glasses. "As if I'd invite you when my beloved Pack plays those nasty Dragons that you continue to love despite their idiotic, bozo management."

Ram snorted a laugh. "Want to move your party game-side? See the game in person?"

"They're at Lambeau. Could you really get tickets?"

"Uh huh. But there's a catch."

She raised one eyebrow. "What is it?"

"You have to sit with the Dragons' fans."

"Phhht." She blew out through pursed lips. "When hell freezes over."

He grinned. "How about if your job depended on it?"

Scowling, she said, "Of course I'd sit there like I used to, if you were playing..." She harrumphed and then repeated, "When hell freezes over."

"Well, hell is a block of ice. I start against your team a week from tomorrow."

"Holy shit!" she screamed lunging out of her seat.

She flew around her desk and nearly knocked him over as she flung herself at him open-armed.

Laughing Ram hugged her and then held her shoulders at arm's length gazing into her eyes in amusement.

"Hell, yeah, I'll sit in Dragons territory. I have to call Alan and tell him the news." Beaming a smile, a wicked glint in her eyes, she exclaimed, "Go Pack!"

Chapter 17

Nikki's cozy flannel pajamas called her name. Weary to aching, she counted the minutes until finishing the kitchen clean up so she could change into pajamas and, hopefully relax. A heavy thump sounded overhead. She jumped, threw the dishcloth on the counter and bounded up the stairs two at a time. Jack's bedroom door was ajar. Breathless she charged inside his room.

"I'm okay, Mommy," he said through clenched teeth, a steely glint in his eyes. "I dropped my stupid backpack."

She stooped to help him pick up the books that had toppled out onto the floor.

"I. Can. Do. It. Myself." His robotic, staccato delivery registered like a slap in the face.

Rising from a crouch, she let him collect the books unaided. "I was just trying to help you, Jack," she said defensively.

"You're always trying to help. But I want to do things *myself.*" His voice rose in exasperation as he tossed the books into the pack and then struggled with the zipper.

Her fierce instinct to assist Jack had her straining against the desire to zip it for him. But, as commanded, she allowed him to struggle while her heart twisted.

Lingering a few moments, she observed his labored

movements feeling impotent and useless while he ignored her. Jack's moods were unpredictable and wildly fluctuating. Jodi had advised that the ALD symptoms array included mood swings and that Nikki should be prepared for his erratic moods to worsen as the disease progressed, with no expectation of improvement.

Depressed, she backed out of Jack's room. Down the hall, Rocky stood silently in his doorway. His forlorn expression and the deep sadness she read in the sag in his shoulders prompted her to tend to her baby.

"Hey sweetie," Nikki sang out cheerfully as she approached him.

He spun around and she followed him into his room closing the door behind her. Reflexively she gathered up the clothes, toys and papers strewn on the floor. Perpetually Rocky's room contrasted dramatically with Jack's: disaster area versus military inspection ready.

Nikki glanced at Rocky. He wore a hangdog expression. "What's up?"

"Nuthin'." He knit his eyebrows.

"I know something is bothering you, honey. You can tell me anything."

Sitting on the edge of his bed she twisted a rubbery Spiderman figure in her hands while praying silently. *Please God. Please let Rocky be all right. I don't think I can handle anything more.*

Weak with dread she eyed him head to toe for telltale signs of illness. Although dispirited, Rocky's color seemed normal, healthy. But Jack's outward appearance still concealed the devastation nibbling away at his life.

"Don't tell Jack I told you," he implored, his eyes huge.

"I promise, I won't."

He sat next to her on the bed and quietly stared down at his hands curled in his lap. Nikki put her arm around his shoulder and waited.

"Jack is getting worse and he doesn't want you to know. He cries sometimes at school. He is so unhappy, Mom. Does he have to go to school?"

"Are they picking on him?"

"Nah. I watch out for him. He told me how much it hurts to walk sometimes and when he can't see good, he gets really scared." He paused. "Can't Grandma and Poppy stay with us so he doesn't have to go to school anymore?"

Nikki squeezed his shoulder. "Thank you, Rocky."

"For what?" Confusion swam in his eyes.

"For being such a good brother. For protecting Jack. And, most of all, for listening to him. He needs someone to talk to. I'm thankful he has you."

"You're not going to tell Jack I told you, are you, Mom?" he whined.

Crisscrossing a finger over her chest she swore, "Cross my heart, I won't say a word."

"Are you going to ask Grandma and Poppy to stay longer?"

She automatically rejected the idea. "I don't think so."

At a loss for how she'd go about it, she reassured him, "Don't worry. I will take care of Jack and school."

"Is Poppy still coming to watch the game tomorrow?"

"Yep. Grandma told me that they're leaving New

Jersey at five in the morning. Poppy said he wouldn't miss the game for anything. And Grandma will make you her oatmeal cookies. Have you decided what you want me to fix you for dinner?"

"Whatever Jack wants is fine with me."

"Nope." She ruffled her knuckles along the top of his head. "I want to make what you want."

"Can we have nachos?"

"You bet. One huge platter. We'll stop at the supermarket after church in the morning."

"Oh, and maybe some crock pot hot dogs?"

She made a mental shopping list of the healthy substitutes needed to grant his requests. "You bet. Let's make a huge buffet. We can eat it on the blanket, just like our Super Bowl feasts."

Rocky beamed a smile and impish dimples bloomed on his cheeks. "Even *better* than the Super bowl with Ram playing. Thanks, Mom."

She hugged him, his solid little body warm and comforting. Satisfied that she had found a way to put a smile on one of her boys' faces, she left Rocky's room, hurried down the hallway and closeted herself in her bedroom.

Clutching the flannel pajamas that she had set out on the pillow of the king-sized bed, she fixated on the wedding picture on the dresser.

John, how could this nightmare be true? We need you. Tears streamed, and she brushed them away, furious that she still had tears left to cry over him. *Why did I tell Ram my darkest, shameful secret?*

Done with self-pity she jerked her gaze away from the photo. What would wallowing in the past solve? Would it make Jack's existence easier at school? No.

160

She had to find solutions without relying on a man.

The doorbell rang.

"What now?"

She tossed the pajamas on the bed, hustled downstairs, opened the door and peered through the locked screen door. In the early evening shadows, a delivery truck idled at the curb and two men stomped up the path wrestling with a large box.

A third man stood on the porch clutching a clipboard. Consulting the paperwork, he inquired, "Mrs. Lambert?"

"Yes." She eyed him suspiciously.

"We have a delivery for you."

"I didn't order anything."

"It says right here, 'Delivery and set up paid for by a…'" He licked his thumb and rifled through the sheets of paper, "Mr. Ram Delaney." He paused a minute. "*The* Ram Delaney?"

Widening his eyes, he gazed at her. "You know Ram Delaney?"

At her nod he said, "I'm impressed."

Chuckling she unlatched the screen door and held it open so that the pair of workmen could lug the box into the hallway.

Perspiring freely the burly pair set the carton down on the floor. "Where do you want it?'

"I don't know. What is it?"

"It's the best television we sell, and one of the biggest," the guy with the clipboard said.

Rocky slipped down the stairs as the men removed the big-screen TV from the box.

"Oh cool! It's *huge*. Wait 'til Jack sees it." He ran off yelling, "Jack!" at the top of his lungs.

"Guess we'll keep it," she muttered.

An hour later Nikki and the boys stared in awe at the television that dominated the family room. A member of the Geek Squad had magically arrived after the men set the TV up on the stand that Ram had also provided. The deliverymen had moved the old TV into the framed-out new room addition before they left taking all the packing materials with them.

The Geek Squad technician had connected the satellite dish and various components, and then sat cross-legged on the floor with the pajama clad boys demonstrating the use of the biggest remote control that Nikki had ever seen.

He had patiently reviewed all the features and functions of the remote. "The tricky part is toggling between HDMI2 and HDMI1 if you watch a DVD, and then want to watch TV," he explained. "You have to hit this little star button, here. And then hit devices, and choose TV. Then you have to scroll until you find the screen listing HDMI1. Choose that and you're set."

Unable to make sense of a single word, Nikki had sputtered, "Um," in response to the pointed look the technician gave her after he finished his explanation.

Jack had sung out, "I've got it, Mommy."

Rocky had declared the instructions, "Easy."

Dubious, she had offered the man a tip as he entrusted the remote control to Rocky and sprang up from the floor.

He had waved it away saying, "No thanks, ma'am. The tip was included in the pre-payment."

Overwhelmed, Nikki had marveled at Ram's generosity and foresight.

****

On Sunday morning Rocky carried two grocery bags bound for the kitchen. As Nikki hefted two more bags out of the trunk, Jack remained stubbornly seated in the back of the car.

"Come on, honey," she urged. "Poppy and Grandma will be here any minute."

"No," he huffed out; exhibiting the same crabby intractability he had at church.

She sighed rather than argue with him, reconciled to yet another bad day. Leaving him to sit in the car, Nikki carried the heavy bags through the front door. On her third trip outside she was relieved to find Mickey leaning into the back of the car. He talked to Jack while Kay unloaded bags from their trunk.

"Let me help you, Mom." Nikki rushed over to her car.

Kay handed her the bags and smiled when Nikki kissed her soft, papery cheek.

"It's so good to see you," Nikki said, meaning it.

Kay's delighted grin gratified her and affirmed her decision to invite them to watch Ram's game with her and the kids.

Mickey said something that made Jack giggle. And then Jack exited the car as if the earlier standoff had never occurred. Jack limped toward the stoop with Mickey's meaty arm around his shoulders.

Halting to inspect the new ramp that led to the front door, Mickey gestured with a thumb up and beamed at Rocky who jumped up and down in frenetic anticipation on the top of the stoop.

As Mickey reached him, Rocky begged, "Come on Poppy. Wait until you see the television Ram sent us."

He tugged on his grandfather's hand.

Kay and Nikki trailed the men through the doorway and headed to the kitchen. Nikki plopped the grocery bags on the kitchen table.

Kay's mouth set in a stern line. "You've made some changes." She stepped to the bay window that provided a view of the construction equipment in the backyard.

"The workmen showed up one morning. Ram Delaney hired them and wouldn't let me refuse his assistance." Nikki stared at the back of Kay's head.

Her silence seemed to beg further explanation from Nikki. "And that's not all. A television was delivered last evening. I know I shouldn't accept such expensive gifts from him. But you should have seen Jack's face last night in front of that massive TV."

No response. Kay continued to stare out the window.

Anger flared. And guilt pinched at what Nikki interpreted as Kay's unspoken criticism of her acceptance of gifts from a man. She resented that she had to explain her actions. Wasn't the quest to do anything to make Jack's life better sufficient justification for her decisions?

It doesn't matter to me if she approves or not.

Nikki shifted her gaze and focused on Mickey, Jack and Rocky who clustered around the TV in the adjoining room.

"Do you see Dad's face?" Kay said. "Looks like his eyes will pop right out of his head." Laughing, she paced over to the table.

"And to tell you the truth, I wouldn't mind watching my favorite soap, *Tides of Tomorrow,* on that huge screen. I think I'd feel like I was in the same room with that hunk, Dr. Stone." Rolling her eyes, she sighed.

And then she helped Nikki unpack groceries.

Grateful that she had misread Kay's body language, Nikki hugged her. "Thanks for everything, Mom."

"What?" Her cheeks blushed. "I haven't done anything."

"You've done more than you'll ever know." Nikki squeezed her hand.

****

Fourth quarter, two minutes remaining, and the Dragons were down by seven. A close-up of Ram's face filled the screen. Nikki's heart flip-flopped. The team huddled at the Packers' ten-yard line.

"They have a long way to go." Mickey sat on the edge of the couch.

"No problem, Poppy. Ram can do it." Rocky clapped his hands and rocked on his knees on the floor.

The team broke huddle and lined up on the twenty-yard line.

Jack flipped a page in his notebook, apparently recording Ram's every move on the field. "He can do it. He has to keep throwing to Steele. He's been his hot receiver all day."

Ram hollered out a string of numbers, grasped the hiked ball, stepped back and fired the ball into Steele's hands.

"Hold on to the ball!" Rocky yelled as the Packers defense swarmed Steele and brought him to the ground after a fifteen-yard gain.

Methodically Ram moved the team down the field

as the clock ticked down. The Dragons' field position was third and goal with only ten seconds left in the game. Ram took the snap, pulled back deep and scanned the right and left flanks for a receiver. His head moved rapidly back and forth.

Rocky and Mickey surged to their feet.

"Come on, Ram!"

"You can do it!"

"Go, Ram, go!"

Four defensemen covered the receivers like blankets. The Packers defense bore down on the Dragons' O-line jostling to break through, intent on sacking the quarterback. Ram faked a toss right, and then barreled down the left side of the field. His center, O'Donnell positioned in front of him and blocked each threatening defenseman like a speeding bus. Ram launched off the ground and stretched his body full length. Leading with the ball jutting from outstretched arms, he dove over the goal line.

In Nikki's family room five pairs of arms stretched overhead as they shouted, "Touchdown!"

A hush fell over Lambeau Field. The extra point sailed through the goalpost sending the game into overtime.

Exhausted, the family collapsed back into their seats.

"Look at how cool and calm he looks," Kay said after the commercial break. "My hands are shaking."

Ram stood casually on the sidelines, his arm draped over Coach Beltzer's shoulder, focused on the aerial prints that the coach held in his hand.

Play resumed. The Dragons won the toss and chose to receive because one score would end the game.

The Packers kicked off and Dragons rookie, Spooners, ran the kick back to the fifty-yard line.

"Here we go," Jack said. He clapped clumsily.

The center snapped the ball. Ram took three steps backward and fired the pass to Steele. Downfield, the perfect throw sailed into Steele's hands. He tucked the ball and sprinted furiously toward the goal line. A brutal hit by the Packers defensive end rocked the ball out of Steele's hands before he hit the ground.

Woodson, the Packers All-Pro cornerback, bobbled the ball, secured it, and sped toward their goal post.

Kay and Nikki jumped up shouting, "No, no, no!"

The Packers defenseman crossed the goal line, ran toward the stands and executed the famous Lambeau leap. He landed seated on the wall behind the end zone where ecstatic Packers fans thumped his back and shoulders.

The stadium erupted in noise deafening cheers.

Rocky burst into tears and flopped into the La-Z-Boy chair.

Deflated, Nikki slumped on the arm of the chair and rubbed her hand in circles on Rocky's back. "It's okay, honey. Ram did great today. Look. Look at Ram."

A smile lit Ram's face as he met the Packers quarterback, Rodgers, in the middle of the field. He shook his hand, grinned widely, and made a comment that spurred a laugh from Rodgers who patted Ram on the back. Then Ram walked over to the sidelines where Steele stood dejected and alone. Ram clapped him on the back, mouthed a few words into his ear, and shook his hand.

A mic wielding reporter and his cameraman

surrounded Ram. "Ram, great to see you back on the field."

"Thanks, Bruce, good to be back."

"You went 30 out of 32 with 450 yards. One of your best games ever. How's the arm feel now?"

"Feels great." Ram paced toward the tunnel with the reporter trailing him.

"Any comment about Steele's fumble? Not exactly the Cinderella finish I'm sure you hoped for."

"I can't single anyone out for the loss. We win as a team and we lose as a team. The Packers are the reigning world champions. It was an honor to play here at Lambeau Field again."

"He is a gentleman," Mickey said. "Other players are quick to throw teammates under the bus, but not Ram. Have to respect a man like that."

Mickey piled the food-smeared, paper plates and napkins on a tray and carried them into the kitchen.

As the game wrap-up continued, Ram stepped away from the reporter, waved to a few diehard Dragons fans braving the hostile Lambeau crowd, and then approached the reporter again.

"Something to add, Ram?"

"Yes." Ram looked directly into the camera lens and Nikki's heart skipped a beat.

His blue eyes twinkled, his sandy hair matted damply around his chiseled face. "Hi, Jack and Rocky. Miss you guys."

"Whoa!" Rocky yelled. "Did you hear *that*, Jack?"

Rocky launched off the chair and plopped down on the floor next to his open-mouthed brother.

Excited for the boys, and yet again grateful for Ram's thoughtfulness, Nikki stood up and lifted a couple platters off the coffee table watching Ram's huge body disappearing down the tunnel ramp.

As she entered the kitchen carrying the dishes, the Dragons theme song sounded faintly.

"Mommy, that's your phone," Jack said.

"Can you please grab it for me, Rocky?" she called. "It's in my purse on the table in the living room."

"Hello, Nikki Lambert's phone," came Rocky's husky voice. "Hi Ram! Oh, wow! Mom, it's Ram."

Kay and Nikki deposited the platters into the sink and hurried into the living room. Mickey scooped Jack up into his arms and followed.

"Sure, Ram. Here she is."

Nikki took the phone from Rocky, and greeted him with, "Hi. Let me put you on speakerphone? Dad and Mom are here, and Jack wants to say, hi, too."

Pressing the speaker button on the phone, she laid it on the coffee table. The family clustered around the table staring at the phone.

"Hi, everyone. Hi, Jack."

"Hi, Ram. I'm sorry you lost the game," Rocky said, with a catch in his voice.

"Ah, buddy, it's okay. It was so much fun to play again. I feel like a winner today."

"That was so cool that you said hello to us on TV," Jack said. "I hope those dorks at school were watching."

Rocky and Nikki exchanged glances as they all leaned closer to the table hanging on Ram's every word.

"I had to say hello to my favorite people," Ram said. "Sorry, Nikki. I thought I'd say hello to you privately instead of national TV."

"Thank you, Ram." Nikki's cheeks burned and she purposely avoided looking at Kay, certain that she wore her infatuation with Ram like a purple and orange Dragons flag.

"Thank you for the new TV," Jack added. "It felt like we were right on the field with you."

"You're welcome. Maybe soon when the Dragons have a home game you can come and really be on the field with me."

"Me too?" Rocky chimed in.

"Everyone. You and Jack and your grandpa and grandma and your mom. Okay, guys I have to go. I'll catch up with you all in a few days."

"Ram, can you hang on a sec for a private word?" Nikki asked.

"Of course."

After everyone yelled good-bye and drifted out of the room, Nikki picked up the phone, disconnected the speaker and nestled it against her ear. "Thank you so very much for the TV. The boys are over the moon." She chuckled. "And my in-laws and I enjoyed it more than I would have thought possible. I left a message on your phone last night."

"I got it, but it was too late to call you back."

"God, Ram. What am I going to do with you? I can't keep taking these extravagant gifts. I repeat, it's way too much."

"No, sweetheart. It's not enough. I wish I could keep talking, but I have to run. Someone from ESPN is waiting for me. I'll call you tomorrow. Pleasant dreams."

"You, too." She ended the call and slipped the

phone in her pocket, his endearment lingering in her mind like a tender caress.

"Hey, guys. Put on ESPN," she directed to the crew in the family room. "Ram said someone was waiting to interview him."

Nikki returned to the kitchen and set to work at the sink, her mind reeling.

I can't fall in love with Ram. It's crazy. It's too soon.

The realization hit her that it was already too late.

Chapter 18

Winter

Rummaging through his dresser drawer, Ram dug out the crimson, cable knit sweater that he annually reserved for the Christmas holidays. Shrugging into the sweater, he scanned the surfaces of the bedroom furniture until he found his cell phone. As he pocketed the phone, Ram ambled into the living room to collect the presents for Nikki, Jack, and Rocky. What a difference a year makes. Last Christmas he had sent his parents on a cruise and spent Christmas Eve and Christmas Day in front of the television watching game tapes and eating cold pizza. This year he looked forward to watching the boys open their gifts. He couldn't wait to be with Nikki. Day by day Nikki became more comfortable with their relationship. He wished he could tell her how in a few short months she and her sons had become his whole world. Nothing else mattered.

Multi-colored lights twinkled on the boughs of the ten-foot, fragrant fir tree in the corner of Ram's family room. Luci had set up the tree and decorated it full out while he was on the road with the team. She had apparently bought every Dragons ornament in the NFL online store and had, also, hung one galling figurine in a Packers uniform on the topmost branch of the tree. Despite the dig, she had touched him with her thoughtfulness and he intended to give her a hefty raise in the New Year. In addition to her contributions to Ram's personal life, she virtually had run the GSC single-handed the past six weeks.

Ram left the house to celebrate Christmas Eve with Nikki and the boys, light-hearted and brimming with holiday spirit. A new dusting of snow provided the storied white Christmas, and he whistled that song, his breath visible in steamy puffs. Despite the sub-freezing temperature, Ram didn't wear a jacket; his usual custom no matter how frigid the weather. He had a racing metabolism that super-heated his body like an enveloping heat lamp. That trait came in handy during games played on outdoor fields in December and January—like the next day's match against Florida on home turf. He sincerely hoped that those Miami guys' blood was nice and thin.

After loading the trunk, he jumped into the car that he had parked on the garage apron. The Hummer's engine turned over with a roar, and he switched on the windshield and rear defrosters full blast de-icing the glass.

Pressing the Bluetooth call button on the steering wheel he dictated, "Call Pop."

When the connection clicked he boomed, "Merry Christmas, Pop."

"Merry Christmas to you, son."

Ram flicked the wipers on. The wiper arms dislodged enough slush to clear the windshield. He shifted into gear and navigated down the driveway.

"I'm pumped for tomorrow. When are you and

Mom leaving for the airport?"

"In about a half hour. We get into Logan just before midnight. That's too late for you to meet us, right?"

Nodding on reflex he said, "Yep, I don't want to break training. I ordered a car for you. You'll see the driver holding a sign in the baggage claim area."

"Thanks. We'll be quiet when we get to your house. I'm looking forward to the game."

"Me, too, Pop. My Christmas gift to you and Mom is watching the game from the owner's suite. A fully catered Christmas dinner with all the trimmings."

"No kidding." He rumbled a throaty laugh. "The private jet ride and the limo tonight would have been more than enough, Ram."

Ram grinned. "I hope you enjoy it."

"You bet I will. See you in the morning. I'll call Mom to the phone."

Although Ram imagined that his father moved the phone away from his mouth, he blasted, "Mavis!" in Ram's ear anyway.

"Pop." He waited a beat before repeating, "Pop."

"Uh, yes, Ram?"

"I'm leaving at dawn tomorrow for the stadium, so I may not see you before the game. All the car keys are on hooks in the cabinet next to the wine cooler. Take your pick and enter the stadium at the usual place. They'll direct you to parking and private elevator access to the owner's suite."

"This is going to be great," Pop said. "Can I take the Ferrari?"

"Sure. I think the roads will be clear enough."

"Here's your mother…"

A couple dull knocks sounded as the phone presumably changed hands. "Merry Christmas, darling."

"Merry Christmas, Ma."

"Ramsey, your father has a question for you..." Mom's voice trailed off.

In the background Pop said, "No, I don't."

"Oh, okay. I guess I'll have to ask then." Mom cleared her throat. "Ram, is there something you want to tell us? About your...love life?" she asked hesitantly.

He considered telling her everything about Nikki and his feelings for her, especially since his parents would likely meet her the next day. "Not on the phone, Mom," he decided.

"Who is Nicky?"

Stunned, he responded, "How do you know about Nikki?"

Paper rustled. "It says here that you're an item with a woman named Nicky Dahlman."

Relief flooded through him that, as was frequently the case, the press had it wrong. The last thing he wanted was for his parents to learn about the love of his life from the media. The last thing his Nikki needed was the press on her doorstep. "What newspaper are you looking at, Ma?"

"The headline 'Ram's Woman Revealed. Wedding Plans Rumored' is in bold print in *The Carolina Tattler*," she said with conviction as if bold print in the rag sheet denoted reliable information.

He hooted a laugh. "Since when do you read that stuff? I never met the woman."

She sniffed. "Ram, there's a picture of you together."

"Really?" *When the hell did that happen?* "Honestly, Ma, I don't know her. I think she's a star on a television show. Where was this picture taken?"

"I can't tell, exactly. Maybe outside somewhere…yes, it looks like a palm tree in the background."

Rolling to a halt at a red light, Ram wracked his brain over when he might have inadvertently clued in the mosquito swarm of paparazzi that stalked him to the name, Nikki, and how he had wandered unaware into the same photo frame with Nicky Dahlman.

"Maybe at the L.A. or San Diego game," he suggested. "There's nothing to that story. But…"

"Yes, dear?" she prompted.

"I wouldn't propose to a woman without your meeting her first."

He accelerated and drove down the nearly deserted street lined with Cape Cod style houses trimmed with Christmas lights.

"You might meet a lady at the game tomorrow. Ironically her name happens to be Nikki. I'm inviting her and her two sons to go when I see her this evening. She's…special to me. So are her boys. Maybe you can tell me your impressions of her tomorrow night?"

A brief pause preceded her exclamation, "I'd love that. I can't wait to see you, honey."

"Me, too. Love you, Mom."

"Oh, I love you so much. Pop says, 'Have a game.'"

Ram grinned at the traditional "break a leg" wish Pop had wished him since he played junior high football. "I will."

****

Arms piled high with presents, Ram rang Nikki's doorbell.

"I've got it!"

"No, I've got it!" sounded from inside.

The door swung open revealing Jack seated in a tricked-out motorized chair. Purple and orange bunting fought with the lighted artificial Christmas garland that wound around the arms and backrest.

"Hey, Jack," he said, toeing the door closed. "That's one fine ride you've got there."

"I'm getting pretty good at driving it now." His sunny grin robbed Ram's breath.

His eyes widened. "Are those presents for *us*?"

"Nope." He laughed at the boy's crestfallen expression. "I'm teasing. Of course they're for you. And Rocky and Mom. Should I put them under the tree?" he asked, glancing into the living room that was ablaze with lights.

Ornaments and strings of white lights weighted down the branches of the Christmas tree. Lit snowmen and Santas of varying sizes glowed from the floor and the top of an end table. Pre-lit ropes of garland hung off the mantel and framed the front window. The surface of the coffee table disappeared beneath a gleaming snow-globe collection.

"Wow," Ram said striding into the room where Nikki and Rocky joined them.

He stacked the presents under the tree and then stood admiring the decorations. "This looks better than a department store display."

"A little over the top?" Nikki laughed as his arm circled her shoulders.

"Not at all. It's perfect." He wholeheartedly meant

it. Being here with this wonderful family *was* perfect.

"Thanks, Ram. Merry Christmas." Nikki rose up on tiptoes and pecked a soft kiss on his cheek.

Self-conscious with the boys looking on, but aching to draw her close and breathe in her tantalizing scent, Ram brushed a chaste kiss on her forehead, and then freed her from the hug.

She surveyed the room a half-smile on her face. "I went all-out this year."

A myriad of emotions swam in her brown eyes. As if Ram heard her thoughts, he understood her unspoken reasoning. *Because this is Jack's last Christmas.*

Ushered into the kitchen, also decorated to the hilt, Ram savored the smells of roast turkey, baked sweet potatoes and clean Christmas pine.

Like starved cannibals, Jack, Rocky, and Ram flew through the meal in less than a half hour. He'd bet that it had taken Nikki all day to prepare the food. And that cleanup would take three times as long as chowing down. Ram was probably just as eager as the kids to finish eating and proceed to gift giving.

Rocky zipped into the living room when Nikki fired the starting gun with a smiling, "Yes, Rocky. We can open presents now."

Jack scooted along in his chair and Ram followed as strains of a Christmas instrumental drifted from the music channel on the TV in the family room.

Ram took presents out from under the tree and placed gifts on the floor where Rocky directed. And then he sat down behind his stack of three gifts.

Nikki, Jack, and Rocky ringed the tree in positions on the floor next to him. Ram scooted closer to Nikki, their legs touching intimately. "Who's first?" he asked.

"Me," Rocky declared as he tore off a corner of wrapping paper.

Laughing, Nikki contradicted, "No. Ram's our guest. He goes first."

With a shake of his head Ram insisted, "The three of you go first. Just open everything at once."

Paper ripped and littered the floor as the kids whittled down their wrapped piles: game balls, official number seven jerseys and athletic shoes for both, a set of leather-bound journals for Jack and cleats for Rocky. Assorted exclamations rang out: cool, wow, awesome, thanks Ram.

"Oh, Ram, it's stunning," Nikki declared as she fastened the delicate vintage watch on her wrist.

Her eyes gleamed with affection warming Ram. He had wanted to give her something permanent to mark their first Christmas together...hoping they'd celebrate decades of holidays in the future. He leaned over and kissed her lips. The boys were too involved with their gifts to notice. She melted into the kiss, a sweet surrender that tested Ram's restraint to the max with the boys nearby. He ended the kiss reluctantly, and she gave him a dazzling smile that had him beaming back at her.

"I have one more gift for all three of you," he said. "Can we save it for last?"

"Sure," she said. "Your turn."

Rocky nearly burst with pride as Ram admired his handmade gift. The pale gray fired-clay, eight by five inch, rectangular "dish" bore Rocky's lumpy thumbprints. Pinched at the four corners, it resembled a giant, unfilled half-ravioli.

"It's for your dresser," he explained. "You can put

change or keys in it."

"Thanks, Rock. I can really use this."

Next, he opened the gift tagged from Jack. "I helped Jack make his present for you, too," Rocky noted.

Under the cover of the purple three-ring binder, a title page read, "NFL Dragons, QB Stats, Number 7, Ramsey Delaney."

Thumbing through the binder Ram appreciated the effort involved in creating the book. Each page heading documented the game date and opposing team. And Ram's stats for passes attempted, passes completed, yards gained, touchdowns, and interceptions were recorded in blue ink. "Thank you, Jack. Not too shabby a record, huh?" he joked.

"You see the blank sheets?" Jack asked.

Continuing to turn pages, Ram nodded.

"I'll try to fill those in for you, too."

Nikki stirred next to him. Ram didn't dare to venture a glance at her as the word, *try*, clanged in his head.

"What a great gift, Jack. Thanks again."

Jack's cheeks dimpled with a shy smile. "You're welcome. Open the one from Mommy."

Glancing at Nikki, he picked up the small package. Her pretty blush had him ripping off the paper with one tug.

Ram snapped open the jewelers' box. A small circular medal hung on a sterling silver chain. Loosening it from the velvet covered cardboard inside, he peered at the engraved image of Saint Sebastian.

"He's the patron saint of all athletes," Nikki said. "There's a little prayer card inside."

Digging under the cardboard he extracted the card that read, "May athletes be always as strong in their faith as their Patron Saint so clearly has been. Amen."

Undoing the clasp, he strung the chain around his neck and fastened it. He yearned to thank her with a heartfelt kiss, sweep her into his arms and waltz to the Christmas carol playing in the background. Lost in her shimmering gaze he wanted to say, I love you.

Instead he said, "Thank you. I'll never take it off. This means a lot."

"I'm glad you like it."

Ram read the dreamy expression in her eyes as conveying, I love you, too.

"Why don't you open that last one, Nikki?" Ram suggested. "It's for you, Jack and Rocky."

Smiling she unwrapped the package that contained Ram's hand-written invitation to the Christmas Day game.

Holding the card in front of her she read, "Nikki, Jack, Rocky, please watch my game tomorrow from the Owner's Suite in Dragons Stadium."

"Holy cow," Rocky sang out. "Is this for *real*?"

Chuckling, Ram said, "Yes, sir. A motor coach will pick you up at ten AM. My parents will be there, too." He cast a poignant glance at Nikki. "They're looking forward to meeting…"

"Stop *whispering*!" Jack screamed.

"What?" Ram sputtered.

Agitated Jack spun the chair in circles. "I can't *hear* you!" he shouted.

Nikki bounded to her feet and attempted to show Jack the invitation as he spun wildly. "Stop, sweetie." She rocked, imbalanced while trying to impede his gyrations.

Nikki managed to position the card in front of his nose and he swiped her hand away. "I can't *see*!"

Ram lunged toward the chair and grabbed the armrests forcing the wheelchair to remain stationery while the motor whirred. Jack's hand flopped off the control button and into his lap. Twisting his head from side to side he moaned.

On his knees in front of him Ram tried to break through, "Jack. Jack! It's okay, buddy. I'm here."

Jack's jerky movements continued as he blubbered. Ram couldn't tell if the spell was subsiding or worsening. Ram's vision tunneled on his small form, shrunken in the grasp of the terrifying experience. All he could think to do was cradle Jack in his arms. Rising, he released Jack from the confines of the chair, clasped him against his chest and rocked him.

Her face ashen, Nikki stood in front of Ram pressing Rocky against her side.

"Jack! We won't whisper anymore!" Rocky bellowed.

Nikki winced, and then Jack's thin voice broke through Ram's scared senseless state. "Yikes, Rocky. Don't scream."

Shaking, Ram shifted Jack in his arms so that he could see his face.

He scowled at him. "Put me down, Ram. I'm not a baby."

Lowering him back into the chair, Ram gaped at him. "Feeling better?" he ventured.

The glint in Jack's eyes held a foreign meanness. But his reply was even-toned. "I'm okay. Mommy, what does that card say?"

As if the past five minutes hadn't transpired, Nikki injected delighted excitement in her reply, "We're going to see Ram's game tomorrow in person."

"That's cool," Jack said. "But I want to go to bed now."

At a loss, Ram gazed at Nikki for direction. He had envisioned some private moments with her later that evening. Maybe a chance to spin out fantasized embraces and deep, mind-blowing kisses. But her flickering concern-laden gazes at Jack told him otherwise.

"I should go," Ram said.

"Oh, Ram, I so wanted you to stay…"

"I need to go to bed now," Jack whined.

Nikki frowned and cast a crestfallen gaze at Ram.

He winked at her and then said, "Good idea, Jack. Sweet dreams."

"Rocky, can you please see Ram to the door? I'll help Jack upstairs," Nikki said.

Rocky paced toward Ram as Nikki's gaze locked on him. He read the conflict in her eyes. She wanted to be with him, he could see that, but Jack's needs without question took precedence.

"It was wonderful having you here with us, Ram. I love my watch." She twirled her wrist. "I'm really looking forward to meeting your family. I'll see you tomorrow after the game?"

"Count on it."

Christmas Eve with Nikki forged Ram's resolve to carry whatever portion of her burdens she'd allow. No matter the obstacles or self-sacrifice, he wouldn't disappoint her. That was his naive intention.

Chapter 19

Flat on her back in the middle of her bed, Nikki pressed a pillow over her face and sobbed. Loneliness mounted and she missed John's strength. Handling Jack was too monumental a burden to handle without her husband, especially on a traditionally joyous holiday. No choice. Soaking her pillow with tears seemed her only option at that moment.

The exhaustion and emotional roller coaster exacted a heavy toll. After Ram had left, Jack had begged to open the rest of his presents in a fit of contrariness before agreeing to sleep. Of course, Rocky had echoed his brother's request. Jack's earlier tantrum had evaporated once Nikki agreed, and despite earlier chaos she had fun with the kids.

Now she remained wrung out from seesawing between sweet togetherness and despair.

Done with the useless crying jag, she switched the bedside lamp on and propped her damp pillow behind her back, resigned that she couldn't force sleep no matter how much she needed rest. She had resumed sleeping in her bedroom again to be near Jack at night. Although the king sized bed beat the couch in comfort, she mostly slept with one eye open.

Gazing at the Christmas gift from Ram on the nightstand, she picked up the watch, fingered the filigree around the dial and then fastened the clasp around her wrist. She moved her wrist back and forth in half circles and delighted in how the tiny diamonds adorning the face caught the light and sparkled. Unique and seemingly one of a kind, the watch symbolized her opinion of Ram. And had her hoping that he had chosen the gift because he felt the same way about her.

What would life be like if Ram were in bed next to me? Would he hold me in his arms and kiss away my fears? With Ram I'd never be lonely again.

Suddenly her body tensed at the sensation that she wasn't alone. For an instant she feared that John had materialized there in response to her fantasizing about another man.

Holding her breath, she darted her eyes. Her gaze lit on Rocky peering into the room as he stood in the doorway.

"What's wrong, honey?"

"Jack."

"What's wrong with Jack?" She swung her legs out from under the covers and perched on the edge of the bed ready to speed to Jack's room.

"Nothing. Just sometimes he gets scared at night, so I go and sleep in his room. For him, ya know?"

Straight-faced, Nikki didn't contradict him even though she knew that Rocky was afraid of the dark, not Jack.

"But tonight when I went into Jack's room he yelled at me to get out." He hitched a breath. "He's never done that before."

"I'm glad you came to me. I can't sleep because I'm feeling scared tonight. Do you think you could sleep in my room instead of Jack's?"

His face brightened.

She scooted over and patted the mattress next to her. He bounded into the room and hopped into bed. Leaning over his wiggly body, she switched off the light and snuggled under the covers with him.

"I didn't know moms get scared."

"Sure we do. Remember when that huge beetle got into the house? I was petrified."

"Daddy said he could hear you yelling all the way down the block." Rocky hooted a laugh.

In the darkness the bedside clock ticked, the pipes knocked and she could almost hear Rocky thinking in the silence.

His husky whisper came, "I miss Daddy. Christmas Eve was sorta sad without Daddy, Poppy and Grandma, Nana and Grandpa."

Rubbing his arm she agreed, "I know, sweetie. I missed them, too. Poppy and Grandma wanted to be here more than anything. If it weren't for that darn ice storm in New Jersey they would have come. And Grandpa is still sick. Nana has to take care of him."

"I know…" He pulled the quilt over his shoulders.

Her heart ached for her little boy. He was too young to be without his father, and too young to watch his big brother die.

"Thanks for the Nintendo DS. It was my favorite gift this year."

"Really? I thought the invitation to see Ram's game was your favorite gift."

"It's gonna be awesome. But I like my DS the best. Did you know Ram has one and he plays games when he is on the team plane? He said he has some extra games that he'll give to Jack and me to share."

"That's awfully kind of him. Ram is a very nice

man."

"He's cool." Rocky butted up against her side, his firm little body swathed in his Spiderman flannel pajamas warming her.

Smiling, Nikki kissed the top of his head and then said, "Good night, Rocky. Big day ahead of us tomorrow."

"Good night, Mom. Love you."

His toasty warm, small hand slipped into hers, trusting and soothing.

"I love you, too, honey." She squeezed his hand.

Soon Rocky snored raspy kitten purrs.

Relaxed as she held her boy's hand, she stared at the ceiling and thought about how Ram had changed everything for her sons. *Thank you, God for bringing Ram into our lives.*

Her eyelids drooped, and she drifted peacefully to sleep.

****

The luxurious coach that Ram sent to her house Christmas morning had a satellite dish on the roof, plush seats, a flat screen television and a mini bar with cut crystal tumblers. Ram's agent and self-declared best friend, Brad arrived with the driver at ten AM as promised. The Lambert family traveled the forty-five minute route to the stadium in first class style and awed anticipation.

A buffet breakfast was set out on the countertop along the left side of the bus. The boys dove into the egg and bacon muffins. Nikki drank two cups of delicious coffee and ate the taboo bacon she diplomatically pilfered off Rocky's sandwich.

Jack had a good morning and swallowed the food

with ease, so she let him gobble the bacon praying Rocky wouldn't balk at the inequality. Whisked into the stadium's inner parking lot where the players and coaches parked, the driver pulled right up to the door and lowered the lift gate for Jack's chair. Trailing Jack as he motored along expertly, Nikki and her family magically glided past door attendants and ticket takers without a single pause.

Like celebrities, they followed Brad to a private elevator. "Push the button for the top floor, Rocky," he requested.

A quick hydraulic zip upwards and then they followed Brad down a dimly lit hallway lined with doors that led to the players' and owners' private boxes.

"Ram's folks and a few college buddies are in our party today," Brad said as he opened double doors into the owner's suite.

An extremely large man, presumably one of Ram's college friends, stood up when Rocky and Nikki entered following behind Jack's scooting chair.

"Wow," Rocky exclaimed. And then he stood speechless in the middle of an interior doorframe in the apartment-like space that might have contained the same square footage as the first floor of her house.

She gaped at the spacious, formal dining room—so incongruous in a sports stadium. Eight, linen covered, round tables, which would easily seat ten people each, fronted the mahogany bar that dominated the space. Two large screen TVs hung on the wall over the bar: one tuned to ESPN, and the other tuned to the national coverage of the game.

Trancelike, Nikki roamed into a separate room that contained a sectional sofa and ample couches to seat twenty. Another TV on the wall nearest the furniture grouping displayed the live feed from the field. L-shaped linen-skirted tables, laden with every kind of finger food imaginable, abutted the opposite walls. Beneath a retractable enclosure, two rows of leather recliner chairs faced the glass wall above the panorama of Dragons Stadium.

Jack drove his chair over to the giant standing near the couch in the corner. "Hey, Caboose. I didn't know you were going to be here."

"Wouldn't miss it," he rumbled. "Especially when Ram told me that you and Rocky would be here. He didn't say anything about a beautiful woman coming, too."

"That's not a beautiful woman. That's our mom," Rocky introduced her.

"Thanks a lot," Nikki joked grinning.

Extending a hand she said, "I'm Nikki Lambert, this little charmer's mother."

Smiling, he ruffled Rocky's hair and then shook her hand. "I'm Neil Roberts, but my friends call me Caboose. A real pleasure to meet you. Anyone special to Ram is special to us."

Her heart swelled hearing him singling her out as special to Ram. *Unbelievable, but I think it's true.*

The two other men jumped to their feet and each shook Nikki's hand.

"I'm Luke 'Diesel' Murphy."

"And I'm Chris 'Engine' Simmons. Ram said you were pretty, but he didn't tell us *how* pretty. Guess he was afraid of competition."

"You're too kind." She blushed at the compliment—and at the information that Ram had described her to his friends.

"Jack come here," Rocky invited. "You've *got* to see this. I can see the *whole* field."

He jumped up and down, his palm on the glass, as he gazed down on the football field.

"I think I see Ram. That's him there by the bench, isn't it?"

Jack maneuvered his chair forward, but had to halt behind the row of seats, lacking enough space to squeeze the wheelchair between the recliners. He strained his neck to see above the chair backs.

Caboose grasped the arms of the chair, hoisted it off the floor and carried Jack, seated in the chair, toward Rocky, as if toting a piece of paper. He placed Jack down practically nose to the glass.

There are unforgettable moments in life that reach your soul, Nikki thought. The sheer gratitude shining in Jack's eyes as he smiled at Caboose was etched forever in her memory.

Caboose faced Nikki. She smiled and mouthed, "Thank you."

He nodded and flashed a toothy grin.

"Can I get anyone something to drink?" Brad surveyed the shelves of a fully stocked refrigerator.

A man's voice, and then a woman's higher pitch sounded from the outer room...Ram's parents, Nikki surmised. A shimmer of nervousness brought a shiver as Ram's dad entered the room and sped straight past her.

"We didn't miss kick off, did we?" He positioned next to Rocky and Jack and leaned against the glass.

"Nah," Rocky said. "Just Ram talking into that lady's microphone down there."

"Good." He straightened, glanced down at the boys and introduced himself, "Hey, guys. Harold Delaney, Ram's dad."

Patting the boys on the back he added, "But you can call me Gramps."

"Of course we didn't miss the kick off, Harry. Have I ever missed a kick off? Brad, darling, can you please grab my coat?" Ram's mother slipped off a hooded mink coat.

She sported the identical Dragons jersey that Nikki, Rocky, and Jack wore. Statuesque and although sweet-faced, Mrs. Delaney's presence seemed to polarize the men and powered up the group to kowtow mode.

Brad fell all over himself to take her coat.

"Why are your other guests still wearing coats?" she asked, the implied command even more effective in the soft tone of her voice.

Engine sped into action, relieved Nikki and the boys of coats and helped Brad hang them in the closet.

"Mom, did you bring me anything?" Diesel bent down and pecked her cheek.

"Now, would I forget my boys?' She laughed. Slipping plastic bags that brimmed with chocolate chip cookies out of a shopping bag, she arranged them on the buffet.

"Why do you think we almost missed kick-off?" Harold asked as he removed his coat and tossed it on one of the leather chairs.

He wore the same jersey as his wife—evidently Ram's one-stop Christmas gift. Nikki smiled thinking about Ram's arranging every detail of this event. Right down to introducing her to his parents.

"We had to visit the locker room before we came

up here," Harold said.

"You got to go to the locker room?" Rocky asked wide-eyed.

"Sure I did. You can, too. I'll take you there after the game." Harold squinted through the glass.

"Really? Thank you." Rocky bumped a hip against Jack's chair. "How cool is that, Jack?"

"Way cool." Jack rose unsteadily and corrected his balance by gripping the arms of his chair.

Leaning heavily on his hands he gained purchase on one of the recliner chairs and plopped onto the edge of the leather cushion.

If the exertion bothered him, he didn't let on. The glowing delight on his face as he scanned the field below was pure magic.

"You know that the coaches count on my bringing home-baked cookies to the game. How could I disappoint them?" Ram's mother directed the rhetorical question to her husband.

Casting her gaze at Nikki she said, "You must be Nikki."

Smiling Mrs. Delaney advanced toward her and hugged her to her ample chest. Enveloped by her arms, Nikki breathed in a heavy dose of baby powder scent.

Freed from the bear hug, Nikki said, "It's nice to meet you, Mrs. Delaney."

Waving her hand, she retorted, "You're lovely to be so polite, but please call me Mavis. Ram told me you would all be here. I am so excited to meet you."

"Now, which one of you is Jack and which one is Rocky?" Mavis sang out as she strode toward the boys.

Each disappeared temporarily within her hug and froze as she kissed the top of each head.

"I'm Rocky," he mumbled.

"Ah, so you're the football player Ram told me about. It won't be long until we'll watch you play for the Dragons from this box."

The breezy prediction rendered Rocky speechless.

"Ram told me that you keep the best stats." She sat next to Jack and pointed to the notebook on his lap. "When Ram was in high school I used to keep his game stats in notebooks just like yours. I still have them. I'll show them to you the next time I see you, if you like."

"I would. Thank you, Mrs. Delaney."

"Oh, please call me Grammy." She rose and retraced her steps back to Nikki. "Just adorable. I remember when Ram and his older brother were that little. Aren't sons just the best?"

Nikki nodded as Brad chimed in, "Yes we are, Mom." Grinning, he bit off a chunk of chocolate chip cookie.

Harold sat between the boys in the front row. Mavis and Nikki took seats behind them.

Brad picked up the phone and addressed the room at large. "I'll order the food now so we can eat at half time."

Casting a glance at the barely touched feast on the buffet table, Nikki thought they had more than enough food already.

Cheers arose when the announcer's introduction blared and the Dragons took the field. Nikki alternated viewing the TV and the field during the plays. The Chicago Bears defense blitzed repetitively as the Dragons O-line fell short of protecting Ram: three tackles and two sacks in the first quarter.

"Damn, the line has to tighten up," Caboose

muttered pacing back and forth behind the seats.

The scoreboard read seven to seven at half time. Mavis, Jack, and Nikki claimed they were too nervous to eat the sumptuous dinner Brad had ordered. Rocky joined the men and filled a plate high with food. Dwarfed by the members of Ram's former O-line seated at the table, Rocky's Cheshire grin and uninhibited glee were palpable.

"The wife will skin me alive if I don't eat her Christmas dinner when I get home," Diesel said before he forked up a helping of food and shoveled it into his mouth.

"Mine, too," Caboose said, following suit.

Jack stared vacantly at his brother gobbling down food to keep up with the men.

"How about a shake, Jack? They make the best chocolate shakes here." Harold picked up the phone at Jack's nod.

Did Ram tell him about Jack's problems swallowing?

Nikki's heart melted at the tender caring and consideration this special man lavished on her.

The score hadn't changed by the end of the third quarter. Mavis had abandoned her seat two minutes into the second half, and had joined Caboose pacing behind the viewing recliners.

"Look we're on TV!" Rocky shouted, pointing to the JumboTron on the field.

"I see that Mavis and Harold Delaney are at the game today, along with the rest of Ram's family," an announcer said.

Rocky waved and laughed, watching his image on the screen.

"Ram's mother never misses a game," the other announcer added.

"I wonder if she kept up the tradition of supplying the team with her delicious cookies today? Since Ram started playing high school ball she has baked cookies for the team and coaches. Ram's teammates considered the tradition a good luck charm. I was fortunate enough to be in the locker room after the game in Green Bay, and let me tell you—those cookies are wonderful."

"Such nice men," Mavis said. "Brad, do me a favor, honey, and get me the announcers' addresses? I'll send them a couple of tins."

The fourth quarter wound down. The defense sacked Ram again, and Nikki could barely breathe as he lay on the ground after the whistle. Mercifully, he bounced up when the referee walked toward him.

"For goodness' sake, Ram, throw the ball!" Mavis yelled as the Bears defense broke through the Dragons line, chased him around the field and he slid to avoid another sack.

The ball was on the Bears forty-yard line, third and eighteen. Ram broke the huddle, paused, and looked up at the owner's box. A close-up on camera showed his wide smile as if he acknowledged his mother's heated play call.

The center hiked the ball. Ram stepped back beyond the reach of the Bears middle linebacker, who bore down on him like a speeding bus. He waited until the defenseman was inches away and then launched the ball downfield. Ram took the inevitable hit and crashed to the ground.

The stadium went wild. Jack, Rocky, and Harold surged to their feet, bristling with excitement. Nikki should have followed the ball, but her eyes remained on Ram willing him to get up. After he did she shifted her gaze in time to see the perfectly thrown pass sail into Darrin Laborski's outstretched arms.

Avoiding two tackles, Laborski charged toward the goal line.

"Go, go, go!" The floorboards pulsed with the cheering.

Laborski hurtled into the end zone. Ram lifted his arms over his head, gazed up at the box and pointed. The boys waved their arms over their heads.

"Keep waving, Jack. He sees us." Rocky jumped up and down.

Jack's legs buckled, and he stumbled backward against the chair. Harold smoothly extended a hand and helped Jack stand. "Put your arm around me, son, and hold on," he said.

Nikki fished her cell phone out of her purse, clicked the camera function and shot a photo of Jack and Rocky viewing the game of their lives, tilting toward Gramps Delaney.

The game clock ticked down the seconds and the stadium erupted in a clamorous countdown. "Three, two, one!"

The Dragons held on to the lead as the final whistle sounded.

"Heavens above." Mavis laid a hand over her heart. "They clinched a spot in the play-offs. I can breathe again."

****

Harold led Jack and Rocky into the Dragons' locker room. Nikki waited with Mavis on a bench outside. Team family members and several celebrities mingled in the packed hallway. The din of conversation didn't permit Nikki's chatting with Ram's mother.

Harold and the boys reappeared ten minutes later. Star-struck and speechless, Jack and Rocky gawked at the overwhelming spectacle outside the locker room. Rocky sprang up each time the door opened, no doubt anticipating Ram's emergence.

Mavis greeted exiting players and coaches by name. She inquired about children and wives, complimented players on the game, and presented the Lamberts with a whirlwind of introductions.

The center, Mike Clark, emerged through the door and spied Mavis. Wearing a chagrined expression, he lumbered over to her. "Sorry, Mom. I tried to protect him but, damn, that Bears defense is good."

"You did a fine job, Mike. Go home and soak those knees. Say hi to little Mike for us." She reached up and patted the huge man on the back.

Nikki leaned against the wall, her hand resting on Jack's chair. His head slumped, and he dozed, a serene expression on his face.

Moments after Ram strode through the doorway a willowy blonde wrapped her arms around his waist, stood on tiptoe and kissed his cheek, branding him with a vivid red lipstick mark.

"Great game, Ram," she cooed, her voice husky and suggestive.

"Thanks, Roberta." A quick maneuver and her arms hugged air. He advanced to shake Harold's hand.

The spurned woman pouted as Ram neglected her. Nikki enjoyed the inward surge of victory.

"You had a game, son," Harold said as he pumped Ram's hand. "How's the side?"

"It's fine, Pop," Ram apparently lied as his mother's hug drew a flinch.

Ram laughed as she jumped away from him as if scalded. "No problem, Mom. I'm fine."

"How did you like the game?" Ram squatted down next to Jack's chair and put his arm around Rocky.

"It was awesome. Did you see us waving to you?" Rocky asked.

"I sure did."

"Me too?" Jack asked, rousing from his doze, his eyes glazed.

"Yep. You, too." He patted Jack's arm.

"We were on TV and everything. Thank you, Ram." Rocky wrapped his arms around Ram's neck.

"You are very welcome." He grimaced as he rose from the crouch.

"I hope you enjoyed the game, Nikki." His blue eyes twinkled, capturing her in his thrall.

"Oh, I did. It was great watching the TV in the suite, too. I didn't know where to look half the time," she rambled, off-center from his magnetism. "Are you sure you're all right? You took some nasty hits. They hurt just to watch."

"I'll be much sorer later, but right now I feel fantastic."

Nikki's surroundings receded as she hung suspended in his gaze. Fringe conversations broke through and she blurted, "Um, thank you for inviting us, Ram. We better go."

"Would you like to join us for dinner?" Mavis asked.

"I'd love to, but thank you, no. I have to get the boys home. Jack needs to rest, and I have a feeling that it will take a long time before I can calm Rocky down enough to sleep tonight."

Jack, however, already slumped sound asleep in his chair.

"The bus is waiting at the back entrance," Brad informed her, his cell phone to his ear.

"Good, that's where we parked the cars," Ram said. "I'll walk you out."

A crowd huddled in the parking lot, braving the cold, hopeful of catching glimpses of football heroes. A cheer went up as Ram stepped into view.

The mass of people surged toward him clamoring for his autograph.

"Hey guys," Ram greeted the fans. "Thanks for waiting. If you give me a minute to get my family settled, I promise I will sign all your autographs."

He moved around the fringes of the crowd, wheeled Jack to the coach, and helped the driver secure the chair on the lift.

"Thanks again, Ram," Rocky said scrambling onto the bus.

Nikki mounted the first step and turned around to face Ram. "Thank you seems so inadequate. This was an amazing, unforgettable experience for us."

You've stolen my boys' hearts. And mine.

"I'm glad you had a good time."

The autograph hounds inched closer while Ram gazed deeply into Nikki's eyes. Transfixed, she hoped that her deepest affections mirrored in her eyes.

"Hey, Ram. Kiss her. It's getting cold here," one of the fans shouted.

"I better go. I'll call tomorrow." He leaned forward and warmed a spot on her chilled cheek with his kiss.

And then he left to accommodate the fans. The crowd burgeoned as Ram's presence attracted a growing swarm.

Through the bus window, she witnessed a sultry, young woman freezing a pose, her lips plastered on his cheek as another woman took a photo with her cell phone. The two women changed places and reenacted the scene.

Ram's a football star. I'm just a mom and office worker. I can't believe he'd turn down beautiful women for me.

Ram shifted his gaze toward the coach. She smiled when his eyes met hers. He puckered his lips and sent her a kiss. Then he winked.

Nikki nestled in her seat as the bus pulled away, elated that Ram had apparently chosen her.

Chapter 20

Nikki was often unavailable during the days leading up to the play-offs, but never absent in Ram's mind. His record spearheading the team to a shot at the league title had upped his eligibility quotient with women, and he had received numerous propositions, veiled and *really* explicit—all meaningless to Ram. The rag sheets ridiculously paired him with starlets, George Clooney rejects, strippers, European royalty, and a couple political candidates. Nikki's family's fleeting exposure on air and in the parking lot at the Christmas Day game had created an investigative flurry as to her identity. Brad had effectively squashed conjecture by insinuating that she was a blood relative.

Ram's off the cuff request to the fans in the parking lot to "settle my family" before signing autographs had added heft to the detour Brad created for journalists. And it was close to the truth. Ram considered Nikki and the boys the family of his heart. No suggestive overtures from beautiful groupies competed with Nikki's appeal.

When Ram was in his early twenties, his father had predicted that the love of his life would bring him to his knees. Nikki had blotted out any interest in other women for Ram with a single kiss. He savored fleeting intimate, blood-boiling encounters with Nikki, and he was happier than any other time in his life. Mystifying, but true: he considered phone conversations and the occasional family dinner at her house with rare opportunities to be alone enough.

His parents had loved her and her sons at first sight. Despite Ram's long-standing independence, their opinions meant a lot. Mom, never one to beat around the bush, advised him to propose immediately.

Pop had suggested, "Mavis, let the boy alone."

And then he had winked and added, "But she's a wonderful girl. And her kids are great, too. I could eat 'em up."

Pop's sentiments matched Ram's exactly. And Mom's advice wasn't that far off the mark, either. But if he were to propose less than six months after she had lost her husband, he suspected she'd shoot him down. For the first time in his career, his head was in the game, but his heart was with Nikki, Jack, and Rocky.

"Hey, Luce," Ram called out. "Can you spare a minute to go over some things before I leave?"

"Yep." She appeared in the office doorway cradling in her arms a stack of folders topped by a legal pad, a pencil poking out from behind her ear.

"I was just about to beg you for some time." She perched on a chair in front of his desk. "The commercial broker in Chicago called. He has a site scoped out for a GSC campus there. Want the particulars?"

"Hmm," Ram stalled considering possibilities. "I think we have to put the plan to go national on hold until the season plays out. What do you think?"

"I agree. I have my hands full with the pool construction project here. Want me to tell the Realtor that you'll contact him directly when you're available to check out properties in the Midwest?"

"That's good," he agreed. "Anything pressing right now before I go on the road?"

"Oh yeah." She dumped the folders on his desk, opened the first on the stack and looked inside. "First off, can you approve the bid from New England Construction for the aquatics facility? That will get things rolling with permits and such."

"Sure." Ram accepted the document she passed over, signed it and handed it back.

Filing it she positioned the top folder underneath the rest and opened the next in line. "David Cry wants your permission to use some photos of you for promotional purposes. I told him, yes, but I can retract permission if I thought wrong."

"Nope, you thought right. What else?"

She shuffled the order of the folders again, head bent over the paperwork. "Coach Harriman wants to organize a community flag football league, an outreach program using GSC kids as mentors. Any objection?"

The idea appealed a lot. "I like that. But do we have issues with liability? I assume he wants to play the league here?"

"Uh huh. I have a call in to James at the law firm. If he's okay with it, should I tell Harriman it's approved? Even if the decision ups your liability insurance premium?"

"Yes. If there's a budget shortfall, I'll cover it personally." Ram folded his hands on the desk. "What else?"

Luci gazed at him over the rim of her reading glasses, a devilish gleam in her eyes. "One more thing. Harry DeSanto from the *Boston Ledger* wants you to call him."

"Does he now?" He grinned back at her. "For a spot on the Features Page about doings at the GSC?"

Luci wagged her head. "No, sir. He wants you to give him an exclusive interview to appear on the front page of the Sunday Sports Section. I kind of like the headline. 'Harry DeSanto and Phil Beltzer Share a Crow Sandwich.' " She cracked up.

Snorting a laugh, he directed her with great pleasure, "Tell him to work through Brad."

"Ha. Yessir. I hope that gets his goat." Scooping up the folders in her arms, she rose from her seat. "That's all I've got. Good luck in the playoffs, Ram."

"Thanks. A couple other things?"

She propped a hip on the corner of the desk and regarded him quizzically.

"First you'll see a fifty percent raise in your January 15th paycheck."

Widening her eyes she sank back down onto the chair in front of the desk. "Good Lord, I can't believe it. Ram, you're crazy. I mean, I *really* appreciate it, but...are you sure?"

"Positive. You deserve it."

Pressing a hand over her heart, tears welled in her eyes. "Thank you, Ram. I'm speechless."

Chuckling he quipped, "If I knew a raise was all that it took, I'd have given you one every month."

Her eyes narrowed to slits. "Hilarious," she said dryly.

"Not that a higher salary is connected to this, but I have a personal situation..." He paused, determined to phrase the request perfectly.

She leveled her gaze into his eyes. "Just tell me

what you need, Ram. I'd do anything for you."

"Luce, I'd be very grateful if you'd take care of the Lamberts while I'm on the road."

Her brow furrowed. "Well, sure boss. I'll take care of all the kids while you're gone."

"That's not what I mean. Could you call Nikki Lambert every day, see if she needs anything…like errands run, or maybe some girl talk? I'd like you to volunteer to drive Jack and Rocky home every evening. Maybe save her the trip. I've been trying to do that when I'm in town."

The crease in her brow deepened. "Okay, I'll be glad to. But…are you trying to tell me something here?"

"I guess I am. I love Jack and Rocky. And I'm in love with their mother."

She bit her lip and her eyes clouded. "Oh, sweetie. I'm so glad and so sad for you at the same time. Jack…"

"I know," he said reading her mind. "I'm afraid Jack won't make it."

"Odds are…" She trailed off, her eyes glistening with tears. She sniffled and swiped at the corner of one eye with a crooked index finger. "I'll take really good care of all of them. Don't worry about a thing."

"Thanks, Luci." Ram stood, rounded the desk and opened his arms.

Rising from her seat, pressing the folders to her chest, she circled her free arm around his waist as he hugged her tight.

On her way back out to her desk she casually tossed out, "Maybe I'll even root for the Dragons against the Packers in the playoff rounds this year."

He burst out laughing. "My God, Luci. Has the earth tipped on its axis?"

The clincher came. "I said *maybe*. Probably not."

"Ha, that's more like my girl."

After he organized his desk, Ram left his office to say goodbye to Jack and Rocky. Entering the gym, he inhaled the tangy, stale scent of overheated kids. Rocky lazed on the sideline of a basketball game in progress. Jack was nowhere in sight.

Sidling up to Rocky he squatted and sat down on the gleaming floor next to him. "Hey, Rock. You don't feel like playing today?"

"Nah. I'm taking a rest."

"Oh. Okay." Ram watched the back and forth motion of the kids' gameplay a few seconds. "Where's Jack?"

Rocky's jaw set, and his breath rasped in and out of his nostrils. "I don't want to tell you," he said, the words clipped.

Stunned, Ram tried to process his evasion since Rocky was an open book with everybody. "Why's that?" he probed.

"Because…" He scowled. "If I tell you, I'll cry like a sissy."

Ram's ears buzzed as alarm quickened. Lunging to his feet he held a hand down toward him. "Come on. Let's get out of here."

He took hold of the offered hand and Ram towed him to his feet. Still clasping his hand Ram strode out of the gym and stopped in the empty hallway outside the doors.

Stooping to Rocky's eye level he assured him, "Crying doesn't make you a sissy, Rock. Where's

Jack?"

His face scrunched up and he declared, "My dad said men don't cry."

"Well, I am sure your dad meant they don't cry often. I cry."

"No way. Really?"

"I sure do. And I'm not ashamed to tell you. What's bothering you, Rocky? I really want to know."

Ram's heart splintered as Rocky's eyes filled with tears.

"Jack is home sick. He can't come here. Mom's talking about keeping him home from school, too." He panted a few breaths before he blurted on a sob, "He's never coming back here, Ram. He's not Jack the Whack anymore."

Rocky dissolved in tears. Ram embraced him, clasped him to his chest and hauled him up off the floor as he stood. Holding him in his arms, his sneakers dangled and bumped Ram's thighs. Rocky's body quaked as he cried his heart out.

"It's okay, Rock. Go ahead and get it out. It's going to be okay," he soothed as tears tracked his cheeks.

His phone vibrated in his vest pocket, a tickling sensation that Rocky sensed, too.

"Your phone's ringing," he said.

"It can go to voicemail."

He raised his head off Ram's shoulder and said, "You can get it. I'm all right now."

Ram lowered him to the ground and fished the phone out of his pocket. Before he connected the call, he extended his hand to Rocky and said, "Come on. I'll drive you home."

Walking briskly toward the coat rack, Rocky in tow, he answered the phone, "Ram Delaney."

"Where the hell are you, Ram? I just boarded the plane," Brad groused.

"I'm on my way. No more than forty minutes." He disconnected the call before Brad could protest, and ushered Rocky outside.

On the way to Nikki's house, he hated witnessing Rocky's dispirited slouching in the Hummer's passenger seat. Even though Rocky was disease-free, ALD's ugliness sapped the life out of him, too. Ram desperately wanted to say or do something magical to talk Rocky out of his funk.

He couldn't begin to devise how to do that without all the facts, so he continued to question him. "Is Jack resting at home?"

"Yeah."

Waiting a beat for him to elaborate, Ram pressed on when he didn't, "Did he have another seizure?"

"No. I wish my dad was here. He would know what to do to make Jack better."

"Rocky, your mom and the doctors are doing everything they can for Jack. Even your dad wouldn't be able to do anything differently. You understand that right?"

"I guess so. I just miss him so much."

Ram's heart broke for the little boy. "Can you tell me what's going on with Jack?"

The floodgates released.

"He can hardly see anything and he keeps yelling at me and Ma to talk louder. I'm screaming at him and he screams back, talk *louder*. He doesn't want to eat, and Ma doesn't make him. He's lying around in a cool bed downstairs in the pool room, but he won't let me push the buttons to make the bed go up and down. He won't play with me anymore."

"He can't help those bad moods, Rocky. He doesn't mean it, and I'm sure he's sorry," Ram said.

"I know. Ma says that, too." He heaved a sigh. "But," further unburdening he continued, "I can't really fit in the bed downstairs, so he won't let me sleep with him. Even though I told him I could scrunch up real small at the bottom, he says get out…"

His complaints petered out, and Ram still hadn't concocted some magical or tide-turning response.

"Is he going to die, Ram?"

His plaintive request for information provided the moment of truth Ram hadn't faced squarely himself.

"I don't know, Rock." He wouldn't give him false hope, either. "He might."

"I don't want him to leave me like daddy did." Rocky blubbered.

Pulling up in front of Nikki's house, Ram bolted out of the car, raced around the front bumper and whipped open the passenger door. Leaning inside he wrapped his arms around Rocky and somehow found the tide-turning response, "I don't want him to die, either. But for now, he's with us. And I think we should enjoy every minute that we can with him, even if he's not himself sometimes."

Rocky's upturned eyes held unbridled trust and mature understanding. "Well, yeah. I can do that. Thanks, Ram."

Rocky scooted out of his seat and stamped on the slush piles that lined the curb and the walk leading up to the house. Climbing the stairs behind him, Ram stopped two steps short of the top of the stoop when the front door opened and Nikki poked her head out.

Rocky nudged past her, explaining, "Hi, Ma. Ram drove me home."

"Hi," she said as Rocky disappeared inside the house. "I thought you'd have taken off by now."

She swung the door wide. "I was planning to pick Rocky up in a couple hours."

Brushing her hands down the sides of her jeans, she invited. "Do you want to come in?"

He did, especially after hearing Rocky's take on Jack's condition. *Should I miss the first play-off game? Would Beltzer fire me if I did? Probably.*

"Do you need me to stay? Jack's not doing well according to Rocky."

Heaving a sigh, she responded, "He's having a bad day."

She stepped out onto the top stair and pulled the door closed just short of latching. "But I wouldn't think of preventing your going to the play-offs. We're all so excited for you. I have a lot of arranging to do because I can't let Jack go to school anymore, but it's under control."

She shivered, crossed her arms and rubbed them briskly up and down from shoulder to elbow to stave off the cold. "The ladies at work and a few students will split shifts and take turns watching Jack during the day. Everybody is so wonderful to me."

Her smile had him reeling with impotence. He wanted to stay and take some shifts, too. But he had to catch that plane. "I don't want to go." He traced the dark circles under her eyes and then pulled her close into a tight embrace.

She snuggled against him and he kissed the crown of her head, content to keep her close to his heart.

"You have to go," she said softly.

"If you're sure you'll be okay." He held her at arms length gazing at her beautiful face.

"I'm positive. Watching you play is one of the few things Jack enjoys these days," she said breezily.

"Can I run in and say goodbye to him before I leave?"

She wagged her head. "He's sleeping."

Before she backed into the house she pecked a kiss on his lips. "I'll tell him you stopped by."

"I'll leave him a note," Ram said as he dug into his pockets for a pen and something to write on. The sharpie in his right pocket and his itinerary in the vest pocket suited.

Working off the top of the Sharpie with his teeth, he flattened the paper against a house shingle and jotted down a couple sentences. Snapping the top back on the marker and pocketing it, Ram handed Nikki the note.

Accepting it, she smiled and said, "Good luck, Ram. And be safe. Don't get hurt, okay?"

"I promise. I'll call you every day." He jutted his head through the doorway and gave her a tender kiss.

She smiled and nodded.

"Oh, and my assistant, Luci Baldwin will be in touch, too. She can help out with groceries, errands, anything you need."

Frowning, she said, "Oh, I don't want her to go to any trouble. I'm fine."

"Don't be stubborn, Nikki. Give me this. I think it's the only way I can leave right now."

Her soulful, brown eyes gleaming, she agreed, "All

right, if it makes you feel better."

"Thank you. It does." Ram couldn't tear his eyes away from her beautiful face. "I'll miss you."

Her eyes soft, she said, "I'll miss you, too."

Chapter 21

"I don't want you," Nikki heard Jack say as she walked through the back door.

"I want my mom!" he crabbed at full volume.

Hurrying toward his converted bedroom within the new room addition, Nikki dumped her purse on the kitchen table and sang out, "I'm here, honey."

She left a trail of ice chunks and muddy boot prints in her wake as she bolted to his bedside. Cupping his hand in hers, she squeezed it tenderly. "What's wrong, Jack?"

His body rigid, he strained his head off the pillow, stared at Nikki unblinking as if he saw straight through her, and scowled.

Nikki cast a questioning glance at Debbie, one of the student volunteers, who stood at the foot of Jack's bed, a distressed expression on her pale face.

"I'm so sorry, Mrs. Lambert. I tried to help Jack out of bed and into his chair, but he started yelling at me and said he didn't want my help. I explained every step to him before I touched him, but I don't think he heard me."

Debbie heaved a shaky breath. "I'm really sorry," she repeated.

"I'm here now, Jack. Mommy can help you into your chair," Nikki said in a raised voice.

His tension released, and he relaxed back on the

pillow.

"Hi, Mommy." The quirky smile she knew so well creased his thin face.

The sporadic vision impairment, loss of coordination and the hearing deficits that Jack experienced were difficult to deal with, but his mood swings were impossible.

"I'm going to go now, Mrs. Lambert. If you want me to come again tomorrow, just text me." Debbie backed up a few paces.

"I'll see Debbie to the door, Jack," Nikki said as she gave his hand another squeeze. "And then I'll come right back to help you into your chair."

Trailing Debbie out into the hallway, Nikki plodded behind her lithe form whizzing toward the coat rack. Debbie yanked her coat off the hook and swung it around her back like a toreador cape stuffing her arms into the sleeves in a split second maneuver.

Nikki empathized with her apparent zeal to escape.

"I'm sorry." Tears brimmed in her eyes. "He was okay today. Better than usual. He could see his notebook and he wrote quietly in it all morning. Then all of a sudden, he couldn't see and...well...I understand. I think he gets scared."

Laying a gentle hand on her shoulder, Nikki consoled the student. "When he's scared, he only wants me. Don't take it personally."

"Oh, I don't. It just...my heart breaks for him." She gave a little whimper as tears streamed.

Nikki hugged her as a dull headache blossomed into a pounding throb in her temples. Releasing Debbie she gazed into her red-streaked eyes. "Thank you for your help, Debbie. I really appreciate it."

A frigid wind blew into the hallway, an icy blast of reality, as Debbie rapidly let herself out the door. The latch clicked with jarring finality.

Shivering, Nikki hung her coat on the rack and toed off her boots. She sat on the bottom step of the staircase and buried her face in her hands. The volunteer caretakers from the college, who helped Nikki to continue working, although generous, wouldn't suffice much longer. Although she considered herself blessed beyond her wildest expectations by the kindness and selflessness of so many people who loved her family, Nikki had to face reality. Jack wanted and needed only his mother.

She shuffled in her stocking feet back to Jack's room, intending to assist him transfer to his chair. He slept, his breathing raspy. A glance at her watch prompted a frustrated huff of breath. *It's almost time to pick up Rocky. Now what do I do?*

On tiptoe into the kitchen, she searched her cell phone contacts and then dialed the Good Sports Club. Luci answered the phone on the first ring.

"Hi, Luci. It's Nikki Lambert. Sorry to bother you."

"You're not. In fact you must be psychic. I just opened Jack's file to find your home phone number. I was about to call you."

Nikki's breath hitched and her knees went weak. "Is something wrong with Rocky?"

"No, no. Rocky's fine. Ram asked me to keep in contact with you while he's out of town. I wanted to touch base to see if you needed anything."

"That's so kind of you and, of course Ram, too. There is one thing, if you don't mind? Could you please keep an eye on Rocky after dismissal until I can arrange for someone to pick him up? Jack isn't doing well today and I can't leave him."

I could kick myself. I should have asked Debbie if she could drive Rocky home. Maybe I can catch her on her cell phone before she's back to the dorm.

"I just have to make a few calls," Nikki added.

"Don't bother. I can bring Rocky home."

"I hate to impose…" She did. Much as she appreciated outside assistance, she had juggled all childcare tasks by herself in super-mom style before Jack's illness—a former source of pride.

"You're not. I wanted to leave early today anyway," Luci assured her.

"Thanks so much. I really appreciate it."

"Consider it done. Anything else? Do you need anything from the store?'

"No, thank you. I have everything we need."

"If you think of anything, please call me. Do you have a pen to write down my home and cell phone numbers?"

Nikki found a pen in her purse, but no paper, so she wrote the numbers Luci supplied on the palm of her hand.

"I'll see you in a little while," Luci promised.

After she broke the connection Nikki continued to hold the phone against her ear, lost in thought.

We do have everything that we need. We have our faith and we have love.

She hurried back to Jack's room. Carefully she positioned next to him on the bed. Nestling her head on his pillow, she cupped her hands around his right hand, so small and fragile, like when he was a toddler.

"I'm here, Jack," she whispered. "I'll always be here."

She lay next to him and watched him sleep until the doorbell chimed.

While she bustled to greet Luci and Rocky at the door, Nikki decided to impose on Luci's good nature one more time.

Opening the door she said, "Hi, Luci…"

Rocky zoomed past her and up the stairs. "And Rocky," Nikki said to air.

Grinning, she invited, "Luci, can you please come in?"

Stepping over the threshold, Luci smiled as she glanced around. "You have a lovely home, Mrs. Lambert."

"Thank you. But please call me Nikki. I feel bad asking, but could you stay here, maybe for about an hour while I run to work? I have to arrange some things with my boss, and I don't want to do that over the phone."

"Of course. Take your time," Luci said breezily as she strolled with her toward the back of the house. "My husband, Al, is bringing home pizza so I don't have to rush home to start dinner."

Luci followed Nikki and peeked into Jack's room. Overhead Rocky thumped around in his room, more than likely playing video games.

Back in the kitchen, Nikki wrapped a scarf around her neck and put on her coat. "Make yourself at home, Luci. Help yourself to a snack or something to drink."

"I'll be fine."

"I won't be long," she predicted.

Shivering outside, Nikki hurried to the car. Every

year in memory, she yearned for spring as soon as the calendar turned to a new year. She missed sunshine mired in frigid and slate gray New England winters. That winter she didn't wish away one bone-chilling second.

Outside Elizabeth's office, she paused and rapped on the doorjamb.

Seated behind her cluttered desk, the boss held up the palm of her hand without an upward glance. "One second," she said as she continued reading a document on her desk.

Impatient, Nikki shifted from foot to foot.

A minute or so passed before Elizabeth raised her eyes and glanced toward the door. "Oh, Nikki. I didn't know it was you. Come in. Sit down. Is everything okay?"

"Honestly. Nothing is okay." She sat on the leather chair next to Elizabeth's desk and unbuttoned her coat. "I knew this day would come. I just didn't realize how soon. I'm sorry, but I have to quit my job."

Elizabeth furrowed her brow. "Oh no. Are you sure? Is there anything I can do to help you work through this? Anything I can say to make you change your mind? I hate to lose you."

"Thank you for saying that, but I'm certain about this. Jack needs me at home with him. But, more importantly, I realized this afternoon that I need to be with Jack."

"I understand." She opened her desk drawer, extracted a manila folder and placed it on the edge of the desk in front of Nikki. "I wish I could tell you that I haven't anticipated this. I've done my research on ALD."

Her eyes clouded and she paused, gazing out the office window a few moments before adding, "I know you need the insurance benefits. I've come up with an idea." She pointed to the folder. "Have a look."

Leaning forward, Nikki opened the folder and leafed through the pages inside. She finished reading and sat back stunned. Elizabeth had created a job description for a virtual position that involved posting financial aid and scholarships to the university database. She could do the job entirely from home.

Nikki's heart leaped. "You will do this for me?"

"Before you agree, you have to understand that there will be a cut in your pay. I couldn't convince the CFO to increase the department's budget, but you will keep your benefit package."

"I would do the work just for the benefit package. You don't have to pay me a salary, too."

"Bite your tongue." She laughed. "Never let the CFO hear you say that. If there is anything else we can do for you, you let me know right away."

Shocked, Nikki gaped at the tears glistening in her boss's eyes.

"I like to think that we are family here," she pronounced as she stood and skirted the oak desk.

Rising to meet her, Nikki flung her arms around Elizabeth, her heart overflowing with gratitude and affection. "Thank you so very much," she said.

Facing Elizabeth, Nikki continued, "I seem to spend the majority of every day thanking people for their kindness lately."

"I believe that you receive more in return when you give to someone else. I'll have Jerry the tech give you a call, and he'll download the programs you need to your home computer."

Grinning Nikki joked, "I'll have to keep Rocky away from it."

She gazed into Elizabeth's eyes, "I'm overwhelmed. Thank you can't express my gratitude."

"I wish I could do more." The apparent heartbreak mirrored in Elizabeth's eyes broke Nikki's heart.

"One more thing," Elizabeth continued, her face sober, a pugnacious expression in the set of her jaw.

There's the bulldog I know and love.

"Don't mention this to any of the others. I'll have hell to pay if they *all* badger me to let them work from home."

"I won't say a word. Thank you again."

The wind whipped Nikki's face as she trudged to the car. She buckled her seatbelt, pumped up the heat and rested her head on the steering wheel. The cell phone in her coat pocket vibrated.

She glanced at the caller ID and greeted her mother, "Hi. I intended to call you tonight. How's Daddy?"

"Hi, honey. He's doing very well. I tried you at your office number, but they told me you left for the day. Is everything all right?"

"I'm sitting in the parking lot outside the college. I just quit my job."

"Oh, honey, I'm so sorry."

"It's okay. I want to be home with Jack. I'm so blessed, Momma. Elizabeth created a virtual job for me. I'll still get paid with full benefits."

"That's wonderful. How is Jack?"

"Not good. That's why I planned to call you tonight. You said to let you know when you should come." Nikki had a hard time speaking over the lump in her throat. "I think you should come as soon as you can."

Silence on the other end of the phone.

A few seconds later Mom's quavering voice sounded in Nikki's ear. "Daddy is being released from rehab in two weeks. I'll call Aunt Patty tonight and ask her to come here to take care of him for a while."

"Mom, if you can't come I'll understand."

"I *have* to come," she declared, and then she broke down crying. Her sobs tore Nikki's heart to shreds. "I'm sorry, Nikki," she wailed.

"I know, Momma. I know…" Nikki sobbed.

"I'll call you tomorrow after I speak to Aunt Patty."

"I love you, Mom."

"I love you and the boys *so much*, darling."

The connection clicked off.

She dialed her mother-in-law's work number before she left the parking lot.

"Kay Lambert," she answered.

"Hi Mom, it's Nikki."

"Hi dear. What's up?"

"Would you and Dad like to come for the weekend and watch the play-off game with us? Weather permitting, of course."

"We'd love that. I bet the boys are beside themselves with the way the Dragons are playing. If they win this weekend, they play in the Super Bowl. Listen to me…" Pausing she chuckled. "Who knew that I would become a rabid football fan?"

"Me, too. It helps when you know someone on the team." Nikki smiled as Ram's handsome face came to mind.

"Is there anything I can bring?"

"Just yourselves."

"Thanks for inviting us."

"You don't need an invitation, Mom. Come whenever you can."

"We'll see you Friday night."

"Drive safe."

****

Luci stayed a while after Nikki returned home. Rocky continuously beat her by wide margins playing one of his video games.

"I'm not leaving until I win one game," she said with a roll of her eyes.

"Mom, Luci is sleeping over tonight." Rocky smirked.

Nikki burst out laughing and Luci winked at her as she left them to their game and checked on Jack. He continued to sleep.

Satisfied that he didn't need her, Nikki entered the kitchen and started dinner.

"I have to go, but I want a rematch, young man," Luci called up the stairs.

Nikki met Luci in the hallway. "Thank you for watching the boys."

"I had fun. If Rocky needs a ride tomorrow... You know what? I'm going to drive him home every day."

"Oh, no..."

"Yep." She gave Nikki a quick hug and then she left, cutting off further protest.

After she finished dinner prep, Nikki climbed the stairs, declared video game playing over for the day and helped Rocky with his homework.

Later, Rocky and Nikki ate dinner in front of the television. Rocky had his bath and she tucked him in bed for the night. Jack hadn't stirred the whole time. Clad in her flannel pajamas and robe, she lazed in the doorway of Jack's room observing his still form in the bed.

"Hi, Mommy." His soft voice startled her.

"Hi, honey," she said. "I didn't know you were awake. Are you hungry? I have some chicken soup and pudding."

She willed him to agree to eat since his lack of appetite had shrunk his body visibly on a daily basis.

"Nah, I'm not hungry," he said predictably. He held his notebook in his hand.

"Working in your notebook?" Elation filled her at the possibility.

"Yep. I can only work on it when I can see." His matter of fact tone jarred her. "I'm almost done with it. I just hope I have enough time left to finish it."

They had never talked about the end. Just thinking the word "death" made Nikki want to scream on the top of her lungs.

"I'm scared." His crystal blue eyes widened and his terror-stricken expression stabbed her.

"Oh, sweetheart," she cried rushing toward his bed.

Nikki propped a hip up on the side of his bed and drew him close. Easing back to lean against the headboard, she hugged him to her heart. "I know. This disease is so scary."

He shifted out of the embrace and lay on his side facing her. "I'm not afraid of dying, Mommy. I know Jesus loves children, so he will be happy to see me. And I get to be with Daddy. And I am almost done with my plan. As soon as I finish it, I will be ready."

Ready? Dear God, give me strength. She clasped his hand and inquired, "Then why did you tell me that you're scared?"

"I'm afraid for Rocky. You might not know this, but he's afraid of the dark. He tries to be tough, but I've heard him crying in his sleep. He misses Daddy, and I am afraid he is going to miss me more."

Any response lodged in her throat.

God, why are you taking this angelic soul home? Please, God, please don't take him. We need him more than you do.

But if God's will stole Jack away from her reach, he would still, forever, *always,* be *hers.* She could answer God's will with equal opposition. Jack might be taken, but she would *not* let him suffer one single scary thought.

"Maybe you've heard the saying, God never gives us anything we can't handle. When Daddy died, I didn't think I could go on without him. But here I am, maybe even stronger than I was before Daddy's accident. The truth is, if you go to heaven it will break our hearts. But God will give us the strength to go on, and someday we will all be together again. I will take good care of Rocky. And we will be strong for you."

His peaceful smile warmed her wildly beating, aching heart.

Jack remained silent for a moment, and she wondered what he was thinking.

"Can I skip the soup and just have the pudding?" he asked, his eyes twinkling.

Chapter 22

Jack

Before the ladies from the college stopped taking care of me, I asked one lady, who said she was the librarian, if she could bring me some books about death traditions in different cultures. She burst into tears and called me, "You poor, poor lamb."

I don't remember her coming over again. I never got the books, so I Googled it. I found out that the Eskimos, or Inuits which they like to be called better, do *not* put sick people on ice floes and send them away to die floating on the water. If somebody did that, I wonder if it would be good to die that way? I mean, if you're gonna die anyway, like me. Would you just curl up on the ice and rock to sleep, and then freeze to death without knowing it?

That would be good. For a while I thought about a plan to die on an ice floe floating on Heron Lake, near my house. But even if I could get there without Mommy finding out...I stopped thinking about that plan. Because I couldn't get anywhere by myself, Rocky couldn't drive, and even if he could, he would never take me somewhere to die. He still thought that I could whack ALD.

I couldn't.

Instead of writing down a death tradition for me, I

kept writing down my plan to change the world. I was tired, but really happy when I finally finished. I tossed my pencil on the table near the right side of the bed and it rolled off and landed with a pinging sound on the floor. Mommy came into my room and picked the pencil up and put it down on the table.

"Hey, sweetie," she said smiling into my eyes. "Want me to put your notebook in the drawer?"

"Uh uh," I answered. "I keep it right here all the time when I'm not writing in it."

I showed her by tucking the notebook away behind my pillow. "And this is important, Mommy, okay?"

Her forehead wrinkled like she didn't understand, but she said, "All right, Jack."

"No, I mean *really* important! Don't forget, Mommy, *please*."

I grabbed her hand and gave her my most serious face. "I don't want anybody to read my notebook."

Only Ram could read it now. I couldn't wait to give it him.

"Okay, Jack." She fluffed up my pillow. "Can I get you anything?"

I squeezed down hard on her hand and say, "Promise."

"Ouch."

I opened my hand, feeling guilty that I hurt her, and she slipped her hand away and shook it a couple of times.

"Sorry," I said.

"It's okay."

"But you still have to promise," I said again, all strict.

She raised her right hand like she's swearing on the

Bible. "I promise. Feel better?"

"Sure."

I didn't feel better. Things I saw got blurry and then not, like I was on a ride at Hershey Park, where we went once and I wished I could go again. Sometimes everything went black, like I was in a deep hole. I had to think real hard not to be scared. I told myself that I'm not dead, because if I were dead I'd see light, not dark.

My ears rang or sometimes it was like they were moaning, "Yaw yaw."

Or sometimes Mommy and Rocky moved their lips and no sound came out at all. That scared me so much I usually couldn't help screaming at them.

Mommy moved her lips just then.

"What?" I yelled.

"I. Said. The pregame. Is. On. Ready?" she said, her mouth wide making each sound.

Nodding I lay still while she took off the blankets. Poppy came over and lifted me straight out of the bed. Up high in his arms my stomach felt like it was falling out of me and I jerked around trying to stop it.

Poppy said, "Whoa. Steady, kiddo. I've got ya."

I closed my eyes when he carried me so I didn't feel like I was flying around in space like an astronaut fixing his space capsule just connected by one of those long hoses. When we got into the TV room I opened my eyes again. Poppy looked down at the floor where Mommy had a blanket picnic set out. Then he looked straight at Mommy like he didn't know what to do next.

"I can't sit down there," I said.

And then I started crying because I wanted more than anything to sit on the blanket with Rocky and watch Ram play.

"I'm gonna bring his bed in here," Rocky said as he jumped up off the blanket and ran into my room.

Mommy followed Rocky real fast and Poppy said, "Come on, kiddo. We've got this covered."

The next thing I knew I was back in bed staring at the ceiling moving in a big blur. Over my feet I saw Grandma and Rocky shoving away the coffee table and dragging the ends of the blanket with bowls of food on it to clear a path for me. Mommy was huffing behind me as she pushed the bed, and Poppy was on one side steering. In a couple of minutes the motor in the bed whirred, and I was sitting up looking at Ram's team photo on the TV screen. The announcer was talking about Ram's stats in the play-off games so far.

"Where's my stats notebook?" I asked.

"Got it right here," Poppy answered.

He lifted it up so I could see it. "Want me to help keep tabs of Ram's performance during the game for you?"

I nodded and then I remembered that I didn't have Ram's note. "Where's Ram's letter?" I asked, all worried that if I didn't hold the note during the game it would be bad luck.

"I'll get it," Mommy said like she's out of breath.

She was back again in like two seconds with the wrinkled paper in her hand.

Smoothing the note open on my bed next to me, I put my right hand on it and then everything goes dark. Not scary black, but calm like swimming in the pool with Mommy or lying back in a warm bathtub. I could hear the ref's whistle, the announcers talking like one long word with a million syllables, and Rocky and Poppy cheering. Mom and Grandma talked sometimes and it sounded like the wind chimes on the porch in the summertime.

"Want something to eat, Jack?" Mommy said real soft like my ears are stuffed with cotton.

"Nah uh," I said with my eyes still closed in the peaceful dark.

But then I realized my eyes were *not* closed. "I can't *see!*"

I heard rumbles, "Wah, wah, wah!" And I was so scared that I thought I went away to some worst place.

My bed shook and Rocky said in my ear, "Move over a little."

He shoved against my side and I moved over, dizzy, my head spinning. I clapped my hands over my cheeks and Rocky wrestled one hand away and held on tight.

"The game's almost over, Jack. They're on their forty-yard line, three points behind. Third down, four to go for first down." His breath in my ear felt hot and smelled like grape jelly.

"The game's almost *over?*" How did that happen? "Quick, Rock, read me the note again."

"I don't know where it is."

I thought real hard. And then I laughed. "You're sitting on it."

Rocky let go of my hand, and the bed moved a lot, and his butt whomped into my side. "Got it."

Paper crinkled and he said, "Mommy, can you read this to Jack? I don't know all the words."

I heard nothing. And then Mommy, who smelled like flowers, said, "You were sleeping when I left, so I couldn't get your good luck handshake. Cheer for me when you watch the games, okay? I'll hear you and

Rocky and Mom cheer in my heart. Everything good I do on the field will be for you."

"Go Dragons!" I yelled with all my might.

"Go Dragons!" Rocky hollered.

"Holy cow!" he screamed.

He grabbed my hand again and banged it up and down on the bed. "Ram threw the ball downfield. It's flying, Jack!"

My heart pounded along with our hands whacking the bed.

"Catch it! Ruuuuun!" Rocky hollered. "Ooooooooooooh! Touch down!"

A blast of hot air filled my ear when Rocky said, "He heard us Jack. He's pointing to the camera! He's pointing to *us*! Wahooooo!"

Rocky rolled over on top of me, squishing me down into the bed. He hugged me around the neck, his stubbly hair tickling my nose. He smelled like shampoo and stinky socks. I grinned and hugged him back as hard as I could.

How lucky was I? This was the best day. I was in no hurry to stop hugging Rocky thinking that it felt even better than floating in my pool. When he let go and climbed out of my bed I started feeling lonely again.

All of a sudden I was sure I heard Mommy crying. My heart hurt. "Mommy, are you crying?" I said in the dark.

She sniffled, and I smelled her perfume. Her breath in my ear smelled like toothpaste.

"I'm crying happy tears," she said. "Ram's going to play in the Super Bowl now."

"Wow, that's right," I said amazed. "Awesome. I

can't wait to watch that game."

Mommy cried harder. *She must be really happy and excited. Just like me.*

Chapter 23

I won't win the mother of the year award, Nikki thought. She kept Rocky home from school without acceptable excuses, according to Green Briar Elementary School policy manual, most days during the two weeks preceding the Super Bowl. He wasn't ill, thank God, but she couldn't stand to let him out of her sight. Even if she had overcome her paranoia and insisted on "normal" for Rocky, she couldn't pry him away from his brother's side, anyway.

The homework delivered each day by Rocky's sympathetic teacher went untouched. He missed tests, and Nikki didn't care. There would be plenty of time for school after…

The word "after" burrowed in her brain like an evil parasite. *Not today. Please, God, another day.* She lived in the moment, because she would go insane if she thought a second beyond now.

Ram called a few times from the road and frequently she let the phone go to voice mail, although she missed him terribly. His exciting, celebrity-filled life had nothing to do with her life: a vacuum centered on a hospital bed. The days blended into each other. At times she couldn't extinguish between day and night because Jack's sleep patterns reversed: wakeful and twitchy by night, slumbering and frightfully still by day.

Rocky and Nikki zipped into sleeping bags spread on the floor by his bed for sporadic rest. She dozed when the boys slept, and then roused to hold Jack's hand when he awoke. Zombie-like she lacked the strength to maintain any normalcy, even for Rocky's sake. The battle Jack waged to hang onto life sapped her energy. Despair consumed her. If Rocky wanted to eat junk food, she permitted that with a smile. She usually forgot to eat at all.

Her in-laws' pending visit over Super Bowl weekend provided Nikki's sole motivation to shower and to straighten the house.

****

A light snow fell as Rocky, Kay, and Nikki huddled in the car outside Our Lady of the Angels Church on Super Bowl morning waiting for the windows to defrost. Mickey had volunteered to remain at home with Jack so they could attend mass. Rocky had negotiated to staying behind with his grandfather and brother, but a promised pancake breakfast after church had him stomping to the car without serious fuss.

Rocky had brought a dollar of his allowance savings to light a candle for Jack. As she gazed at the fragile, flickering flame, another fissure had opened in Nikki's heart.

The windshield cleared, and Nikki drove to the supermarket, crawling along the icy streets. It seemed the entire town had caught Dragons fever. Team insignia banners hung from the lampposts that lined village streets. The bakery displayed a mountain of purple and orange cupcakes in the front window. Dragons' colors balloon bouquets batted against two columns outside the elementary school, and the high school had held a bonfire and pep rally in honor of the contending Super Bowl champs the day before.

The purple and orange flowers on the altar at mass earlier hadn't surprised Nikki. The multitude of Dragons jersey-sporting members of the congregation made it seem like the team themselves had gathered in the pews. Father Chuck's eyes had twinkled when he had removed his cassock after the service to reveal the bright purple Dragons sweatshirt that he wore.

Apparently the rabid fan disease was contagious. Nikki stuffed the shopping cart with purple napkins, orange streamers and assorted team mania utensils, plates and paper cups.

The snowstorm had worsened while she shopped and Nikki spent fifteen minutes brushing and scraping the car windows after she had squeezed the grocery bags in the trunk.

"I'm so glad we decided to come last night or we would never have made it today." Kay peered out the window. "If this storm keeps up, you might have house guests for a few days."

"Stay as long as you want, Mom." Nikki reached over the console and patted Kay's gloved hand. "I'm really glad you're here."

"How lucky is Ram?" Rocky crowed from the back seat.

Stopping at a traffic light, Nikki glanced at Rocky in the rear view mirror. The Sunday papers tented over his lap, he waved the Sports Section in his hand.

"Look, Ma," he directed pointing to the picture of Ram squinting in the Miami sun. "He doesn't even have to wear a coat. Boy, I wish we could be at the game."

Nikki hadn't told Rocky that Ram had invited them to the game, offering a private plane, and even round-the-clock nurses for Jack—anything so that the boys could be there to watch him play. She had refused the tempting, amazing offer. Jack couldn't travel, and at that point she was terrified that removing him from the bubble she had created in the house would expose him to germs or other unforeseen threats.

So, Nikki spent way too much money at the supermarket and secretly attempted to compensate with purple ice cream and Dragons paraphernalia.

Mickey wouldn't permit Nikki to carry the groceries inside the house. He slipped and slid back and forth along the ice-encrusted driveway during his repeat trips inside until he had covered the kitchen floor with brown paper bags. Kay fixed Rocky's pancakes bribe while Nikki crammed the food into the refrigerator.

Soon the homey smells of cooking on the stove and in the oven filled the air. Kay prepared her special meatballs. Nikki made a bubbly, hot cheese dip and Jack's favorite pigs in a blanket. The coffee table sagged beneath platters of the boys' traditional, "blanket" tailgate favorites. Jack sat, eyes closed, in the hospital bed that Mickey had positioned in front of the TV.

Each year the pre-Super Bowl hype had begun increasingly early, and by kickoff the game seemed anticlimactic. Historically, Nikki's family had watched the event while drifting in and out of the family room. Grazing the tailgate buffet on the coffee table, the Lamberts had devoted most of the viewing time to the much-publicized commercials, if not the actual game. John customarily had taken the boys outside for a three-man football game at half time, and most often the boys were tucked in bed before the game had ended.

That year everything had changed. Rocky, too, sat in the hospital bed, his eyes glued to the screen for the hours leading up to the game, alert to the possibility of glimpsing Ram. Mickey dozed on the couch, but snapped to attention every time Rocky shouted out a sighting.

"Wow, Jack. There's Grammy and Gramps." Rocky hopped off Jack's bed, charged toward the television and pointed out the Delaneys.

Returning to his seat next to Jack he asked, "Do you think Grammy made cookies? Do you think they took them to the locker room?"

"I bet. The cookies are good luck," Jack whispered in a hoarse voice.

Rocky kept up a constant commentary on the pre-game show for Jack's benefit, apparently intent on being his brother's eyes for the day. Jack's blindness seemed permanent, although some spotty ability to hear remained.

The Carolina Panthers took the field.

"Oh my. Those are some *very* big men." Kay pointed to the screen. "Our O-line needs to step it up today."

Mickey laughed as he hugged her. "Who are you, and what have you done with my wife?"

Kay chuckled, a girlish blush reddening her cheeks.

"You won't believe this, Nikki," he said. "The other night I came home a little late from work and caught Kay watching Sports Center."

Dragons fever had spread to New Jersey, too.

Kay helped Nikki clear the leftovers off the coffee

table, most of which were dumped in the garbage. Nikki opened a cabinet and took out a cookie tin. Strolling into the family room, Kay trailing her, she placed the tin on the coffee table.

"Gosh, I wish we had good luck cookies to eat before the game starts," Nikki said wistfully.

"Yeah, me, too," Rocky said.

"Oh wait…" She whipped off the cover of the tin dramatically. "We do have some."

"Really?" Rocky scampered toward the table.

He snagged two cookies and retraced his steps back to the bed.

Unselfishly, Rocky set one cookie down on the bedcovers and carefully wrapped Jack's fingers around the other. He waited until Jack nibbled on a corner before gleefully biting off half of his cookie.

"Did you make these, Grandma?" he mumbled finishing off the cookie.

"Nope."

"These are the real deal," Nikki said, a wonderstruck lilt in her voice. "Ram's mom sent them to us in overnight mail."

"I need this recipe," Kay said reaching back into the tin. "I'm so full, but I can't resist."

Jack made a gagging noise.

"I'll get some milk," Mickey volunteered, rushing into the kitchen.

He returned to the room with a gallon of milk, cups and a straw. After pouring a cup for Jack, he tenderly served him, leaning down to Jack's level and placing the straw in his mouth.

"Thanks, Poppy," Jack gurgled.

The television became the focus of attention again

when Ram's image appeared on screen. He knelt, led his team in prayer and then the Dragons burst through the locker room doors out into the stadium tunnel. Emerging through the mouth of the tunnel into the roaring, packed stadium, Ram lifted a hand over his head and the Dragons stormed the field together.

Caught in the electrifying moment, Rocky and the adults stood up and whooped. Suddenly Nikki realized that the noises emanating from Jack were moans, not cheers.

"Mommy, please," he whispered, tears streaming.

Speeding over to him, Nikki gasped out, "What, honey? What do you need?'

"I need to…to…" His body stiffened and after one raspy exhalation, he stopped breathing.

Nikki screamed, "Mom, call 911; he's not breathing!"

Kay tore out of the room.

Rocky grabbed Jack's hand and yelled in his ear, "You have to breathe, Jack. Do it. *Breathe*."

Miraculously, Jack's eyes fluttered open and he gazed directly into Nikki's eyes. "Mommy…" His chest rose and fell spastically.

Her heart in her throat, Nikki clutched his hand and smoothed one hand over his hair. "Be calm, darling. We've called help to make you feel better."

"No…" His head wagged as chills coursed through her. "I'm leaving…call…have to tell Ram."

His breathing hissed, and his legs thrashed under the covers.

Mickey stood at the foot of the bed rubbing Jack's legs while Nikki clung to his hand. Rocky held Jack's other hand and gabbed nonstop, "You're okay, Jack.

The game is about to start. I can see Ram. He's waving to us, Jack."

Tears streamed down Rocky and Mickey's cheeks. Nikki cried blinding rivers, blurring Jack's little face above the covers, droplets dripping off her nose. She distantly heard the opening chords of the *Star Spangled Banner* and then wailing sirens drowned out the music.

Mickey raced to the door and ushered the paramedics into the room. Shivering uncontrollably Nikki made way for the two young men with kind eyes who surrounded the hospital bed and placed an oxygen mask over Jack's face.

At Nikki's request one paramedic contacted Jodi Warner, and then advised her that the doctor would meet Jack at the hospital.

"Ma'am, your son's blood pressure is dropping. He's nearly comatose."

Rocky clamped both his hands around Jack's hands and narrowed his eyes to slits.

"Rocky, let the men put Jack on the stretcher," Nikki requested, her heart hammering in her ears.

"No." She had never seen the combative expression Rocky flashed at her like a figurative punch to the gut.

"Please, honey," she begged. "We have to get Jack to the hospital."

Mickey slipped an arm around Rocky's shoulders, but he jerked it off.

"I can't," he wailed. "If I let go, Jack will leave."

Training panic-filled eyes on his mother's face he screamed, "I have to keep him here! I *won't* let go of him."

"It's all right, ma'am." Sorrow shimmered in the

paramedic's eyes.

"Can you help us move your brother to the stretcher?" he posed to Rocky.

He maneuvered the stretcher abreast of Jack's bed.

"Move on three," he said.

Rocky nodded grasping the end of the bed sheet.

"One, two, three…"

Jack's inert body within the bed linens slipped onto the stretcher. Kay thrust coats and a purse into Nikki's hands. Nikki hung Rocky's coat on his shoulders, tailing him on the run with the paramedics.

"Don't worry about us." Mickey's tremulous voice sounded, and he patted a warm hand on Nikki's quaking back. "We'll follow in the car."

Kay huddled in the open doorway; her face blanched ghostly white.

"Be careful, Dad, it's icy out here," Nikki shouted over her shoulder as she skidded on the path to the ambulance.

"We'll be fine," Mickey hollered.

Rocky and Nikki crammed into the back of the ambulance. Through the window the blue revolving lights colored the faces that peered out of windows as the ambulance sped by houses, sirens blaring.

"We're in an ambulance, Jack. You're gonna be all right," Rocky blubbered.

Jack's sightless eyes fluttered open an instant, and then closed. His forehead wrinkled.

Leaning over, Nikki mouthed in his ear, "I'm here, darling. Dr. Warner will meet us at the hospital."

He tugged weakly at the oxygen mask, and his mouth moved beneath the clear plastic.

She pulled the mask down below his chin.

"Ram?"

His labored breathing terrified her and she repositioned the mask back in place assuring him, "I can't reach him until the game is over. I promise, I'll call then. He'll probably call you after the game anyway."

"Yep, he'll call after he wins the Super Bowl," Rocky announced, his sobbing at odds with the optimistic statement.

Jack furrowed his brow and lapsed into unconsciousness. Rocky tightened his grip on Jack's hand.

****

Jack's V.I.P. reception at Coastal Regional Medical Center as an incoming, critical patient fostered hope in Nikki's tortured heart. Jodi Warner met the ambulance at a private entrance and directed the paramedics through labyrinthine hallways to a private room. Skittering behind the rolling stretcher, Nikki's feet barely stayed beneath her body.

The transfer from the stretcher to the bed reversed the process Rocky had insisted on at home, since he stubbornly remained linked to Jack's hand.

Sizing up the situation, Jodi assured Nikki, "I'll work around him."

Her blue eyes steely, she examined Jack while Nikki stood trembling in the doorway. Fresh panic gripped her at the physician's somber expression and Jack's non-responsiveness to stimuli.

What if Mickey and Kay don't know how to find us? Will they get here in time?

"My in-laws were following the ambulance," Nikki croaked out. "How will they find Jack's room?"

"No problem," Jodi said as she unclipped a phone from her belt. "What are they driving?" She gazed at Nikki, her phone in hand.

"Um…" Her mind went blank. Floundering to recall the simple information, Nikki sagged helplessly against the doorframe until Rocky intervened.

"Poppy's car is a blue Chrysler. His license tag says, 'MAK0921'," Rocky rattled off.

Open-mouthed, Nikki gaped at him while Jodi made a call and directed the person on the other end of the line, "I want an escort for Mr. and Mrs. Lambert to the east wing, room 700, please. Check arrivals routes for them. They're driving a blue Chrysler, MAK0921. Thanks."

Jodi continued examining Jack.

"Rocky, how do you know all that about Poppy's car? Even the license plate number?"

"Easy," he said off-handedly. "Poppy told me it stands for Mickey and Kay, September 21st. That's when they got married."

In the depths of misery, Rocky could still make Nikki smile.

Jodi finished her exam and then cast her a glance so dire-laden that icy chills raced through Nikki like a cascade of razors. "Rocky, I'm going to talk with Mom in the hall a second. Will you stay with Jack?"

"Yes." He bobbed his head. "Can we watch the Super Bowl?"

"Sure," she agreed, picking up the remote control.

She fiddled with the channel selector until the game played on the TV that hung from the ceiling.

"OK, Jack. Still no score. Dragons have the ball…" Rocky said.

Jodi rounded the bed and advanced toward Nikki. As she stepped backwards out into the hall, dread rose in Nikki's throat like acid.

"Nikki, he's comatose."

The tears brimming in her eyes simultaneously scared and touched Nikki. It was a comfort that Jack's doctor cared enough to cry for him.

"I knew he was getting worse, and sometimes he was so still when he slept I was afraid that he wouldn't wake up," Nikki whimpered. "But he does wake up at night."

Wagging her head, Jodi bit her lower lip and then said, "Not tonight, Nikki. His current state is irreversible. I'm powerless to provide any meaningful treatment."

"Oh, *God,*" she whispered sagging into Jodi's outstretched arms. Lost in bottomless sorrow, she sobbed silently, her body wrenching.

Jodi tightened her grip when Nikki managed to ask, "Is he in pain?"

"No," she asserted her thin arms like steel bands around Nikki's back. "And I won't permit him to suffer *any* pain," she vowed.

Consoled the tiniest bit, Nikki stepped out of her embrace. "Thank you."

Nikki pinched her nostrils and then swiped the back of her hand under her nose. "Can I take him home?"

"I want to watch him overnight. Possibly tomorrow. We'll see."

Her heart leaped at the prospect of tomorrow in Jack's life. Maybe Jodi was wrong and maybe Jack would wake up again.

Please, God. Not today.

She prayed the same as she had since Jack had become bedridden to keep him with her one day at a time.

"Possibly tomorrow. We'll see," Jodi said.

"Good." Nikki sighed heavily. "Thank you so much."

Mickey and Kay clamored down the hall toward Nikki with a white-haired woman clad in a pink hospital jacket.

With a kind smile, Jodi retreated bidding Nikki's in-laws, "Hello, Mr. and Mrs. Lambert. Good, you found us."

"How is he?" Kay asked breathlessly, pulling up short.

"Not good," Nikki said, pained at their stricken expressions at the news. "The doctor says he's in an irreversible coma."

"Oh, Nikki…" Kay flattened her palm against the wall and tilted sideways. Held upright with a stiffened arm, her head hung.

"Can we see him?" Mickey inquired so meekly that Nikki hardly recognized his voice.

She led them into Jack's room and the trio fanned out to circle the bed. Maintaining those guardian posts, each robotically stroked Jack's limbs. Unmeasured time passed. Rocky continued narrating game plays in Jack's ear like a sports commentator.

Rocky's voice registered as gibberish as Nikki focused only on Jack's sweet face, drinking in every feature…that would never be enough no matter how many tomorrows God granted.

Rocky's fist thumped down hard on the bed.

"Laborski, catch the ball!"

Emerging from her trance, Nikki focused on the screen to witness the ball spiraling in an arc toward a downfield runner.

"Ram threw a darned near perfect pass," Mickey claimed.

"Ohhhh! He's got it. Go!" Rocky pounded a drum roll on the bed. "Wahooooo! Touchdown! They're winning. Do you *believe* this, Jack?"

Hearing Ram's name triggered Nikki's memory. She walked over to the armchair where she had plopped her purse upon entering the room. Digging inside the purse, she couldn't find her cell phone, even after she dumped out the bag's contents on the bed. Then she remembered that the phone was on a lamp table in the family room anticipating Ram's post game call to the boys.

"Dad, could I please borrow your phone to make a call?" She rolled her eyes toward the television.

Nodding, he slipped a cell phone out of his pocket and tossed it over to her.

Out in the hall near a sign that designated the area for cell phone use, Nikki dialed Ram's number. The ring tone burred four times and a computer voice, preceded by a click, advised, "This voicemail box is full. Please try your call later."

Frustrated, she returned to Jack's room, leaving every ten minutes in an attempt to reach Ram, growing more disturbed each time she received the same recording. Jack needed to tell Ram something; he had made that clear. Despite the fact that he might never fulfill that need, Nikki *had* to bring Ram to see Jack before…

Redialing his number for the twentieth time she nearly had a heart attack when a man answered, "Ram Delaney's phone."

"Uh…hello," she stuttered. "I need to speak to Ram. It's urgent."

"I'm sorry, no can do. He's on the field. And this is the Super Bowl, lady."

"I realize that…" Her head spun. "Could you get a message to him?"

"Yeah, sure. I guess…"

"Please tell him to call Nikki right away. Jack's in the hospital, and he asked for Ram to come. This is *an emergency.*"

"Sure, doll. I got it."

The connection went dead. Relieved, she limped back to Jack's room. Rocky was in a tizzy.

"They won, they won! Mom, the Dragons are world champs! All because of Ram."

"This is wonderful." She noted how Rocky's eyelids drooped and how often he blinked. He needed a comfortable bed and a good night's sleep. She had neglected his well-being for too long. Nikki decided to wait another half hour before insisting on sending him home for the night with her in-laws, hoping the post-game hoopla would wind down and she'd hear from Ram by then.

When the call wasn't forthcoming after the Super Bowl broadcast ended, she directed, "Rocky, I want you to go home with Grandma and Poppy now to get some sleep."

His eyes went wild and he moaned, "Nooooo…"

"Yes," she contradicted him, gently disengaging his hand from Jack's. She knew he wouldn't risk hurting Jack, and he didn't resist.

Tears brimmed in his eyes as he begged, "Please let me stay, Mom. Jack needs me…"

"Jack needs his rest, too," she argued, praying that Jodi was right and there would still be tomorrow to reunite Rocky with Jack.

Rocky would never forgive her if Jack died in his absence. But she would never forgive herself if she didn't demonstrate that when Jack left, it wouldn't matter if Rocky held his hand. Nikki couldn't let Rocky carry that failure, so she held her ground against his opposition.

His body language screaming reluctance, Rocky allowed Mickey to shepherd him home. Kay stayed with Nikki to continue the vigil at Jack's bedside. Bleary-eyed Nikki still expected him to awaken at midnight, like he had recently, despite Jodi's prediction.

Exhausted, Nikki couldn't remain on her feet another second, so she curled up next to Jack on the bed and Kay collapsed in the armchair recliner. She fell into a half-sleep to the rhythmic beeping of the heart monitor. Sweating in the stifling hot room, Nikki fought genuine sleep, terrified at the nightmares that surely would manifest if she lost consciousness.

****

"How's the arm?" The shout-out came from the back of the room.

Fisting and then relaxing his right hand, which hurt like a bitch, Ram stated, "Great. Never better."

He hunkered over one of the microphones on the table in front of him, squinting into the glare of hot lights, the standing-room-only crowd a gleaming blur.

Damn, this is amazing.

The room bulged with press from all over the world.

"Funny, how a win vanishes all the pain," he said.

Friendly laughter resounded, upping his delight in facing the press after the game of a lifetime.

"What were you thinking with that last pass to Laborski? Anderson was bearing down on you. Did you even see your receiver in the end zone?" Ram's "pal" Harry with the *Boston Ledger* rattled off from the front row, his gruff voice familiar.

"Thinking? Did you see that pass? I just let it fly on pure instinct. Thank God that Laborski is a magician and he managed the catch. I swear; I saw my life pass before my eyes when Anderson landed on me. He's one big fellow."

Laborski's miracle catch had won the game for the Dragons while Anderson had almost broken Ram's back.

"What's this I hear about the possibility of your appearing next season on *Dancing with the Stars*?"

"Really, Stan?" Ram snorted a laugh. "You're kidding me, right? The only dancing in my future is on the field."

"So you're definitely coming back next year? Is that official?" Stan asked.

"That's up to management. Whitney's finger will be healed by camp." Ram paused and wiggled his eyebrows.

The group reacted with another round of laughter.

"*If* things work out the way I'd like, we'll get together after a Super Bowl win this time next year." Ram stood and nudged his chair away from the table with the backs of his legs. "Thanks, guys. It's been a great year. See you in August."

Off to Ram's right, Brad nodded his head in apparent approval judging from the shit-eating grin plastered on his face. Approaching him wearing the identical expression, Ram clapped a hug around him.

Slapping Ram on the back he proclaimed. "Son of a bitch, you *did* it. I can't believe you just won the fucking Super Bowl. My phone is ringing off the hook. You can pretty much name your price right now. Nike, Wheaties…oh, and guess what? You're going to Disney World."

"Great. Include Nikki, Jack, and Rocky in the arrangements."

"Will do. How does it feel to be 'the man'?"

"It hasn't sunk in yet. Did Mom and Pop make it back to the hotel okay?"

"Yes, they did. They're planning to order room service if you want to join them. They have an early flight out tomorrow morning."

"Sounds good. Any messages from Nikki?" Ram couldn't wait to speak to her and to celebrate in fine style with Jack and Rocky.

"She didn't call my phone," Brad said on pace with me toward the locker room. "Wouldn't she call your cell?"

"I'll check. My phone's in the locker room."

Brad halted as Ram detoured a few minutes to sign autographs.

"Great game, Ram." The taller, coffee-skinned man gave him a congratulatory back slap and a hearty handshake. "Awesome Hail Mary pass at the end. The Panthers didn't know what hit them."

"Thanks, Mike." Ram grinned and continued on to

the locker room.

Brad gawked, open-mouthed.

"Holy shit. You just called Michael Morgan, 'Mike'," he whispered gaping at Morgan's retreating figure.

"It's unreal, isn't it? I know I'm going to wake up in the morning and this will all be a dream. I'll shower and catch you back at the hotel."

Ram shoved open the locker room door and hustled to his locker to call Nikki. Despite the late hour, he hoped she'd forgive him if he woke her up.

He placed the call observing the roaring pandemonium in the room with a skeptical eye.

I probably won't hear a word she says, but I hope at least she can hear me.

The phone blooped, and Ram frowned at the low battery notice on the screen. And then the damned thing shut off completely. Shit.

Ducking a geyser of champagne, Ram grinned as the spray washed his cheeks.

Damn, we did it.

Stripping off his gear, he wrapped a towel around his waist and strode to the showers. At the hotel he'd call Nikki and *really* celebrate this achievement. He wouldn't believe that he wasn't dreaming until he heard her voice.

The jubilant chaos Ram encountered in the hotel lobby rivaled the game's aftermath in the locker room. Who were all those backslapping, shoulder-punching people sucking down drinks? Gracious and grateful, Ram waded through the well-wishers and signed autographs. Rapidly, he lost steam and dragged his aching body toward the elevators. In the blessed hush on an upper floor of the hotel, he traveled the corridor to his parents' room.

He had just enough energy to accept their beaming congratulations and bid them goodnight. By the time he closed the door of his room in the suite, it was too late to disturb Nikki and the boys. Collapsing on the bed, his last waking memory was a nibbling of dread on the edges of the dream-like victory.

Chapter 24

Although Nikki wanted every precious moment with Jack to last ten years, the night dragged in her surreal waking nightmare. When Rocky and Mickey bustled into the room around seven AM toting bakery sacks and a tray of coffee cups, she rose off the bed, achy and exhausted.

A beaming Rocky replaced Nikki next to Jack as she sucked down coffee as if it were a blood transfusion.

"Do you want to go home for a little while to freshen up?" Kay's face was lined with exhaustion and way too much grief.

"No, I can't leave him." Nikki stretched her arms overhead and yawned widely. "Dad, did you bring my cell phone?"

His brow furrowed. "I'm sorry. I didn't think to."

"That's all right," she assured him, wondering if Ram had called. "Did you notice if I had any messages on the cell or home phone?"

He wagged his head. "I was too busy corralling Rocky. Want me to drive back home now and check?"

"No, we'll get it later. Maybe I should call Ram's assistant. Can I borrow your phone again?"

Nikki placed the call and succeeded in leaving two messages: one on Luci's cell phone and one at the Good Sports Club. Afterward, she wandered the maze of halls a while needing the mind-blanking motion. The morning wore into afternoon without a word from or appearance by Ram.

Hope winged when Nikki spotted Jodi approaching down the hall. Perhaps she'd okay the return to her home bubble. She'd be a better mother to Rocky and concentrate on strengthening herself for Jack. She ducked into Jack's room on Jodi's heels, aghast when she witnessed the expression on Jack's face.

"Jodi." She tugged on the doctor's sleeve. "Is he in pain?"

Jodi gazed at Jack intently for a moment and then turned around and faced Nikki. "Step back outside with me, please?"

Mutely reversing, Nikki faced Jodi in the hallway clutching her trembling hands together.

"I don't have a clinical basis for my assessment," she said. "But I've seen similar expressions on my patients' faces enough to interpret what's going on with Jack."

Heaving a breath, she delivered the opinion that Nikki had already intuited deep in her heart. "He wants to go, Nikki. He needs you to let him."

Nikki's stomach dove as she understood the necessity in Jodi's advice. To be the mother that Jack deserved she'd have to direct him to do the unthinkable.

"At the house after we called the ambulance..." She sputtered and then choked on a sob. Sniffling she continued, "He said he was leaving..."

Jodi's hand brushed Nikki's face and she didn't feel it. She had turned into a block of ice.

"Think about it, Nikki. You'll know..." Jodi's sad eyes pierced Nikki's heart.

As Jodi walked back down the hall, Nikki staggered numbly back into the room. Jack's expression hadn't changed. If anything his little face seemed more deeply frozen in that disturbing pose. Her mind buzzed realizing that the last word her baby had uttered was "Ram."

Fury surged through her like bubbling lava. Where was his big hero? Yammering to the press about his prowess on the field? Of course.

He's now the most sought after quarterback in the world.

How could two little boys and a soccer mom compete with his mind-boggling celebrity? His mailbox was full and his assistant most probably was right there with him doing PR for next season.

Nikki tiptoed over to the bed and lay her head on Jack's pillow, so close that her lips touched his soft earlobe as she whispered, "Ram's not coming, Jack. It's okay to go. I love you always."

Jack's face relaxed. So peaceful. Nikki placed her hand on her baby's chest. So still. Jack left her. And as hot tears poured from her eyes all she wanted to do was scream with all her might, "Come back, darling! I didn't mean it."

****

It wasn't a dream. Ram woke up the next morning, and he was still the MVP of the Super Bowl. The message light on the hotel phone flashed repeatedly.

Scribbling down messages on a hotel pad, Ram wagged his head in disbelief. The man of the hour, he was in demand—ESPN, all the morning shows.

Brad would have his hands full handling the schedule. And he'd be in his glory. He and Brad had dreamed of this for so long, and the reality surpassed their wildest imaginings.

As thrilling as the career pinnacle was, Ram just wanted to soak his stiff, bruised body and fly home to Nikki's doorstep. He picked up his cell phone and then tossed it back down on the night table, frustrated that he hadn't charged it the night before in his exhausted state. Entering Nikki's number on the hotel phone, he settled back against the pillow eagerly anticipating the conversation.

Her voicemail recording sounded and he left the message, "Nikki, it's Ram. I had phone trouble last night and couldn't call. I hope you enjoyed the game. Give the guys my love. I'll call again later. Or you can call me in an hour or so on my cell. I'm going to charge it up now. It went dead last night. I miss you."

Why didn't she answer? His mind spun searching for an explanation. *They must be sleeping in after the late night watching the game.*

He jumped out of bed and made good on his promise by connecting the charger to the cell phone and plugging it into the wall socket.

Padding through the suite, he tapped on Brad's door before opening it. "Wake-up call, buddy," Ram boomed as he entered the dim room.

Brad dragged a pillow over his head and moaned.

Ram drew open the curtains, and brilliant sunshine illuminated the lump on the bed. "C'mon. We have a plane to catch."

"You go ahead. Leave me behind here to die." He rolled over and squinted in Ram's general direction. "I never should have gone out last night."

"You're getting old." He chuckled at Brad's

miserable expression. "Don't make me throw you in the shower. You've got fifteen, or I'll be back to haul you out of there."

Refreshed after a bracing shower and dressed in ten minutes, Ram zipped up a leather suitcase he had bought in the hotel gift shop to contain all the swag he had for Rocky and Jack. He couldn't wait to see their faces when he gave them the stuff; he couldn't wait to see their faces, period.

He unplugged the cell phone and hit the home button. The screen was still inexplicably black. Stuffing the useless thing in his pocket, he opened the door and stepped into the living room of the suite, fourteen minutes after waking Brad.

Brad's bedroom door opened, and he dragged his suitcase through the doorway batting it against the frame. He had slicked back his wet hair and donned light-filtering Ray Bans.

"The bigger the hangover, the better the party," Ram teased.

"I should have listened to you and stayed in. One drink turned into…who the hell knows how many?" His smile inverted to a grimace.

Ram held open the door for him to pass in front of him.

Following him into the hall, Ram mentioned, "I have a slew of messages off the hotel room line for you to sort through. My damn cell phone didn't charge for some reason. Can I borrow yours on the plane before takeoff?"

"Anything as long as you whisper."

A car waited in front of the hotel. Ram ducked inside.

The limo whisked him and Brad to a tiny airport where they boarded a private jet.

"Wow, this is sweet. How'd you swing a private jet for two?" Ram asked as he fastened his seat belt.

"You're the freaking MVP of the Super Bowl. Get used to it. This is your life from now on."

The instant Ram's belt clicked the plane started to taxi as if the pilot awaited the quarterback's every move. A tall, stacked blonde served coffee and Danish. Completely awed, Ram sipped the strong brew and admired the view of the stewardess retreating toward the galley.

Jarred back to his senses as the jet engine accelerated for takeoff and the pressing need to speak with Nikki reasserted, he asked Brad for his phone.

"You can't use it when we're in the air."

"Right. Now I'll have to wait until we land. Have you called Luci?"

"Yeah, I talked with her a few minutes last night, and she nearly screamed my ear off, she was so excited. It must have been one hell of a party wherever she was. I could hear Al cheering in the background. Good thing you didn't beat the Packers…"

Ram huffed a laugh. "Yeah, right."

Brad and Ram relaxed and dozed for the rest of the trip. As soon as the plane landed, Ram turned on Brad's phone. The voicemail message notice appeared.

"Better listen to your messages." He handed the phone back to Brad, and tapped his foot impatiently as Brad held the phone to his ear.

Whether he could reach her beforehand or not, Ram intended to go straight to Nikki's house from the airport.

"Oh no," Brad said.

"What?"

"A message from Luci. You have to go to the hospital right away. Something's happened to Jack. Everyone has been trying to reach you."

Ram's heart galloped as he bounded down the jet's stairway.

Brad tossed Ram his car keys. "I'm parked in the lot to the east. Row E, close to the signpost. I'll take care of the luggage and meet you at the hospital. Just promise me you won't drive like a maniac."

"Promise." He sprinted to the parking lot and jammed himself into Brad's spotless Lexus convertible.

Forced to keep his speed down negotiating the icy roads, Ram longed for his truck's Herculean traction.

He left Brad's car at the curb outside the hospital, intending to reimburse his friend the cost of a parking ticket, and charged through the glass doors.

Stopping at the information desk he fired off, "May I please have Jack Lambert's room number?"

"One second." A middle-aged dumpy woman held her finger in the air as she scanned a magazine in front of her.

"Look, this is really important..." Ram modulated his voice to control his mounting frustration.

"I said, one minute." Again, her finger raised—the only indication the woman actually heard him.

"*Now*," he demanded.

Her lips tightened. Without meeting his eyes her raised finger lowered and hovered over a typed list. "Room 700, east wing. Elevators on the left."

"Thanks." Ram raced to the elevator and jutted his hand in between the closing doors.

"Sorry," he apologized to the group of nurses inside as he squeezed into the crowded car.

"That's okay, Sugar. There's room for you closer to me." A brown-skinned woman with curves in all the right places shifted and sandwiched Ram against her left flank and the elevator wall.

"Oh my God, it's *you*." Her eyes widened and heads turned toward him. "It is you, isn't it?"

"Well yes; I'm me," Ram said with a grin.

"My husband will have a heart attack when he finds out I rode the elevator at work with Ram Delaney."

"Good thing his wife's a nurse," he quipped.

She ruffled through the oversized satchel on her shoulder, no easy feat in the close quarters. Ram took an elbow to his aching rib cage.

"Would you mind signing an autograph for me? He won't believe this without proof."

Chuckling he agreed and jotted what she dictated on her pay stub, "Hi Damian. Best, Ram Delaney."

As soon as the doors slid open on the seventh floor, Ram hopped out of the car and stalked toward the nurses' desk through a corridor lined with primary colored walls and paintings of smiling cartoon animals. A little girl passed him trailing an IV pole while she chattered non-stop to a nurse who kept pace with her.

"May I help you?" Recognition glimmered in the desk nurse's eyes. "Oh my. Football players visit our kids often, but you? The day after the Super Bowl win? Wow, this is a first. Congratulations. We watched every second of the game. You were wonderful. I'm sorry…"

She wagged her head. "Listen to me go on and on, and you a busy man. Are you here to visit one of the children?"

"Yes. Jack Lambert. They told me downstairs that he's in room 700. I'm just going to pop in and surprise him." Already on the move past the desk, Ram interpreted her silence as consent.

"Mr. Delaney, wait." She caught up with him as he reached the door to Jack's room.

Ram peered inside. The curtains were drawn and the bed was empty.

Confused he gazed at her. "I must have the wrong information. Is Jack Lambert here in your wing?"

"I'm very sorry. I...I don't know how to tell you this," she stuttered. "Jack Lambert passed away."

His body stiffened, and his heart pounded in his ears. "No. That can't be..." He grabbed the door jam.

"There's no mistake. My deepest condolences. The family left about a half hour ago."

Rubber-legged, Ram stumbled into the pristine room and sat heavily on the chair next to the bed.

Stupid with shock Ram struggled to finish a complete sentence. "Can I sit here for a moment?"

"Take as much time as you need." Her rubber-soled shoes squeaked as she backed away and closed the door.

The last time Ram had cried his heart out was in childhood after he had learned that his best friend in the world had died—Bella, a yellow Labrador with soft, chocolate eyes. Around the same age as Jack then, he had left that morning for school with his customary view of Bella wagging her tail at the front door as the bus pulled away from the curb. When he had returned home that day, Pop had given him the devastating news. Ram had cried so hard all afternoon and evening that his parents had considered taking him to the doctor.

What had bothered him most was that he hadn't been there with Bella to say good-bye.

Ram doubled over at the waist and sobbed into his hands. *Why? Jack is the sweetest, little boy...an innocent. Oh, God. Jack was...*

His anguish swelled into throat-clogging fury.

Where was I? Twelve hundred miles away playing a game. Playing.

Enraged, he launched out of the chair. Ram kicked the bed with spine-jarring ferocity and then sent the tray cart careening across the room. It crashed against the wall. His chest heaving he looked around for something else to tackle and then upended the cart. The nurse's head poked inside the room a moment, and then disappeared in a flash.

Probably running to call security.

Helpless, he sank back into the chair next to the bed. "I'm so sorry, Jack. I'm so sorry I wasn't here with you." He hung his head.

A splotch of black under the corner of the pillow caught his eye and he moved the pillow aside. Crying harder, Ram's tears dotted the cover of Jack's "always-with-him" notebook that he found there. He opened the composition book and read the inside cover.

Jack had printed in block letters, "FILL THE STADIUM FOR ALD."

Skimming the pages, Ram marveled at the contents. Jack had drawn out his plan to raise money to fund research for the disease that could take...he caught his breath...the disease that did take his life. And according to Jack's narrative, Ram played a starring role. Jack had placed five red star stickers next to

Ram's name on the list of the Highland University Train's names. Next to each team member's name, Jack had stipulated the positions he had assigned each man to play in an off-season, benefit flag football game pitted against the Massachusetts Dragons.

At least thirty pages of notes described promotional flyers, the address of a website about forming charitable organizations, plays for the game, a silent auction dinner the evening after the game, the capacity of Highland U's stadium multiplied by his suggested ticket price: $5.00 each.

The message on the last page robbed Ram's breath. "I'll watch the game from heaven every year, Ram. Thank you for being my friend and helping me to change the world."

Reverently clasping the notebook, Ram rose off the floor, straightened the furniture and went out into the hall. He stopped by the nurses' station, handed the doe-eyed nurse behind the desk his business card and said, "Please send me the bill to fix the wall."

On his way out of the hospital, bone crushing grief and devastation crested at the thought of facing Nikki. She had to suffer Jack's loss without him to hold her, console her. Not that he had any idea how he might have offered her any consolation even if he had been there when Jack died.

Maybe Jack's plan might offer her some relief since Jack had made it clear that he didn't want other little boys to suffer his fate. The MVP, the endorsements, the trappings of victory on the football field seemed utterly insignificant as he bounded through the hospital corridors. The only thing that carried any importance was seeing Nikki.

Chapter 25

For Nikki only scattered memories remained of the events immediately following Jack's death. Someone, probably Mickey, lifted her off the hospital bed while ambient sounds: Jodi's voice, Rocky's hysteria, Kay's high-pitched sobs, sporadic electronic bleeps of hospital equipment buzzed in her ears. Keening she writhed in the grip of the fireman's carry that separated her from Jack.

A prick on her upper arm and a burning sensation preceded her descent into a black void. The rest of her memories for an indeterminate time period formed a kaleidoscope of images as if shutters in her mind opened and snapped shut after varying sessions of consciousness.

She didn't permit active thought until her mother's soft, sugarcoated tones pierced her insensate, voluntary coma on the bed. "Darling, we have to do something about funeral arrangements."

Why hadn't Nikki possessed the foresight to handle that onerous task before then? Did Jodi's prognosis six months before leave any room to doubt that a funeral was in Jack's near term future? No. But obviously she had harbored hope that Jodi would conjure a miracle, that Jack would whack ALD like Rocky had firmly believed or that she would love him fiercely enough to turn back the genetic tide she had supplied Jack at conception.

Hope is dead. "Momma..."

Nikki struggled toward awareness as if nearly drowned and swimming a breaststroke up toward the water's distant surface. It would have been so wonderful to stay on the bottom of that sea of grief and just let the ocean fill her lungs.

"Okay," Nikki agreed, thick-tongued. Unfolding from her fetal position on the bed, she promised, "I'll get dressed."

Nikki approached the task of orchestrating Jack's burial arrangements as if portraying a role. On the surface she acted composed, attentive to details, careful concerning choices fitting a celebration of Jack's life, and deliberate about honoring her son's wishes with limited true knowledge of how he'd shape such a ceremony. While inside she remained a flailing, screaming mess.

On her feet at the head of Jack's open casket for the entire duration of the day of funeral home visitation, she dutifully accepted the hugs of sobbing individuals.

She responded to the endless stream of, "Sorry, I'm so sorry, sorry, sorry, sorry..." with her own stoic litany, "Thank you for coming, thank you for coming, thank you for coming..."

Fleeing to hide in the ladies' room when she spied Ram's imposing figure lining up outside the funeral parlor room, she tagged her mother and requested her assistance. "I don't want to see him, Momma. Let me know when he leaves."

"He came to the house the day..." Her mother bent her head and heaved a sigh. "The day before yesterday. He was crazed with grief and begged to see you. He's been calling around the clock since."

"I don't care," Nikki said. "Please."

"All right." She trained weary, blood-shot eyes on Nikki. "I don't know how to convince him, but I'll try."

Nikki never asked her mom what had transpired between her and Ram during the ten minutes or so that Nikki had remained in the bathroom seated on a red velvet, tufted settee in the foul smelling air. Nikki hardly had the capacity to deal with the heartbreak of losing Jack. She couldn't think about how Ram had broken her heart when he broke Jack's.

When Momma gave her the all clear, Nikki assumed her position by her baby until the funeral director essentially made her go home. The only thing that convinced Nikki to leave that place was the knowledge that she'd see Jack again the following morning before the funeral Mass.

Her final glimpse of her precious son was inscribed in her memory as if his peaceful, sleeping, angelic face burned its contours in her brain. She didn't want to forget that image any more than she wanted them to close that small, white casket.

The funeral service viewed through a veil of tears, and mostly recalled later as nostril-pinching incense odor and choral crying emanating from behind Nikki's seat in the front pew, seemed over in a minute. Rocky maintained a death grip on her hand throughout what Nikki was told was the most beautiful funeral mass in memory, while he incessantly stared at Jack's casket.

Up down, in out, since Nikki had awakened that morning she had shuffled from house to car to one place and then another. The progress of ceremonial movements that divided the inevitable last goodbye into stages anesthetized her from the looming, final knife lash.

Jack didn't share his father's resting place in the cemetery. Nikki couldn't bear the thought of actually burying her little boy in the ground.

That's not logical, I know. Ashes to ashes, dust to dust.

But opting for an above-ground crypt in a cathedral-like mausoleum with stained glass walls provided some comfort. She didn't examine whether or not she symbolically withheld Jack from his father in eternal rest. Probably some lingering bitterness might have influenced her since John hadn't stuck around to comfort Jack during his illness and by default didn't deserve to enjoy Jack's companionship in resting.

Whatever the basis of her reasoning, the weather affirmed Nikki's choice of burial site when the funeral procession reached the cemetery. What had begun as a soft, early morning snowfall had whipped into a full-blown blizzard. The hearse crawled so slowly through the whiteout that John's buddy's limo, carrying Nikki, Rocky, Momma, Kay, and Mickey, seemed parked in a snow globe. The hearse's taillights glowed like reddish pinpricks of light ahead of the family's car.

The nightmarish nature of that day heightened with each passing moment: the protective, useless umbrellas that didn't succeed in shielding Nikki from the icy, swirling storm; the claustrophobic crush of bodies clustered around her seat at the foot of Jack's casket; the doleful, "May the perpetual light shine upon him…" from the mourners' mouths; the shuffling, endless procession of people laying roses on the lacquered white surface of the casket; the awful pending goodbye she'd have to face as the crowd dwindled down...

Nikki remained glued to the rickety seat, a lump with soaking wet hair, wet faced, teeth chattering, Rocky's hand an ice cube in her clasp—nothing but a tear machine.

"Don't cry, Mommy," Rocky implored, his chest heaving with sobs. "Jack doesn't want us to cry, Mommy."

"I know, sweetie," she whispered as she continued to manufacture tears.

Abruptly Rocky broke his hand free and flew out of his seat. Nikki's gaze followed his catapult into Ram's outstretched arms. She stiffened witnessing Ram's outpouring of sympathy and feigned affection. He hoisted Rocky off the ground and held him against his massive shoulder like an infant tenderly cradled in sheltering arms. Rocky's muffled crying and the tears streaming from beneath closed eyelids that rained down Ram's chiseled face affected Nikki's raw nerves like a hot poker to her heart.

She wanted to rip Rocky out of his "hero's" grasp and protect him from the inevitable disappointment that loving Ram Delaney involved. The helium balloon, destined for Jack, tethered to Rocky's right hand clinched Nikki's resolve to end the display.

When Ram's eyes opened and bored into her, Nikki mouthed, "Put him down."

His gaze at her unwavering, Ram bent his knees, gracefully lowered Rocky downward and set him on his feet with his back toward his mother. Crouching at Rocky's eye level he said, "I'll be here for you, Rock. I loved Jack, too. And I love you."

"I love you, too, Ram," Rocky sputtered, his husky

voice saturated with tears.

Insulted to the core Nikki launched out of her seat and advanced toward Ram. "Rocky, please go over there by Poppy. I'd like to speak with Ram for a second."

She strode over to the far corner of the mausoleum, satisfied that Ram followed her as his heavy footfalls sounded from behind. Containing her fury to a church whisper she spat out, "I want you to pay your final respects now and leave, please."

His blue eyes darkened. "Nikki, please...don't be this way. I tried..."

"Whatever you *think* you tried to do wasn't enough. I'll never forgive you if you force me to make a scene at my son's funeral."

He enveloped her in an embrace before she saw it coming. Locked in the vice of his unyielding muscles, pinned against his stone-hard chest, Nikki derived no comfort from those arms that had enticed her before. Surely he sensed her wooden lack of response because his arms dropped and released her.

"I didn't know that Jack was hospitalized until I landed late morning on Monday. Nikki, I would have left the game..."

"No, you wouldn't have," she interjected. "It doesn't matter now."

Snagging Nikki's arm before she could move beyond his reach, he anchored her to the spot. "I found Jack's notebook. It's amazing..."

"You can mail it to me," she tossed out as she jerked her arm free.

Keeping pace with Nikki's determined stride back toward Jack's casket, he said, "Jack set out a plan to change the world." He chuckled. He *actually* chuckled at Jack's *funeral*.

Nikki spun on him, forcing herself to keep her voice down. "It's too late. You're too late. Jack wanted to tell you something before he died. He *asked* for you."

Her heart split open at the memory. She could hardly make her mouth form the words, "Jack's *gone*. And I want you to go *now*."

His defeat blazed from the stricken expression on his face. "If that's the way you want it…"

Turning her back on him, Nikki returned to her seat and stared straight ahead as Ram placed his hand on Jack's casket, bowed his head, closed his eyes and then lumbered away, fresh tears lining his cheeks. Her mother and her in-laws visited the casket in turn, wracked with sobs, and then Rocky and Nikki were left alone with Jack.

The stillness in the chapel calmed Nikki. Soft pastel blotches reflected off the shiny surface of the little white casket strewn with red roses—a pretty greenhouse insulated from the snowstorm and all those people outside. She sat linked to Rocky's hand.

Just the three of us.

"Do you think Jack can see us now, Mommy?" Rocky's question echoed in the cavernous space.

"I don't know, sweetie. I think so."

"Then he sees how sad we are," he deduced.

Tears streaming she said, "Yes. I guess so."

His eyes widened as he faced her. "That would make him sad, too."

She nodded, suffocating on sorrow.

"I want to give him his balloon now." Standing, the helium balloon wobbled upward with him.

"Okay," she said rising from her seat. "Let it go."

Nikki steeled herself for the coming parting.

Rocky's face contorted. Frowning he asserted, "No. The roof will stop it and it won't get to heaven."

Dismayed, Nikki stressed, "But the storm is really bad."

"I *have* to go outside," he demanded.

Appreciating Rocky's brand of logic, she stepped forward and rested her hand on the casket. *Goodbye Jack. I have loved you every second of your life and I will love you forever.*

Staggering to the doorway she ushered Rocky outside—or he ushered her. The storm slapped snow in her face and seized Rocky's red, heart shaped balloon the second he cleared the threshold.

"I love you, Jack," he shouted.

Car doors opened and the funeral director rushed forward to help them into the car. Ice crunching beneath the tires, the limo rolled away from Jack's burial site. Nikki stared ahead through the windshield. Jack wasn't in that building.

"Wow, did you see that, Poppy?"

"What, Rocky?"

"The balloon went *straight* to heaven."

"You bet." Mickey slipped his arm around Rocky's shoulder. "Just like Jack."

"Yeah." Rocky leaned against his grandfather.

There was a restaurant luncheon, sparsely attended and cut short due to the storm. She didn't see the point of the whole thing anyway and was vastly relieved when they returned home. As she floated trancelike into her hallway, an inner switch flipped and she dropped into the abyss that Jack's absence opened in her life.

Time lost meaning—everything did. Her bedroom became a refuge where she could achieve unconsciousness and relive Jack's life in dreams. She resented the wheedling voices that expected more from her than curling up on the bed and blotting out daily life. But she learned that if she cooperated, then she could return to her bedroom haven to sleep.

"Nikki, you need to eat something."

And she'd fork down food that had no taste.

"How about a shower, and I'll change the bed for you?"

And she'd dutifully strip out of sweats, douse herself under the shower spray, don clean sweats and then crawl back in bed beneath fresh sheets. Her pillows mildewed from wet hair and constant crying.

Still the voices came, "We're taking Rocky to the movies? Do you want to come?"

"Do I have to?"

"Well…No. Not if you don't want to."

"Good. Nice of you…Have fun."

Cocooned in the darkness she cradled a newborn Jack in her arms, reveling in the impossible softness of his cap of silky black hair and smiling into his astonishing blue eyes. The garbage truck clanged beneath her window, the TV blared, cooking smells permeated the air, and the vacuum cleaner whirred nearby. She'd draw her knees closer to her chest and ride a roller coaster with Jack or push him on a baby swing.

"Mommy, get up!"

"What is it, Jack?" She rolled toward the sound of his voice and snapped her eyes open to gape into Rocky's saucer eyes.

"I'm *Rocky*!" he bellowed.

"Um…" Nikki swung her legs over the side of the bed and sat up, her head swimming. "I'm sorry, sweetie. I know…"

Squinting at Rocky's belligerent expression, she struggled toward awareness. She felt ill to the core as if she had guzzled ten bottles of champagne the night before.

Rocky tugged on her sweatshirt sleeve. "Get *up*," he insisted. "I'm gonna be late for school."

She couldn't force her brain to function. "Um…Can't Poppy take you?"

Tears welled in his eyes. With another tug on her shirt he whined, "He's not here. *You* have to take me."

He hauled backward and leveraged Nikki to her feet.

Dragged into shuffling motion as he towed her behind him, Nikki gazed at the back of his head. As she finished thumping down the stairs she swiveled her head around dumbly taking in her spotless, empty home. "Where is everybody?"

Rocky spun around, crocodile tears pouring down his face. "They had to leave."

"Nana, too?"

"They *told* you. Mommy. Last night…You're *scaring* me."

His shoulders heaved with his sobbing and he sank to her knees clasping him to her chest. She couldn't remember the conversation she supposedly had with her in-laws or her mom.

"It's okay, sweetie." Nikki hugged him tightly and brushed her hand down his back, over his spiky hair, and along the side of his arm. "I'll take you."

Disoriented she scrambled to find her purse and car keys. Rocky opened the fridge and extracted a brown lunch bag neatly folded on top and then slammed the door shut. She traipsed behind him to the front door, plodded outside, and refrained from voicing her astonishment that there was barely any snow on the ground.

Behind the wheel of the car Nikki's disorientation mounted. Like a student driver, she backed out of the driveway by inches. Rocky sulked in the passenger seat. She had driven this route enough in the past for the engrained routine to empower her.

I can do this.

Negotiating the circle to the drop off spot at Rocky's school, she braked and leaned over for the customary kiss. Rocky's little boy smell filled her senses. Regret pierced her that in withdrawing from waking life so that she could be with Jack in her memories, she had neglected to miss Rocky.

"Have a good day," Nikki said, jittery with guilt and confusion.

What do I do now?

"Do you want me to pick you up after school?"

One hand on the door handle he said, "Nah, that's okay. Miss Luci picks me up and takes me to the Good Sports Club every day."

"She does?"

"Uh huh," he said shoving open the door and hopping out of the car. And then he leaned inside, one arm flung over the doorframe. "Miss Elizabeth says it's okay if you're a little late to work today. See you at dinner, Mommy."

Off center, Nikki blurted out, "Rocky wait."

He raised his eyebrows and gazed at her.

"Why are you calling me Mommy?"

His eyes bore into her, and his lips met in a line—such a grave expression on her little boy's face. "Jack called you that. I thought you'd like it."

"Oh." She paused gathering her wits, her heart aching. "I like what you call me, Rocky. I don't want you to change one thing."

His grin broke her heart a little more. "Okay, Ma. See you later."

The car door slammed with a jarring quake. Shifting into drive, she steered out into the street. Shaky, she returned home, showered, dressed and went back to work at the university.

****

A month later Nikki ferreted out the whole truth after multiple rounds of questioning Rocky. Kay, Mickey and Mom hadn't left town prior to that morning. Rather they had stayed in hotel suites, financed by Ram Delaney. In constant touch with Rocky, Ram, Luci, and her boss, Elizabeth, Nikki's family hunkered down out of sight the rest of that week before they actually returned home to the lives they had put on hold for her for more than a month. The intervention, if she could call it that, forced her to live again.

The adults had refined the plan, but the basic course of action was Rocky's idea. Her amazing Rocky saved her life.

Chapter 26

Spring

The milder temperatures heralded spring. Buds appeared on the trees. Piles of snow melted into muddy puddles. The sun shone brighter and longer in the sky. People emerged from winter hibernation to jog the pathways, ride bikes, or wash filmy windows. Cheerful. Invigorated in the season.

And Ram was miserable.

He had completed all the obligations befitting a Super Bowl "hero" without enjoying a single thing—the television appearances, photo shoots, and interviews. The trip to Disney World and the ride in the ticker tape parade of heroes had been the hardest event to tolerate. He had wanted to share the trip with Nikki and Rocky, but Nikki wanted no part of his life.

She had closed herself off from the world—at least the small part of the world Ram occupied. His telephone calls went unanswered. He stopped knocking on her door. After Jack's funeral Ram knew that Nikki's mother felt sorry for him, but Mama Bear guarded her baby and no matter how heartfelt his pleas, she had repeatedly turned him away.

Rocky remained the one bright spot in Ram's existence. He looked forward to those days when Rocky would show up at the after-school program so

Ram could pepper him with questions about his mother. The sadness in his eyes broke Ram's heart. Rocky was worried about her. The boy had lost his dad and his brother, and Ram suspected that he feared he'd lose his mom, too. Ram spent every waking minute trying to figure out a way to help, but came up empty.

Post season he had worked at the Good Sports Club seven days a week, secluded in his office, until weariness overcame him.

In late-March his lackluster routine persisted. Waiting until everyone vacated the building at the end of the day, Ram left the office and traveled the dark hallways listlessly bound for home.

The drive progressed in a blur. In his funk no anticipation set in as he motored down his street. Simply pulling into his driveway used to fill him with a sense of accomplishment. Ram's home was a showplace that had merited a spread in *Architectural Digest* three times. For him, the house had represented the pay-off for all the hard work. The view of the Charles River from the back of the house had infused him with peace at every homecoming. He had passed countless, pleasant hours lazing on the balcony off his bedroom, sometimes with a date, sipping wine, while the beautiful, flowing river had filled his senses. Nikki had never even walked through his front door.

He inched his truck between the two cars parked in the driveway and pulled into the four-car garage. Switching the engine off, Ram lingered behind the wheel a few minutes, unwilling to socialize. The guys meant well, but he wished that they would leave him alone. All Ram's buddies had keys to the house. In the past he had wanted them to feel free to use the gym, sauna or pool. In the past he had wanted a lot of things…

Lacking an alternative, Ram went inside and plodded downstairs to the bottom level of the house. Grunts, clangs and locker room smell surrounded him as he cleared the stairs. After his injury Ram had converted that entire lower level of the house to a workout room equipped with all the bells and whistles of the Dragons' high-tech facility. As he had rehabilitated the arm, Ram had avoided gapers by working out in private, secretly dealing with his fear of failure in the public eye.

"Hey, Ram." A barbell hovered over Caboose's head in his prone position on the bench. "How's it hanging?"

"Usual." Ram unbuttoned his shirt and headed to the lockers next to the sauna. Changing into a pair of Highland shorts and a thin gray T-shirt, he returned to the gym.

Tracks tossed Ram a bottle of cold water. "Thanks for putting in a good word for me with Highland. They called today. I got the job," he said grinning from ear to ear.

"No shit." Ram slapped him on the back. "Congratulations, Coach Larkin. You'll be great."

"I wouldn't have gotten the position if you hadn't supported me."

"Wrong. You've worked hard. You deserve the job. The Highlanders are lucky to have you as their head coach. I didn't have anything to do with it."

Ram mounted the exercise bike, adjusted the tension and started his daily workout, ready for the mind blanking respite.

Tracks powered up the treadmill next to Ram's bike. "Judy wants you to come for dinner Saturday night, and she said to tell you that she won't take no for an answer this time."

Believing that he was terrible company, Ram had turned down all his pals' social invites. He thought they had gotten the hint when they quit asking.

"We'll see," Ram said softening the brush off.

"She's bringing out the big guns." He laughed.

"Not the pineapple upside down cake?" Ram's stomach growled at the thought of the melted butter and brown sugar treat.

"Yep."

"What time do you want me?"

"Six."

"I'll be there." Hopefully he would come up with an excuse by the end of the week. Even Judy's tempting dessert held no appeal.

Securing headphones over his ears, music blared. Ram pumped the pedals until his legs screamed for relief, then lifted weights and finished the hour-long workout on the treadmill. Caboose and Tracks left for home, and Ram trudged upstairs to shower. Clad in loose sweatpants and a Dragons hooded sweatshirt, he opened the fridge hoping he had remembered to ask his housekeeper to replenish it.

Nope. Nothing new. Just the six pack of imported beer and a container of left over Chinese food.

When did I have Chinese?

He sniffed the container and immediately threw it in the garbage.

In the dark, Ram walked to the living room, grabbed the remote and slumped on the couch. Sinking into the buttery leather, tension released for the first time that day. Channel surfing he settled on the Flyers/Bruins game. Cell phone in hand, he checked voice mail. No message from Nikki.

When will I stop hoping that she'll call?

Everyone had urged Ram to get on with his life. Pop had raised his voice on the phone the night before—something he hadn't done since Ram was a teenager. The frustration in his voice had come through loud and clear as he pleaded with him to snap out of it.

Agreeing with him seemed the least Ram could do out of respect, but he lacked the means to change his behavior.

Right, Pop, Jack wasn't my son. Right again, Nikki and Rocky aren't my family.

But Ram mourned Jack as if he were his father. And Ram's home was empty without Nikki and Rocky, even though they had never visited there. He couldn't explain his feelings to himself, no less to his parents. No matter how unprecedented, he had fallen in love more completely than he had thought possible.

Ram rubbed his face and his stomach growled so insistently that he rolled off the couch and stalked to the kitchen. Grabbing a handful of take-out menus out of a drawer, he tossed them on the granite counter.

The drone of the TV ceased suddenly.

Damn it. What now?

He stomped toward the blank monitor, picked up the remote and jabbed buttons while he aimed the device toward the receiver. The screen lit displaying the hockey game action. Ram turned around and almost fell over the coffee table.

Apparently delusional, Ram rubbed his eyes and

blinked a couple times. But the apparition didn't disappear. Jack Lambert perched on the edge of the recliner. His face glowed blue in the TV's reflected light. Ram scrambled to the wall switch and turned on the lights. Natural color replaced blue on the spectral face.

He gave Ram an impish smile. "You let me down, Ram," he said in his direct style, as if simply continuing a conversation.

Struck dumb, Ram's flagging senses worked overtime.

Did I fall asleep on the couch?

"Jack?" he uttered taking a seat on the couch where he decidedly had not fallen asleep. His eyes glued to the boy, he ventured, "Are you really here?"

He giggled and then replied, "Yes."

"You look…healthy."

"I am. I don't have ALD anymore." He held his hands out, steady as a rock. And then, he folded them in his lap gazing at Ram expectantly.

"I'm sorry I let you down, Jack. I never got your mom's phone call. I didn't know you were in the hospital."

Positive that he was dreaming, Ram still welcomed the chance to voice the apology. "I would give anything to have that day back. I would have been there for you. I would have left the game."

"Oh, Ram, it's okay that you didn't come. You won the Super Bowl! I wanted that so much. I'm disappointed in you for a different reason."

Mute, Ram's guilty conscience pinched and his battered spirits sank lower. Even in dreams, he wasn't forgiven.

Jack tapped his foot impatiently. Apparently, he expected Ram to say something. Ram helplessly continued to disappoint him.

"I left my notebook for you," he said.

"You left it for me?"

"I hid it under my pillow so you could find it."

"I have it. It's upstairs in my bedroom."

"I know where it is." Wagging his head, he gave Ram a closed-mouth, rueful smile. "Why did you put it away in your drawer and forget about it?"

"I meant to give it to your mom. It's been…"

"I didn't leave it for Mommy. I left it for you." He folded his arms and gazed at Ram intently.

"I don't understand. Wouldn't you rather give it to your mom…or Rocky? Why me?"

"Because you can help me change the world. Please Ram. Only you can make it happen. You can raise money and cure ALD."

Jack's eyes filled with tears. "It's an awful disease, Ram. It hurts so much. I don't want any other boy to suffer like I did."

Chills ran through Ram. "I'm so sorry you suffered, Jack."

He longed to hug Jack, but he feared that if he moved, he'd wake up and Jack would leave for good.

"I'm fine now." An angelic smile bloomed on his face. "No pain anymore."

"Have you visited your mom?"

"No. I'm just allowed to visit you this one time."

"Allowed?"

"Uh huh."

"I…" Questions flew through Ram's brain. He sat there gaping at the sweet face that he missed so dearly, and he prayed that he wouldn't wake up for a long time. "Can you please answer some questions?"

He shook his head. "I came to plead with you to read my notebook and make the benefit happen. Please, Ram. Fill the Stadium for Rocky."

"Rocky? What do you mean?"

No response. It seemed the notebook held the key. "Let me go get your book, and we can read it together."

Dashing out of the living room, Ram bounded up the winding staircase to the top floor. Opening the drawer of the bedside table, his hands shaking, he took out the notebook and raced back down to the living room.

The chair was empty.

"Jack!" Ram shouted. "Jack!"

He sprinted from room to room calling Jack's name. He was gone. His head throbbed.

"No," he whispered. "Please come back, Jack."

Devastated Ram plopped down on the couch, incredulous and shaken. The conversation seemed so real. How could he have imagined it? Wide-awake, he knew he hadn't dreamed Jack's unbelievable visit.

Ram opened the notebook for the first time since he had found it in the hospital. *"Fill the Stadium for Rocky"* in bold, red ink labeled the inside cover, written in Jack's precise block printing. His mouth hung open. Certain the original lettering read, *"For ALD,"* Jack's supernatural visit and impassioned request sank in.

Spurred into action, Ram hurried into the kitchen and grabbed a pad of paper and a pen. Seated at the butcher-block table, he pored over each page, jotting down notes on the pad. For the first time in weeks, life held purpose. As if reborn, his body tingled with energy. He remained working in the kitchen until he nodded off a couple times and finally decided to go to bed, dazed with amazement.

Falling into a deep dreamless sleep, Ram awoke a few hours later and jumped into the shower. Ideas whirled in his mind. With a towel wrapped around his waist, Ram stood at the kitchen table again scribbling on the notepad names and thoughts that had come to him in the shower. When he finished, he had filled five pages.

Ram punched Brad's number on his cell phone and connected to voice mail. "Brad. I need you at my office as soon as you get this message."

After signing a few autographs at the bakery where Ram stopped to buy a box of doughnuts and a thermos of coffee, he drove the truck toward the GSC. Switching on the radio, he sang along with Kenny Chesney while he drummed on the steering wheel.

Life is good. The grass is green. The good Lord is smiling on you and me.

The day before he had dragged into the office. Today he couldn't wait to get to his desk.

His truck roared into the parking lot, and he parked next to Luci's car. The Green Bay Packers decal in the window made him smile. Juggling the doughnuts, coffee, and a briefcase, he nudged open his office door with his elbow.

Luci's head snapped up when Ram entered. "Good morning, Boss. You're here early today. What's up?" She rustled the desk calendar pages. "Did I miss an appointment?"

"No. You didn't miss a thing." He set the doughnuts and coffee down on the credenza next to her desk. "I left a message for Brad to come in this morning. He should be here shortly. When he gets here can you come into the office?"

"Ah…sure." Clearly baffled judging from her furrowed brow, she gaped at him.

"I'm sorry I have been such a bear lately." He leaned over the desk and kissed her cheek. "I promise to be better from now on."

He smiled and advanced toward the inner door to his office.

"Oh, thank God. You finally heard from Nikki," she said.

Before Ram closed his door, he faced her and said, "No, I didn't hear from Nikki. Next best thing. I heard from Jack."

Chapter 27

Luci and Brad approached Ram's desk in halting steps after conferring briefly in the outer office.

Luci thinks I've cracked up. I can't blame her.

He would have jumped to the same conclusion if she had claimed that she had heard from a dead child.

Ram grinned at her. She widened her eyes and cast a see-what-I-mean glance at Brad.

"Hey, Brad," he greeted his agent cheerfully. "Thanks for coming on short notice."

"No problem," he said without meeting Ram's eyes. "So...I'm here to discuss...what exactly?"

Picking up Jack's notebook, Ram waved it back and forth a couple times. "Jack Lambert gave this to me."

Smiling he placed the notebook back down on his desk and rested a hand on top of the cardboard cover. "He devised a plan to organize benefit events to raise funds for ALD research. Nothing is more important to me than carrying through on Jack's plan."

"O...kay." Brad gazed at him with penetrating intensity. Worry lines creased Brad's forehead and he snagged the corner of his lips with his teeth. "Ram, I'm worried about you."

Luci rushed to add, "Me, too. You've been under so much stress lately. Maybe you should see somebody?"

That sealed his suspicion that they thought he was a crackpot. Ram threw back his head and laughed. Luci looked like she was about to cry, so Ram hastened to explain, "I haven't lost my mind, guys. Really. I'm fine. Honestly, I haven't been this motivated since Jack died."

Lifting the notebook off his desk again, he handed it to Luci. "Just skim through this. You'll see what I mean."

While she buried her nose in Jack's notebook Ram directed his appeal to Brad, "I really need your help. I've decided to hold the main event, a flag football game, the last Saturday in April. I also want to host a dinner with an auction motif. I thought a silent auction and a bid auction. We only have five weeks to put this together. Are you in?"

Luci raised her head from the book, her eyes sparkling. "Brad, this is pretty amazing."

She passed the notebook to Brad. "What do you want me to do first, Ram?"

Without hesitation Brad said, "If you're in, I'm in. But before we tackle this…Ram, um. What did you mean when you told Luci you heard from Jack?"

The memory of Jack's "visit" replayed so vividly in Ram's mind that he seemed present in the room that minute. He had no explanation for the experience— could scarcely believe it real. But it was real. Jack believed that Rocky's life hung in the balance on Ram's action or inaction to spur ALD research efforts. And he handed Ram the means to change the world for Rocky and other boys with the same genetic legacy. Ram wouldn't betray his trust. He couldn't. Whether Nikki talked to him again in his lifetime or not, Ram forever intended to honor her son's memory and safeguard her Rocky's life.

Choosing his words carefully Ram said, "Last night I took a closer look at that notebook."

He pointed to the composition book dangling in Brad's hand. "I felt strongly that Jack wanted me to do that. As if...I heard his voice directing me. I found the book under Jack's pillow in his hospital bed when I finally made it back from Florida. After reviewing the contents of Jack's notebook, I realized that he intended me to follow through for him. I really think we can make a difference here, Brad. I can't let it go. Whether you help me or not."

Brad's jaw stiffened, and he narrowed his eyes. "You have always been there for me. And I'd like to think I've done the same for you."

"You have."

"I'm not about to stop now." Brad opened the book and thumbed through the pages. "How do you want to go about this?"

Propping a hip on the corner of the desk Ram gestured to the side chairs and said, "Have a seat."

Brad eased into one of the chairs; the book spread open on his lap.

"Hold on," Luci said. "Let me grab my steno pad."

She darted out to her desk, retrieved her notebook and a pen, and then came back to sit next to Brad.

Directing his attention to Luci, Ram said, "First, I'd like you call our pal Harry DeSanto at the *Ledger* and ask him to put together a press release. We want national exposure as frequently as he'll agree to run it." He chuckled. "He owes me for the exclusive I gave him after the big win."

"Sure." She scribbled a notation. "What specifics should I feed him?"

"Let's put our heads together on that."

"Where do want this held?" she posed.

"Good question. Jack said Highland U Stadium. Why not? Turns out that Tracks just landed the head coach job. I'll give him a call."

"Check. You said the last Saturday in April, right?"

"Yes. Let's say kick-off at two PM. We can organize a tailgate lunch and raise money off concessions, too," Ram suggested. "Jack wants to pit my old Highland U Train against the Dragons. Hmmm. I think I'll quarterback for Highland and let Whitney lead the Dragons offense. It's the last time he'll start in any game that I play in."

Brad nodded his head grinning. "Good one."

"I want jerseys made. Take a look in the book, Brad. Jack sketched them out."

Referencing the drawings, Brad huffed a laugh. "What an awesome kid. '*First Annual Fill the Stadium for ALD*,' " he read. " '*Find a Cure and Change the World*.' "

"Yep. That says it," Ram commented. "Brad, do you want to call Beltzer on this, or should I?"

"I'll do it, but wouldn't it be less complicated if we went to the team members directly?"

"Possibly." Ram gave the idea some thought. "But maybe Beltzer would like a shot at coaching his side of the contest. There might be a heart in the old bear somewhere."

Brad snorted. "I'll call him. Do you want Tracks Larkin to coach your team?"

"Nah. I want him on the field. Maybe he'll want to

be a player coach. We'll let him decide."

"Can I handle the auction dinner? Please?" Luci sat on the edge of her chair. Excitement shimmered off her as if she had asked, "Can I open my presents now?"

Laughing, Ram agreed, "Of course. You're sure it's not too much to manage alone?"

She beamed. "Hell, no. I love putting parties together. But you can help beg donations for auction items. You have way more sway with rich people than I do."

"Done. We need to have tickets printed. Who wants to take care of that?"

"Me again," Luci volunteered. "I have connections with printers. How much do you want to charge for admission?"

Pages rustled. Brad stated, "Jack stipulated five dollars. Do you think he did that so kids might be able to afford a ticket?"

"I didn't think of that," Ram said rolling it over in his mind. "Let's print a five-dollar face value on the tickets, but add the words, 'Or larger donation gratefully accepted.' How does that sound?"

Luci took the dictation, curlicues and slanted lines appearing on her steno pad. "Got it."

"I'll take charge of calling as many sports and entertainment celebrities I can think of," Ram proposed. "I'm on a first name basis with Michael Morgan. And apparently I'm engaged to Nicky Dahlman."

Brad hooted. "So I've heard."

Luci pursed her lips and then cleared her throat. "Um, Ram? Are you going to involve Nikki Lambert in planning?" Her eyes darkened. "Maybe Jack would want that?"

He'd give anything if he thought for a second that his relationship with Nikki had survived Jack's death.

"I don't want to approach her about this," Ram replied. "I think Jack expects…uh, expected, me to spearhead his plan.

"You know what, though?" Ram threw out the open-ended question, switching gears. "We need to involve David Cry. I'll call him as soon as we finish brainstorming. I want to ask him about the most promising research out there, and see how we can direct the money that we raise specifically toward those efforts."

Ram rubbed his hands together. "This is really fleshing out, don't you think?"

"I think that this is pretty amazing." Brad stood and handed him Jack's notebook. "I'm itching to get started. You haven't delegated anything to me, except a jersey order and a quick call to Beltzer."

"I want you to do what you do best," Ram said. "I want you to create buzz around the event so that these tickets become the hottest in town. Hey, can you look into sales outlets, like Ticketmaster, Stub Hub, etc.?"

"Great idea. But a face value of five dollars? We'd make squat through those outlets."

"You're right." Ram paused considering options. "How about we sell premium or V.I.P. tickets through retail outlets? And charge crazy prices, like a thousand a pop, or something?"

"Let me explore that," Brad proposed. "I actually like that idea."

"Ooh," Luci said, her face lit with delight. "I want to set the auction dinner table prices and individual plate prices really high, too. Can I?"

"Sure. Let's see that Harry DeSanto gets the word out fast. We have to promote the shit out of this. Let's get to work."

Luci held out a hand. "Not so fast," she said. "My head's spinning here. Um…"

Her face twitched and she sighed. "I assume Nikki and Rocky are guests of honor? Who invites them?"

Her innocent question stole Ram's breath. Would Nikki even come? The thought that she might refuse reduced his exuberance to ashes.

A little help here, Jack?

Brad read his mind with the assurance. "She'll come, Ram. This will blow her away. It has all the makings of a big deal annual event. We'll make her proud. And we'll make Jack prouder. Just like he said on the inside of that notebook, we're going to Fill the Stadium for ALD."

"Huh?" Ram whipped open the notebook and couldn't believe his eyes. Rocky's name was absent, replaced with the acronym ALD, as Brad had unwittingly verified. Stunned, Ram gaped at the red block letters questioning his sanity.

Brad held up his index finger. "One other thing. Who's the spokesperson? You Ram? On Jack's behalf? Or Rocky? Do you think Jack would like that?"

Suddenly Ram questioned his role in addition to his mental health. He didn't want Jack's plan to be about Ram Delaney. Jack had stated that all this was for Rocky. He longed to consult Nikki. He'd never inform her about the "conversation" with Jack the night before. Placing Rocky front and center for the event would scare the shit out of Nikki. It scared the shit out of Ram.

"I think we'll let David and the ALD Foundation

take the spotlight in this," Ram said. "I'll pay the V.I.P. admission price for him, Nikki and Rocky. And...I'll handle the invitations when the time is right. Deal?"

Luci popped up from her chair. "Deal. We have our work cut out for us."

She faced Ram and tears welled in her soft brown eyes. Rushing forward she hugged him. "Thank you so much for letting me do this with you."

Releasing her hold she sniffled. "I'm honored."

"Ah, Luce." Wagging his head Ram smiled. "You're the best."

Brad thumped him on the shoulder. "We make a good team."

Did Ram see a glimmer of tears in his agent's eyes? He gave Brad a head nod and said, "Thanks, Brad."

Alone behind his desk, Ram opened the address book on his computer. Staring at the "A's" he sat lost in reverie. Sometimes he felt a strong sense of communication with God. An idea manifested in his brain and when he embraced it, acted upon it, he'd sensed somehow that heavenly guidance directed him, as many of his actions on the football field testified.

Ram had always thought that football had a lot to do with God's plan for his life. As he picked up the phone to begin lining up donations for auction items, God afforded Ram a snatch of His wisdom in taking Jack so soon and leaving a football player like him behind. Ram was born to follow a plan set forth in bold print in a ten-year-old boy's dog-eared composition book.

Chapter 28

Nikki swept the lace curtain aside and peered out the window noticing that the material was stiff to the touch. She added washing curtains to her lengthy to-do list. Managing household chores had taken a low priority. It took all her strength to just get out of bed each morning and try to live for Rocky's benefit.

She leaned against the wall continuing her vigil at the front room window, waiting, just waiting. The crocuses had fought their way through the soil along the path leading to the street. Spring carried no sense of reawakening in Nikki, however.

An engine rumbled and drew nearer to the house. She dropped the edge of the curtain and stepped backward. Through the lacy material, Edith Kelly's car sped by and pulled into her driveway across the street.

Resuming her post by the window again, her conscience prodded her to do something productive, like straightening the house or starting dinner, instead of anxiety-ridden window watching. But until the car came every day Nikki could not move.

Her pulse raced and her hands shook.

Where is he? Has something awful happened?

Just when she was about to rush to the phone to check on his whereabouts, the familiar sedan pulled up in front of the house. Rocky jumped out of the car, waved to Luci, slammed the door, and ran up the front path. Relieved, Nikki expelled a breath and hurried away from the front of the house toward the kitchen.

"Ma? You home?" Rocky hollered as the front door banged.

"You bet I'm home," she chirped, determined to fake cheerful normalcy.

Grabbing the kitchen towel on her way back to the hallway, she scrubbed her hands with the cloth as if pausing in her work to greet him—his normal mom doing everyday tasks.

"I'm starving. Anything good to eat?" He dropped his coat in the vicinity of the coat rack, and then backtracked as Nikki silently pointed to the crumpled heap on the floor.

"Sorry." He hung the jacket up, grabbed his bulging backpack and followed her into the kitchen.

Nikki poured him a glass of skim milk and heaped a plate with fat free cookies.

Setting the food on the table in front of him, she sat across from him. "How was school today? Do you have a lot of homework?"

"Nah. Miss Peters was out today. The substitute let us finish our homework in class. He was awesome." He popped a whole cookie in his mouth and gulped down half the glass of milk, his cheeks bulging like a hamster storing food.

"I hope Miss Peters is out tomorrow, too," he garbled with his mouth full.

He reduced the plate of cookies to crumbs and then cast Nikki a pointed glance begging more.

She placed the plate in the dishwasher instead. "Save your appetite for dinner," she said with a smile.

"What's for supper?" He drained his glass.

Nikki went to the fridge, hefted the gallon of milk and doled out another glass.

What am I worried about? He could eat the bag of cookies and still claim he was starving at dinnertime.

Rocky's appetite never seemed sated. His legs dangled off the bench, and a good two inches of athletic socks showed between the cuffs and the top of his shoes. He grew over an inch a month and she hadn't noticed.

Mentally adding clothes shopping to the formidable to-do list, she suggested, "How about spaghetti and meatballs for dinner?"

"With garlic bread?"

"Hmm. Possibly." Checking the freezer, she said. "You're in luck. We have some."

After spreading a layer of Texas toast on a cookie sheet and doctoring it with garlic powder and butter substitute, Nikki filled a pot for the pasta at the sink. Rocky emptied the contents of his backpack out on the table while she bustled around the kitchen. She observed his careful handling of two envelopes.

She dumped the defrosted container of homemade sauce and turkey meatballs in a saucepan. *Thank you, Kay.*

Rocky's silence and the expectant expression on his face made her curious. "What's in those envelopes, honey?"

He didn't respond immediately. Her chest tightened at the sadness in his eyes.

Covering the saucepan with a lid, Nikki set the burner light on low and returned to a seat at the table across from him. "Something from your teacher?"

"No. They're from Ram."

Hearing Ram's name jolted Nikki. His absence in her life was an ever-present heartache. She longed to undo the damage her harsh words and actions had done but she didn't know how—the heartbreak of missing Jack consumed her.

Hope flickered in Rocky's widened eyes as she accepted the piece of paper that he extracted from one envelope and slid across the table. Next he upended the same envelope onto the table and dislodged what appeared to be a bunch of tickets wrapped in a rubber band.

Rocky folded his hands apparently awaiting a response, sober and surprisingly intimidating for a just turned eight-year-old child.

She gazed at the paper in her hand. Jack's name jumped off the sheet, and her knees trembled. The handwriting at the top of the flyer riveted her attention. She would know that handwriting anywhere.

"How?" She gaped at Rocky. "Jack wrote this."

"I know. Isn't it cool? Ram had the man at the printers scan it right from Jack's notebook."

"Notebook?" The subject triggered a memory of Ram rambling at Jack's funeral.

Her conscience pricked at her own obstinate refusal to listen to Ram.

"Jack left his notebook for Ram. You know, Ma. Under his pillow. Ram showed it to me. It has all Jack's notes to help Ram raise money for Jack's disease."

Animated, Rocky's face glowed with enthusiasm. "Ram let me see the notebook because he said Jack wouldn't mind. I've been helping him and Brad and Luci with the plans. Ram lets me come to his office every day after school. Luci let me pick the colors for the dinner. I chose green because that's Jack's favorite color."

He took a breath.

Her head swam, uncomprehending. "Dinner?"

"See…" Rocky popped out of his seat, glided around the table, hung over her shoulder and pointed out words on the paper. "Right there on the flyer. There's a tailgate party and a dinner and a football game. Ram said I could do the coin toss."

Rocky's head turned toward her. His warm breath fanned her face. His silence screamed, "This is *important*."

"Ram said I have to ask your permission to go. Please, Ma?"

Tongue-tied Nikki's mind whirled.

"Ram bought tickets for all of us." He pinched the rubber band between two fingers and yo-yoed the ticket bunch.

She stared at him, numb, bewildered, astounded.

"You and me and Grandma and Poppy are invited. Even Nana and Grandpa. Ram said he would fly them to Boston if you wanted him to," he rattled off at a rapid clip as if speed alone might convince her.

"How long have you been working with Ram on this?"

"I don't know. Weeks…"

"Why didn't you tell me before now?"

"I was afraid." He inched away regarding her uncertainly. As if she'd lash out at him.

"Afraid of *me*?"

"I was afraid you would make me stop going to the club. And that you wouldn't let me help Ram." Tears filled his eyes.

"Oh honey." She reached her arms out and drew him into an embrace. "I wouldn't do any of those things. Why would you think that?"

"You're mad at Ram. I can tell. You won't talk to him."

Well, yes and no.

Nikki didn't have a ready response for Rocky. It was way too complicated for that. She obsessed about Ram late at night alone in her bed, aching…regretting. Her life had become a gigantic list of people and things that she missed—a far longer list than to-do, neglected chores.

How she missed Ram's laughter…She missed his daily phone calls, the clean male scent of his aftershave, his sweet touch with her boys, and the fiery, dangerous glint in his eyes when he looked at her. The blame she had thrown in his face for his unavailability the day Jack died seemed misplaced and irrational. But she remained too embarrassed to attempt to make amends.

Maybe this is my chance.

"I think this is wonderful, Rocky." She held out the flyer. "I'm very proud of you for remembering Jack in such a special way. Of course we'll go."

"Thank you *so* much, Ma." Rocky glanced at the clock on the stove. "I have enough time. Can I call Poppy?"

"Sure." She dug her cell phone out of her purse and tossed it to him. "Why are you worried about the time?"

Rocky executed a one-handed catch of the phone. "Ram's gonna be on ESPN at seven, and he told me not to miss it."

Nodding she said, "Okay. Tell Poppy I said hello."

Phone in hand he spun around and sped away.

"Dinner in…" She checked the directions on the box. "Twelve minutes," she called out as he disappeared down the hall.

She emptied the box of spaghetti into the boiling water, and set the timer. Then she sat at the table and opened the second envelope Rocky had left on the table. It contained legal documents laden with "whereas" and "wherefore", nearly a foreign language that would require a lot of study to decipher.

Shuffling through the paperwork, she found a handwritten note from Ram. Her heart leaped recognizing his scratchy handwriting.

Hi Nikki,

You're reading my note, so I'm glad that Rocky was successful in telling you about our plans. He has been a great help. You can be very proud of him.

If you're like me, you won't understand one word of this paperwork. I had my lawyer draft it, but feel free to have your lawyer go over everything before you sign it. With my lawyer's help we set up a 501.3C nonprofit organization in Jack's name. The official name is the John Michael Lambert Foundation to Cure ALD. You are the Executive Director, bottom line you run the show.

I have tentatively set the JMLF team for you, but you can make any changes you want. Again, tentatively, your Director of Development is Brad Ferguson and your Development Associate is Luci Baldwin. David Cry has kindly accepted the position of Chairman of the Board, my lawyer Edward Schotz is listed as Secretary, and I thought your father-in-law would make a perfect Vice-Chairman of the Board. However, I have not contacted him, so that position is blank on the paperwork.

We have already started collecting funds, and I have opened a checking account. I'll give you the checkbook and register when I see you at the dinner...if you decide to go. I'm praying that you will use the tickets Rocky brought home and come to all the events.

I have carefully followed the plans Jack wrote in his notebook. It has been the deepest honor of my life. I hope you'll be as amazed as I am to see his vision come to life. See you there?

I miss you,

Ram

She clutched his note to her heart. *I miss you too, Ram. Oh, God, I miss Jack!*

The memory of her little boy bent over his notebook every day until he couldn't see the pages anymore pierced her heart. She stifled a sob.

Rocky's explosive descent down the stairs had Nikki wiping her eyes with her sleeve. As he landed with a thud at the bottom of the staircase, she stuffed the paperwork back into the envelope to pore over later.

Rocky burst into the kitchen. "Poppy said he couldn't believe his ears. They're coming. This is so cool. Jack would be really happy, wouldn't he, Ma?"

"Absolutely," she replied, certain of at least that statement. "I'm so proud of you for working so hard to make Jack's dream come true..." Her voice cracked and she bit the corner of her lip to prevent breaking down and upsetting him.

She apparently succeeded judging from his casual request. "Can we eat now so we can watch Ram on TV?"

****

While Nikki loaded the dishwasher Rocky bathed and put on his pajamas without a single complaint. She scooped her current version of banana ice cream out of the blender loading a bowl for him to eat in front of the TV.

They hadn't watched TV much since Jack died. Rocky had lost interest in the *Star Wars Saga* and mostly played video games alone in his room during playtime. It seemed a welcome special occasion to sit on the couch next to him waiting for Ram's interview to air.

The anchorman, Jake Walgreen, announced, "After the break, we'll hear from Ram Delaney, quarterback for the Massachusetts Dragons. We have a treat in store for football fans. But first a word from our local sponsors."

Rocky wiggled in his seat, exuding excitement. "Oh *boy,* Ma."

"Welcome back. I'm delighted to host Ram Delaney and the original Highland University Train this evening," Jake Walgreen stated.

"Thank you for having us." Ram smiled into the camera, and the man's spell on her took hold again. Involuntarily Nikki smiled back at his image on the TV monitor.

"My pleasure," Jake said. "If any of my viewers are long standing Highland U fans, like me, you'll be very excited to hear what Ram is about to tell you. The floor is yours, Ram."

"We're all excited, too, Jake, thanks."

His blue eyes mesmerized Nikki as if he spoke directly to her.

"The current Highland University varsity football

team, and my alumni—the infamous O-line Train, face the world champion Dragons in a benefit flag football game next Saturday afternoon at two in the Highland U Stadium. My fellow Train members are here with me today: Neil 'Caboose' Roberts, Casey 'Loco' Mason, Rick 'Tracks' Larkin, Luke 'Diesel' Murphy, and Chris 'Engine' Simmons."

The camera panned the familiar faces seated next to Ram, their huge bodies seemingly overflowing the armchairs on the set. She smiled again recalling the game in the owners' suite and her boys' over-the-top enjoyment.

"Rumor has it that Phil Beltzer will coach the Dragons and that you'll lead the Highlanders as quarterback. Any truth to that?"

Ram grinned. "Both rumors are absolutely true. Larry Whitney's hand is healed enough for him to take the helm as quarterback for the Dragons."

"You're the MVP after the Super Bowl win. Why not play with your team?"

"Highland University will always be my team, too." Ram cast a sideways glance at the Train and pumped a fist in the air. "Go Highlanders, right guys?"

A chorus of grunts and corresponding fist pumps answered him.

"Rick Larkin, aka Tracks, has just been named head coach of the Highlanders," Jake announced facing the camera, and then he turned toward Tracks. "Rick, will you coach against Coach Beltzer?"

"No, Jake. I wouldn't miss playing one more game with these guys for anything. Coach Flynn will come out of retirement for the benefit game."

"Ram, tell us more about the purpose of this

unusual match."

"Proceeds from game admissions, concessions, and an auction dinner benefit the John Michael Lambert Foundation to Cure ALD or adrenoleukodystrophy, a genetically determined neurological disorder that affects 1 in every 17,900 boys worldwide."

"How are you and your colleagues involved with this charitable organization?"

"I met John Michael, nicknamed Jack, Lambert about eight months ago, shortly after he was diagnosed with ALD. Jack was a very special person. He touched my heart." Ram cleared his throat. "In the face of this awful disease that slowly robbed him of his sight, his hearing and his coordination, Jack worked tirelessly on a plan to fund ALD research."

He paused, his eyes downcast.

"One of my greatest regrets is that Jack passed away Super Bowl weekend while I was in Miami. I never got to say goodbye." His voice cracked and his eyes glistened. "But he left me his notebook, so that I could carry out his wishes."

"A notebook?" Jake asked.

"Yes. He documented the idea for the benefit game and the other events we're announcing today in his composition book. We are following Jack's wishes to the letter. He envisioned a dinner after the game including celebrities on the guest list. Confirmations of celebrity appearances grow every day."

"Any hints for fans?" Jake posed playfully.

"Come out and meet stars from every sport as well as television, movies, and music. The greatest basketball player of all time, and one of the most popular captains of the Yankees plan to attend all events."

"It's Michael Morgan, Ma. Ram met him after the Super Bowl, and he is coming. Ram promised I could meet him."

Rocky's voice penetrated Nikki's trance. Awed at the extent of Jack's legacy, she couldn't embrace the magnitude of it all.

The frozen dessert had turned to soup. She took the bowl out of Rocky's hands and placed it on the coffee table.

Ram explained, "Game and dinner tickets are available now through online retailers, in Boston area supermarkets and at both Highland University and Dragons Stadium box offices. If we don't sell out before game time, and with your help we will, tickets will be available at the door."

Jake squinted camera left. "I'm reading the teleprompter, and there must be a mistake. Game admission is only five dollars?"

"That's the face value printed on the tickets." Ram laughed. "I think Jack wanted admission to be affordable."

Gazing into the camera, Ram raised his eyebrows. "Of course, if you can afford to be more generous, please feel free to add some zeros to your check."

"Thank you for stopping by, gentlemen." Jake shook their hands. "Good luck. I'll see you at the game."

"Thanks for having us."

"Tune in next Saturday at one for ESPN's coverage of the first annual Highlanders-Dragons game benefitting ALD research. For more information about the event, please check our website. And to learn more about ALD, please visit www.aldfoundation.org. And now a word from our sponsors."

"Ram was awesome, wasn't he, Mom?" Rocky's husky voice rang with hero worship.

"He sure was."

"It's going to happen, Mom."

"What honey?"

"Jack's dream. Ram is going to fill the stadium."

Chapter 29

On campus, striding through the McKenzie field house door, a wave of nostalgia swept over Ram. Especially when he spied Coach Flynn semi-reclining in his old office chair, his legs propped up on the edge of the desk. Ram had spent so much time in this building as an undergrad that it seemed like he had lived here instead of in the dorm. And he had never entered the place without encountering Coach in his office.

Ram credited the man with his pro career. Tom Flynn had recruited him in high school edging out the big ten schools. He had kept his promises: a starting varsity spot on the Highlanders as a freshman, and a full ride scholarship for the borderline Ivy League quality education afforded by Highland U. Throughout Ram's college career Coach Flynn had talked him up endlessly to pro scouts resulting in Ram's second round draft pick by the Dragons.

Having reached the pinnacle of his career in the game that he was about to play, Ram figured that he owed Tom Flynn everything.

"Hey, Coach," he greeted him swinging by the open door on his way to the lockers.

"Delaney," came the greeting in his throaty, bass voice.

Coach rose and ambled toward him. "Big game,

son. It isn't every day my boys take on a team like the Dragons."

His ear-to-ear grin was contagious.

Ram mirrored his smile and gave him a hearty handshake. "Your boys up for the challenge?"

He snorted a laugh. "They're quaking in their cleats. I don't know what intimidates them more: facing the world champs, or suiting up with you."

"Ha. I'll be gentle." Ram tilted his head toward the locker room. "Are you coming in for the pre-game pep talk?"

"Sure thing."

"Good. See you in there."

He halted with one hand on the locker room door when Coach called out, "Hey, Ram?"

Facing him, he said, "Yes, Coach?"

His expression sober, he said, "I'm honored to coach you again today."

The penetrating gaze of his green eyes riveted Ram's attention.

"Today is special. Thank you," Coach Flynn added.

It sure is. "No, thank *you*."

As Ram shoved the door open, the distinctive atmosphere of the Highland U locker room pervaded his senses: the musky smell of sweat, the thunderous sounds of lumbering heavy bodies, metal meeting metal as locker doors slammed, and the rumbling din of deep voices.

"About time, Ram," Caboose joked.

"Hey, big man." Ram clapped him on the shoulder. "Not much to suiting up today. I don't need much time."

Sitting next to him on the bench Ram removed his shoes and tied up his cleats. He scanned the room and noted the sea of green jerseys with white lettering that Jack had sketched in his notebook. Ram's heart twisted as he read the letters screen-printed across a Highland U kid's back: "*Find a Cure and Change the World.*"

"Okay, men, listen up."

All eyes turned toward Coach Flynn. "Do your best and make me proud. The university made the one hundred dollar donation for each of you to play today. But the school won't pay the double-up, so I advise you to play to win."

"I'll cover the double-up," Ram offered.

Coach didn't crack a smile. "Well, that's kind of you, Ram, but that doesn't give the Highlanders permission to lose. So go out there and do the impossible today. Let's save Ram some money."

Now his face lit with a grin. "I never thought I'd say this in my career."

He shook his head before he added, "Let's take that field and beat the Dragons. Go Highlanders."

Thirty hands met in the center of the locker room as the players shouted the battle cry, "Go Highlanders."

At the mouth of the entry ramp cleats scraped concrete where the team herded, chomping at the bit to take the field. The band started up the nearly forgotten strains of the HU fight song.

"And now…" the announcer boomed. The Highland Uuuuuuuniversiteeeeee Highlanders!"

Rocketing out onto the turf Ram tagged Tracks on the arm. "The same guy is still announcing the games as when we were in college? He must be eighty by now."

"Eighty-five," Tracks huffed out running beside Ram.

On the sidelines the panorama of the stadium bowl blurred as Ram spun around to face the stands behind the fifty-yard line, searching only for her. He zeroed in on her beautiful face in a second. She looked down from a couple rows up, dazzling him with her smile. Flanked by her parents, in-laws and Ram's family, she slowly raised a hand and waved.

Stillness came over him as he beamed her a smile and gave a head nod in acknowledgment. The rightness and the privilege of the moment filled him. Turning to face the field, Jack's landmark event began as David Cry, standing alone at the center of the fifty-yard line, made the introductions.

"Ladies and gentlemen. My name is David Cry, and my lifework is finding a cure for adrenoleukodystrophy, or ALD. Today is a very special day in the fight against ALD. Welcome to the first annual JMLF, Fill the Stadium!"

He spun a slow circle and said, "Look around you. There isn't a single seat left in this great stadium. You know what that tells me?

"Not that you love football, even though I'll bet you do."

He paused as cheers erupted.

"Not even that you're Dragons or Highlanders fans, although I'll bet you are."

David paused again, as the crowd roared.

"No. This stadium is full to the brim because you good, generous people have come forward to fight the disease that claims the lives of special boys, like John Michael Lambert. Amazing Jack Lambert.

"Jack visualized many treats to reward your generosity. In a few moments Ram Delaney will lead his alma mater in a flag football contest against the Super Bowl champion Dragons. What a sight to see, right folks?"

The crowd shouted, "Right!"

"Have you sampled the delicious food at the concession stands compliments of B.good Restaurants? Every selection is a treat, and every cent you spend at the stands goes to ALD Research. That goes for T-shirts, souvenir items, and programs sales, too. Some of the most famous people on the planet are here today, and they'll pose in front of the camera with you, and even autograph keepsake photos for you to take home. For you lucky folks who have tickets to dinner later, one of a kind items will go on the auction block—not to mention the superb food you'll enjoy prepared by celebrity chef, Nick Corello. Again…every penny raised during these events goes *directly* to ALD research. Jack Lambert thought up all these things.

"Yes, folks, you're here today to join me in my lifework. And that wouldn't be possible without the vision of one small boy who lost his battle against ALD in February.

"Jack, a ten-year-old boy, planned every minute of all that we stand to enjoy today. Fill the Stadium is Jack's lifework.

"And I'll bet Jack would want me to say two things to all you good people in closing. So for Jack, number one, thank you for filling this stadium.

"And, number two, are you ready for some football?"

The deafening roar enveloped Ram, Rocky, Larry

Whitney, and the officials, as they approached mid-field for the coin toss. Utterly thrilled, Ram had never experienced anything like that overwhelming reception.

His eyes huge, Rocky clasped Ram's hand, and the heart swelling moment nearly broke Ram down.

In position, nose-to-nose with Whitney, Ram shook the rookie quarterback's hand and tossed out, "How's the hand, Lar?"

"Great. How's the arm, Ramsey?" he sneered.

Ram chuckled. And, for the first time in his pro-career Ram wanted to be the reason why the Dragons lost.

The ref's monotone came, "Official collegiate rules apply to game play today with one exception. The penalty for tackling is loss of possession. The stakes in the game today are also exceptional. Both teams have made a one hundred dollar donation per man on their rosters today. The losing team doubles up the total donation."

"Call it," he muttered to Larry.

"Tails."

He dropped the coin in Rocky's hand with a gentle smile. "Now, Rocky," he encouraged.

Delight dancing in his eyes, Rocky launched the coin up in the air.

The ref followed the coin drop, eagle-eyed. Then, eyes downcast, he read the toss, and asked Larry in a low voice, "Receive?"

Ram's opponent nodded.

"The Dragons…" The ref gestured with a swing of the hand toward Larry. "…won the toss, and elect to receive."

Trotting off the field, Rocky's small hand wound

around Ram's again. Exuberant, he hoisted the boy up onto his shoulders and continued to charge toward the Highlander's bench.

"That was the *coolest*," he said as Ram set him down on the turf.

"Want to watch the game from the sidelines?" Ram invited.

"Nah," he said scanning the stands.

Following his line of sight, Ram homed in on Nikki. Although she smiled, even from the distance between ground level up to her seat, he could tell she was also crying.

Happy tears?

Ram was misty-eyed, too after David Cry's heart wrenching opening address and the sight of Rocky, so much a part of Jack, living out Jack's wishes. But, Nikki's glistening eyes exhilarated him, affirming every move he'd made the past few weeks to secure Jack's legacy.

"I want to go sit with Ma," Rocky continued.

"Okay, buddy. I'll catch up with you later. Don't forget, you're sitting with me at the dinner. I have a few people who you'll want to meet."

"Great. See ya."

Both teams ran out on the field and the crowd went wild. Ram paced the sideline as HU kicked off. A great kick and a slight bobble on the ten-yard line had the Dragons backed up near their end zone. Ram cheered the defense on along with the screaming voices in the stadium. The underdog ruled. If one small boy's dream could come true then anything was possible—even college kids prevailing in a contest against pro-players.

Dragons quarterback Larry Whitney dropped back

on third and long and fired a bullet that was tipped by the line and fell into freshman Isaiah Katz's opened arms. He danced into the end zone scoring on the interception. The Highlanders were on the board.

Instead of kicking the extra point, Coach Flynn sent the offense onto the field to go for two. Ram called for the ball and scored the two points with a quarterback sneak.

The young Highland U players increasingly gained confidence from the early lead forward and played the game of their lives, frustrating the Dragon players all four quarters of the game.

Highland U won the game. In retrospect Ram concluded that Jack wouldn't have allowed for any other outcome. Ram felt Jack's presence during each play, almost as strongly as when he had sat in his living room, and forced him to focus on that day. His day.

The alumni Train functioned like the well-oiled engine of college glory days. The Dragons defense never touched Ram's flag no matter how hard they pushed the blitz. Ram couldn't wait until dinner when surely his former college O-line would flaunt the pummeling in the Dragons O-line's faces. Ram had blasted two Hail Marys downfield to a jet-footed nineteen-year-old running back who scored crowd-screaming TD's.

After the game Ram pulled Laborski aside and introduced him to the kid who was so turned upside down with hero worship that the single words he croaked out to the Dragons running back were, "Um, hi."

Trekking across the field toward the locker room after the game, the stillness Ram had experienced pre-game blanketed him again. Absolutely content, it took him until he set eyes on Nikki later that evening at the gala dinner to define that sensation as peace.

Chapter 30

The chairs on either side of Nikki at the table remained vacant for the first hour of the dinner. Tinkling glassware, conversations, and laughter in the banquet hall instilled a sense of peace in her heart that she hadn't thought she'd ever experience again. A strung-out, emotional mess during the most stunning day in her life, she now felt fabulous. Everything seemed right, perfect. Like Jack. And Ram.

Ram's parents and Nikki's in-laws chatted amicably, new friendships cemented. The excitement of the game had proven too much for Nikki's dad, and her mother had taken him back to the hotel against his protests. So Nikki had time to sit alone and savor the wonderful, unexpected, remarkable memories of what Jack had conceived and what Ram had accomplished.

Jack's hero had become Nikki's.

The seats next to her still remained empty after the appetizer and salad courses were served. She spotted Rocky and Ram across the room moving among the green linen covered dining tables. Ram kept a protective hand on Rocky's back as he steered him from table to table, apparently intent on introducing Rocky to every single celebrity in attendance.

Nikki sensed Jack's spirit everywhere: in the sunflower centerpieces—the kind of flowers he had bought her for Mother's Day last year—and in his drawing of a boy holding a red, heart-shaped balloon on the cover of the program. Nikki hoped that Rocky considered that drawing the proof that Jack had indeed received his balloon. Jack's uniqueness lived on. She closed her eyes and pictured him.

I am unbelievably proud of you, sweetie. I love you so much.

"Ma, Poppy, look at *this*." Rocky's breathless exclamation broke Nikki's reverie.

Smiling she glanced at the baseball card that he placed on the table as if presenting the Holy Grail.

Eyes wide in amazement, he explained, "Pedro Martinez signed his card just for me. Can you believe it?"

He lovingly picked up the card and showed it around the table. "See Gramps…"

Excitement shimmering in his eyes, he pointed to the bottom of the card. "He signed it, 'To my best friend Rocky.'"

Leaving the memento with them, he abandoned the table and scampered away to rejoin Ram in the far corner of the banquet hall.

"I'm amazed at all the sports personalities attending this dinner." Mickey darted his eyes around the room. "I swear I saw Arnold Palmer in the vestibule as we walked in."

"Why don't you go join Ram and Rocky?" Nikki suggested.

He gazed expectantly at Kay who smiled and nodded her head, granting him permission.

As if supercharged, he plopped his napkin on the table and made a beeline for Rocky and Ram.

"Who do you think is more excited?" Kay

chuckled. "Rocky or Mickey?"

"It's a toss-up," Nikki joked, amazed that she could feel genuinely light-hearted.

"It's incredible that Jack envisioned this event." She reached over the table, clasped Nikki's hand and squeezed it gently, tears brimming in her eyes. "He was such a special little boy, and I am not saying that because he was my grandson."

Silent a few moments, Jack's dear face swam into Nikki's consciousness again. *Oh baby. You are incredible.*

"I'll never find the words to thank Ram," Nikki admitted.

The lights flickered. Rocky and Mickey hurried to the table as Ram stepped up on the dais in front of Nikki's table. Standing behind a lectern, he waited for the room to quiet down. His eyes met hers, a tender gaze that thrilled her.

"Thank you, ladies and gentlemen, for coming today. I think I can say that the tailgate party and the game were a huge success. Especially the game."

He huffed a laugh and acknowledged Coach Beltzer who was seated next to Larry Whitney at one of the front tables, "No hard feelings, right, Coach?"

"Rest up in the next few months, Delaney. I'll run your tail off come August," the Dragons coach said, soliciting hearty laughter from the dinner guests.

"Noted, Coach." Ram nodded wearing a crooked grin. "Now to get down to a bit of business."

He clasped the edges of the lectern with his hands. "I need to acknowledge several, very important people this evening. First, I want to thank my right hand man, actually a wonderful woman who organizes my life

317

every day. She single-handedly ran the Good Sports Club during football season and somehow found the time to arrange this evening's silent auction and this beautiful dinner. Luci Baldwin, can you please stand?"

Luci complied rising a few inches off her seat and giving a quick wave of her hand as she sat back down.

"Not so fast, Luce." Ram beamed her a smile. "Please come up here for a moment."

Furrowing her brow, she rose and joined Ram on the dais.

"I don't understand why, but anyone who has ever met you knows that you're a diehard Green Bay Packers fan."

Nodding her head, she gave Ram a sly grin. The crowd reacted noisily, the cheers outnumbered by boos.

"As you know, Luci, Aaron Rodgers donated a signed jersey for the auction. I understand that you asked your husband, Alan to bid the house, if necessary, to win that auction item for you."

Laughter erupted as Ram ducked his arms down behind the lectern, and then revealed a Packers jersey. "Rodgers provided this autographed jersey for you, Luce. Alan, your house is safe."

Luci plucked the jersey out of Ram's hands, hugged it to her chest and kissed Ram's cheek.

Leaning toward the mic, she said, "It was an honor to work on this project with you, Ram. Thank you all for your kind response to my endless badgering phone calls. See you all next year."

She hugged Ram and then stepped off the dais, toting her apparent treasure.

"This event would not have been possible without the help of Brad Ferguson, my brother by a different mother," Ram continued as he leveled his gaze on his agent. "Thanks, Brad."

Brad saluted from his seat at Luci's table.

"I need to thank one more very important person. Without his help and input we would never have been able to make Jack's wishes come true." Ram's gaze fixed on Rocky. "Rocky, can you please stand? Please join me in applauding Rocky Lambert, Jack's brother."

Rocky's face blushed beet red as he pushed his chair back and stood next to Nikki engulfed by deafening applause.

When the ovation ended Ram said, "Volunteers will stop by your table selling raffle tickets. Please visit the silent auction tables frequently to keep those bids going. And please continue to be as generous as your means allow. Thank you so much for your kindness.

"Chef Nick Corello has prepared a feast for us this evening. I can't speak for you, but I'm starving."

Applause erupted again.

Grinning, Ram invited, "Father Chuck, can you please say grace, so we can dig in?"

The priest rushed forward, stepped up on the dais, smiled calmly at the audience and said, "Knowing John Michael Lambert was a blessing to me. I remember the sight of Jack's smiling face from his seat in the pew, nestled between his parents, every Sunday with great fondness. So much has changed for the Lambert family this past year."

Nikki's eyes filled with tears as Kay and Mickey hung their heads.

The priest continued, "God's plan is a mystery, and in our grief, it's hard not to question Him. But I know that Jack and his dad are looking down on us all tonight and smiling. We can only have faith that someday we will understand the glory Jack and John Lambert enjoy now.

"Please bow your heads to receive God's blessing. Dear God, look down on the angels in this room and bless them with your grace. Please give the scientists the strength, stamina, and instruments they need to find the cure for ALD.

"Bless this delicious food and especially the brownie sundae that Jack requested for dessert."

A smattering of laughter sounded.

"In Jesus's name we pray. Amen," Father Chuck concluded.

"Amen," echoed in the huge room as the wait staff carried trays of silver-domed dinner plates to the tables.

Ram left the dais and sat next to Nikki, his emanating warmth blanketing her.

"Great job, son." His father patted Ram's arm.

"Thanks, Pop. But all I did was follow Jack's directions."

His huge hand covered Nikki's. "I only hope that Jack is happy with how the day went."

"Oh Ram." Her voice cracked. "I'm sure he is."

On the verge of tears, she added, "I'll never be able to thank you for this beautiful memorial for Jack."

"You're pleased?"

Nikki raised her gaze to his face and read the uncertainty in his eyes. "Pleased? I'm stunned, thrilled...amazed...I don't have enough words to tell you what this means to me."

"You don't have to say another word." His captivating, boyish smile stole her breath.

Ram's gaze shifted on Rocky. "What's your take,

Rock? How's it going so far?"

"Sweet." Rocky gaily shoveled a forkful of mashed potatoes into his mouth.

"I couldn't have said it better," Mickey agreed. "This whole day has been ideal."

Rocky blossomed as four "grandparents" doted on him throughout dinner. Nikki relaxed, sat back and sipped a glass of wine. In a few short months, her family had apparently bonded with Ram's into a blended unit without Nikki's knowledge or involvement.

It felt right to Nikki. They belonged to each other. She belonged with Ram. Her devastation at Jack's death had blinded her to that simple fact.

Rocky seemingly forged his own identity without his brother. Life moved on…

Later that evening the bid auction brought in an obscene amount of money. People stopped by the table to wish Nikki and company goodnight. One star after another singled Rocky out with personal attention. He had the time of his life.

"Mickey, would you mind bringing Rocky home?" Ram inquired. "I have a few things to handle here, and I really need to give the foundation checkbook and paperwork to Nikki."

"No problem. Okay with you, Nikki?" Mickey asked as he helped Kay shrug into her jacket.

Ram faced Nikki. "Yes, is it okay if I drive you home?"

Elated at the suggestion, a telltale blush warmed her cheeks. "That's fine—if you don't mind, Dad."

"Not at all, dear," Kay answered for her husband.

Was Kay aware of Nikki's feelings for Ram? It

seemed so. And it appeared to Nikki that she had John's mother's blessing.

Rocky yawned as he zipped up his jacket.

"I'll leave the door unlocked. I think we'll all be fast asleep five minutes after we get home." Kay covered a yawn with her hand.

Walking them to the car, Nikki helped carry some of Rocky's celebrity loot. After his seat belt clicked, she leaned inside the back seat and gave him a peck on the cheek. "I'm so proud of you, honey. You did an awesome job today."

"Thanks, Ma."

She closed the car door and stood watching Mickey drive out of the parking lot.

Invigorated in the fresh air, Nikki sat on the top step outside the banquet hall annex to the athletic field house, and gazed at the sky. The moon cast a honey glow on the stadium in the foreground and the stars twinkled in the midnight blue heavens.

"Jack, I miss you more every day. I wish you were here today to stand up with Rocky and receive your applause. You did it. You changed the world. Your message touched every life in that stadium there. I am so proud to be your mommy."

The door creaked behind her, and she blew her nose in the drenched tissue that she clutched in her hand. Ram sat down next to her, clasped her left hand and cradled it on top of his thigh.

His silent consideration of the emotions that swirled inside Nikki deeply comforted her. She tilted toward him, and he released her hand, circling his arm around her shoulders instead.

Resting her head against his chest, Nikki

whispered, "Thank you."

"My pleasure." He wrapped both arms around her.

"Jack took a piece of my heart with him that I'll never get back. But after today…my heart aches a little less. Because…I feel him. It's crazy, but all day it seemed as if Jack were right beside me. Half the time I expected to look up and see him. His presence is so real. I feel it now." She snorted a laugh. "Maybe I am crazy."

"Nope. You're not crazy. I feel the same way. Nikki, Jack *is* here with us."

Nikki shivered, and his arms tightened around her.

His consoling embrace didn't avert the crushing agony of reality. "I don't want this night to end. I don't want to go back to…not feeling Jack here with me."

He stroked her hair as he said, "I can't promise you that you'll feel Jack's presence tomorrow, or ever again. But I can promise that I'll keep his memory alive through the foundation, and I won't stop raising money until they cure the disease that took Jack away from us."

She sat silently within Ram's sheltering arms until the outdoor lights flickered off one by one and the last of the service staff vacated the parking lot. Hand in hand with Ram, she strolled to his truck. Always the gentleman, he held the door open and waited for her to settle in the passenger seat before he closed the door, swung around the front bumper and slid into the driver's seat.

Stretching an arm over the console, he reached into the back seat. He placed a large envelope in Nikki's lap. "That's the checkbook and Jack's notebook," he said.

Ram switched on the ignition.

Opening the flap of the envelope, she extracted the composition book. "Jack would want you to keep this," she said extending the notebook toward him.

He grasped the notebook in both hands, gazed at it and smiled. And then he faced Nikki and gave her a crooked grin. "If it weren't for this book," he said, "We wouldn't be together right now. You'd still be mad at me."

His soft gaze pierced her heart. "I'm so sorry for the way I treated you, Ram. I was so...I couldn't..."

Laying the notebook in his lap, he clasped Nikki's hand. "I'd like to think that I have Jack's blessing. I know it's too soon to ask...you've been through so much. But, please, Nikki. Please give me a chance to be part of your and Rocky's life? I'm in love with you, Nikki. I'll always be in love with you."

His declaration held her spellbound. He tightened his handclasp sending delicious shivers through her. In the midst of her fears and sorrow, Ram's strength had held her and the boys steady. Gratitude had long since given way to secret desire.

"It's not too soon, Ram," she whispered.

She brushed the side of his face tenderly. "I can't imagine a life without you. I love you, too."

Leaning over the console, Nikki laced her arms around his neck and kissed him.

Straining to press closer to each other, Ram ended the kiss on a deep-throated chuckle. "Hold one sec." He opened the driver's door.

He jogged in front of the Hummer's headlights over to Nikki's side of the truck. The door whipped open, and Ram gathered Nikki in his arms and lifted her into a bear hug.

Dangling her one foot off the ground, he launched into a spin. Dizzy and elated, Nikki burst out laughing, her eyes raised to heaven.

Chapter 31

Spring, Three Years Later, Rocky

"Hi Jack," I say keeping my eyes closed so I only see a line of light at the bottom of my eyelids. Maybe if I stay this way with my head on the pillow a little while longer, the ache will stop.

"Rocky, are you almost ready?" Ma yells up the stairs.

"Couple of minutes," I yell back.

And then I open my eyes and stare at the blurry ceiling while I talk to Jack like I always do before I get up. "Big day today, Jack. The fourth Fill the Stadium."

Rolling off the mattress I put on the clothes Ma laid out for me on the bottom of the bed last night: black jeans and the green *JMLF for ALD Research* T-shirt.

Find a Cure and Change the World.

Sitting down on the edge of the bed I think about how cool Jack is for thinking the whole deal up.

"Can you believe it, Jack? So far Ram has sent millions of dollars to the scientists. And ten more boys are cured!"

I like sleeping in Jack's room. Ma let me move in here a couple of months after Jack died. I asked her a bunch of times until she finally said yes. I left things pretty much the same as when this was Jack's room.

Except for my football trophies and the two pictures on the dresser: one, when I was nine, of me, Ma, and Pop at their wedding; and the new one of the three of us at Disney World.

Ma and Pop took me there three weeks ago for my eleventh birthday. He said it was a *big* birthday since my checkup with Dr. Jodi was A-OK. And he said he owed me one from the first Super Bowl win. I don't know what he meant by that, but I had the most awesome time.

"Did you see me on Space Mountain, Jack?"

We went on that ride so many times it gave Ma a stomach ache. And Pop said he needed a massage. Ha. And that wasn't even my favorite.

Soarin' Over California. Now that's an awesome ride.

"I kept thinking that's what the world looks like to you now, flying over mountains and over the ocean. It must be so cool, Jack."

"Hey Buddy, I need you down here in five." Even without raising his voice I can hear Pop from anywhere in our house. Even when he's way out back mowing the lawn or something.

We could have moved to his big house by the river, but I didn't want to, and they didn't make me.

"I couldn't leave you, Jack."

I still can't believe that Ram is my stepdad. After he married Ma I asked him what he wanted me to call him. It seemed weird to call him Ram, but Dad didn't work for me, either. We only have one Dad, right Jack? He said I could call him anything I wanted. He calls Gramps, Pop, so that's what I chose. The first time I said, "Hi, Pop," when I walked into the GSC he smiled like I had given him a present.

"Boy, if you were here now, Jack, you'd like it a lot. Every kid in school wants to be my friend ever since Ram became my stepdad. Even that jerk, Rick Cooper."

Nobody would bother Jack anymore.

"Heck, you'd be in high school now."

But he isn't.

"I wonder if you'll stay ten forever?"

Wow, now I'm the big brother. I can't believe it.

"We have to leave, Rock. Get a move on, please," Pop says even louder than before.

I can't be late because I get to do the coin toss with the refs, like usual.

I open the bedroom door and start to race out into the hall when it happens again. My legs kind of fold and I nearly fall on my butt. Grabbing a hold of the doorknob, I wait until the weird, tingly feeling goes away.

First I stand on one foot and then on the other. Solid. I walk over to the bookshelf testing if I wobble or not. Pretty good. Before I leave, I take Jack's old notebook off the shelf and open it.

Inside the cover it says, FILL THE STADIUM FOR ROCKY.

"I'm coming!" I answer Pop.

I won't tell them about the headaches or my legs today. Tomorrow.

At the top of the stairs, I feel pretty good. I stop a second because I just had a funny thought. Ha. I'm the Whack now.

"Thanks, Jack," I whisper. "I'll whack it. You'll see."

A word about the author...

K.M. Daughters is the penname for team writers and sisters Pat Casiello and Kathie Clare. The penname is dedicated to the memory of their parents, "K"ay and "M"ickey Lynch. K.M. Daughters is the author of eleven award-winning romance-genre novels.

The "Daughters" are wives, mothers, and grandmothers residing in the Chicago suburbs and on the Outer Banks, North Carolina.

Visitors are most welcome at:

http://www.kmdaughters.com

~*~

Kudos for K.M. Daughters

AGAINST DOCTORS ORDERS (The Sullivan Boys, Book One) took Third Place in the Romantic Suspense category of the 2009 Lories

BEYOND THE CODE OF CONDUCT (The Sullivan Boys, Book Two) was a Finalist in the 2010 Borders Books Readers Crown, took 2nd Place for Romantic Suspense, in the 2010 Lories, and was #6 in The Book Connection's Top Ten Books of 2009

IN THE ST. NICK OF TIME was voted #4 Best Romance Novel in the 2011 P&E Readers Poll

Voted #6 Best Author, 2011 P&E Readers Poll